SOUL UNIQUE

Praise for Gun Brooke

Fierce Overture

"Gun Brooke creates memorable characters, and Noelle and Helena are no exception. Each woman is "more than meets the eye" as each exhibits depth, fears, and longings. And the sexual tension between them is real, hot, and raw."
—*Just About Write*

Coffee Sonata

"In *Coffee Sonata*, the lives of these four women become intertwined. In forming friendships and love, closets and disabilities are discussed, along with differences in age and backgrounds. Love and friendship are areas filled with complexity and nuances. Brooke takes her time to savor the complexities while her main characters savor their excellent cups of coffee. If you enjoy a good love story, a great setting, and wonderful characters, look for *Coffee Sonata* at your favorite gay and lesbian bookstore."—*Family & Friends Magazine*

Sheridan's Fate

"Sheridan's fire and Lark's warm embers are enough to make this book sizzle. Brooke, however, has gone beyond the wonderful emotional explorations of these characters to tell the story of those who, for various reasons, become differently-abled. Whether it is a bullet, an illness, or a problem at birth, many women and men find themselves in Sheridan's situation. Her courage and Lark's gentleness and determination send this romance into a 'must read.'"—*Just About Write*

By the Author

Visit us at www.boldstrokesbooks.com

SOUL UNIQUE

by

Gun Brooke

2015

SOUL UNIQUE
© 2015 By Gun Brooke. All Rights Reserved.

ISBN 13: 978-1-62639-358-5

This Trade Paperback Original Is Published By
Bold Strokes Books, Inc.
P.O. Box 249
Valley Falls, NY 12185

First Edition: July 2015

Credits
Editor: Shelley Thrasher
Production Design: Stacia Seaman
Cover Art by Gun Brooke
Cover Design by Sheri (graphicartist2020@hotmail.com)

Acknowledgments

Oh my, I was scared and apprehensive to write this story. I never thought I'd manage a whole novel written in the first person, but that's the only way I could write this story about a woman falling in love with someone who has Asperger's syndrome. It would never have worked without the support of my friend Laura in Texas. She encouraged me, nagged me, cheered me on, read everything, and commented LOUDLY in the margin…So, Laura, thank you for loving this story and really getting the characters. Your advice was invaluable.

Rad, aka Len Barot, owner of Bold Strokes Books—thank you for providing a home for me as a writer. Ten years and counting…

Shelley Thrasher, editor and friend—thank you for making the editing phase fun and quite easy to follow. After all these years, we work together smoothly and I wouldn't have it any other way. You challenge me, and when I come back with other ideas, you are always generous about it. The times you point out sentences that stand out more than usual, in a good way, you make my day.

Sandy Lowe, senior editor—you are a miracle. Always fast to respond, always so nice, and always THERE. Thank you for your patience and professionalism. You totally rock.

Cindy Cresap, Stacia Seaman, Lori Anderson, Connie Ward… and all of the nameless (for me) proofreaders and editors who make up this BSB family—you are unsung heroes in my book. Thank you.

Then there are the people I love and who by their mere existence encourage me to continue writing. Elon, of course, who holds my heart and whom I could never be without. Malin and Henrik, my children, who aren't children anymore—except to me and their father. My grandchildren, who inspire me endlessly by making me laugh until I need my inhaler. Son-in-law Pentti, brother Ove, sister-in-law Monica, nephews, nieces-in-law…the list is long and yet we're a pretty small family. I am ever grateful to have you all and I don't take you for granted. Each day is precious and I try to pour this sense of family into my novels even if it is perhaps only between two or three people. The sense of belonging. So important and so precious.

The last, but most important group for me to thank is my READERS. You are entirely awesome and so sweet with your comments on my Facebook, Twitter, Tumblr, email, and so on. I cherish every single word you write me and try to respond in a timely manner. I've received such humbling notes from some of you, it has brought me to tears. I know very well that what I write isn't rocket science. But the way you've described how some of my stories have been just what you needed to escape and regroup to face yet another tough day is amazing. That gives me courage to take more pride in my work. Knowing that a story I wrote made a difference in someone's life is bewilderingly wonderful.

Thank you all. I hope you like this story, and if you want to write me, I promise to reply. ☺

To Elon, with all my love

Chapter One

G reer Landon! Finally you're here. I'm so delighted you could make it." A compact woman in her late fifties approached me with a broad, toothy smile. Dressed in a pink skirt suit, a pale-pink blouse, and with beads around her neck, her wrists, and in her ears, she looked like a little girl's dream birthday cake. "The students have prepared an exhibition for you. I think you'll be impressed." Her nasal Martha Stewart voice was already grating on my nerves.

I moaned inwardly. It was beyond impolite to answer "don't be so sure," but that was how I felt. Leyla Rowe, richer than most and careful to mention just how old that money was, had laid siege at my office for the last four months, begging me to visit her establishment. In the end, India, my assistant, had threatened to take a permanent leave of absence if I didn't get Mrs. Rowe off her back. So here I was, ready to be "impressed."

"Nice to see you again, Mrs. Rowe." I gave her my best alligator version of a smile, knowing full well it put the fear of nameless deities into most people, but not this individual.

"Oh, do call me Leyla. This way, this way." She waved her hand as if I were a reluctant tourist. "The students are on the second floor. As you might be aware, Rowe Art School is most selective when we screen applicants. We choose only the very best of the best."

"Imagine that." A groundbreaking business idea if I'd ever heard one.

"Excuse me?" Leyla's smile was still in place, but a small frown appeared between her expertly drawn eyebrows.

"Good strategy." Clenching my jaw, I wanted to turn and walk out of there, but no doubt the woman would chase me and drag me back. She looked like the type.

I followed her through the old, impressive hallway, up a winding, broad marble staircase. At the top, enormous mirrors with pompous gold frames lined the entire corridor. I glanced into them, wondering who in their right mind thought this gothic style would be inspiring. They confirmed that I looked the part of a wealthy, powerful gallery-chain owner. Soft gray slacks, white shirt, a darker-gray trench coat, and my signature messenger bag slung over my shoulder. A second quick glance assured me my short, strawberry-blond hair was still flawless.

"Here's where we hold our advanced courses. Maestro Gatti is teaching this particular class." Leyla motioned toward a closed double door.

"*Maestro* Gatti?" I couldn't keep the cynicism out of my voice. "As in Frederick Gatti?" If it was the man I had come across when I lived a year in Rome, this art school was in for an unpleasant awakening.

"Yes, yes. He's new to our faculty and quite popular among the students. Of course, being such a handsome fellow, he's surely making some of the girls' hearts throb a bit extra, but he's most professional about it."

Leyla had no idea how much effort it took for me not to laugh out loud. Frederick Gatti, womanizer and wannabe painter, had already tried in Rome to pass himself off as a *maestro*, which didn't fly with the Italians. Many of them knew their art very well, and for this man to cut corners and invent himself a career just hadn't worked. So he was in Boston now, trying the same thing here.

"Let's pay them a visit," Leyla said and knocked on the door.

"Oh, yes. Let's." Things were looking up. I wondered if Gatti would remember me and the part I'd played in his exit from the Rome art scene.

Leyla swept into the classroom where eight students stood behind their easels. They all focused on the man on the dais in front of them. Dressed all in black and with a classic beret to add to his maestro image, Frederick Gatti also boasted a becoming goatee. I was chuckling inside my head again. Of course he knew to dress the part. Pity he couldn't paint.

"Madame Rowe," he said in what even I had to concede was a charming Italian accent, and rushed to greet Leyla. "You are like the angels. I need you to solve a matter of importance."

"What on earth has you this upset, Maestro?" Leyla took his hands in hers.

"It's that—that *girl* of yours. She barged in here, frightened my students, *questioned* my teaching. Nobody—nobody—treats me in such a rude manner. It just isn't done!"

So, I hadn't been forceful enough with him in Rome. I looked around, trying to spot said rude girl, but the eight frozen-in-place students who stood there didn't look ready to criticize anyone. Nobody moved or said anything.

"Oh, Maestro, I'm so sorry. I'll talk to her. She's not supposed to come down here and disturb the classes, but she forgets. You know she can't help herself." Leyla tapped her right temple and smiled.

"How about a guardian, or a *key*?" Gatti said, showing off his white veneered teeth in a snarl. "I simply cannot work under these circumstances. It's impossible."

Leyla looked furious now, and something told me that Rude Girl, and not Gatti, was the reason. "Leave it to me, Maestro. In the meantime, I have a surprise to cheer you up. I've tried for months to get *the* most influential art-gallery owner in the U.S. to visit us. I'm sure you've heard of Greer Landon."

"Hello again, Maestro Gatti," I said in my best silky voice and stepped into his field of vision.

"Madame Landon." He blanched and turned to Leyla. "This is insanity. You are trying to drive me out of my mind. You allow that girl to roam the halls of this school, and then you bring *her*. That woman," he said, pointing at me with a shaking finger, "has gone out of her way to destroy my good name all over Europe."

"Aw, come on, Maestro," I said, making sure my voice was scathing as well as playful. "I don't have that much influence. I merely questioned some pieces you worked on in Rome. That was ten years ago. Water under the bridge."

"You made me into a laughingstock."

"No, no. I can't take credit for that." I raised my hand to stop his flow of words. "You did that all on your own."

"What are we talking about here?" Leyla asked, smiling too broadly. "I don't understand."

"Frederick Gatti is not a good artist. He's an even worse teacher, Mother. These students are good, but since he started working here, they haven't developed their skills," a beautiful alto voice said very matter-of-factly.

I turned around to face the newcomer. A young woman, perhaps in her mid-twenties, stood in the doorway. She regarded us all with serious, dark-gray eyes and seemed unimpressed with Gatti's enraged growl. The woman looked over at me instead, raising her eyebrows as if my presence was a surprise, which I surmised it was.

She wore blue jeans, a black, sleeveless button-down shirt, and sneakers. I wondered if she was a disgruntled student, but Gatti's reaction suggested this just might be Rude Girl.

"Hayden, how dare you talk to Maestro Gatti that way?" Leyla said, her anger dissolving the veneer that she was a perfect, amicable host. "Leave the school area at once and return to your wing."

I cringed, something I never do, at the way Leyla talked to Hayden. "This girl's right, you know," I said, not sure if that would help. Fascinated, I saw Hayden whip her glance my way.

She seemed to scan me, inch by inch, and then she left without another word.

"You have no idea what you're talking about!" Gatti bellowed. "This girl is crazy. Absolutely crazy."

"She seems like she knows enough to determine the level of your so-called expertise." I was getting tired of this charade. "Mrs. Rowe, Leyla, is this screaming match what I came here to witness? So far I haven't seen any semblance of talent."

"These students, they're my most advanced—"

"Yes, you keep saying that," I said, not interested in prolonging this pain. "Yet none of them has anything remotely interesting or indicative of talent sitting on their easels. Perhaps that *is* Gatti's fault, to a point, but if this is your best, I don't see any reason for me to continue the tour. I'm sure you realize I'm very busy."

Leyla pulled her pink lips back in a grimace of a smile. "Your lack of interest will no doubt have an adverse effect on my willingness to endorse your galleries. I've always sent true art lovers your way, used my good *name*, because I was hoping—"

"You were hoping to draw more business your way if I endorsed your art school." I shook my head. "You show poor judgment on so many levels, and employing people like 'Maestro' here is just one such mistake."

I couldn't care less what this woman thought of what I said. I did, however, feel a little bad for the poor students who stood there like statues, no doubt seeing their dream careers as painters vaporize before them. "Keep in mind that I'm basing my opinion on what I see on your easels right now. You may have decent artwork displayed elsewhere, but if I were you, I wouldn't use any of the techniques or advice Mr. Gatti has taught you."

A young man standing to my far right stepped closer. "Ma'am? Ms. Landon? We do have an exhibit we want to share with you, if you would like to stay for just a moment longer?" He blushed a saturated pink. "We would value your opinion, even if it stings." Smiling crookedly, he shrugged. He seemed like a nice young man, and I do care about painters, no matter what my reputation states.

"Very well." I didn't even glance over to the frantically whispering Gatti and Leyla. "As I did make time to visit you, I might as well."

The young man looked relieved and motioned for me to walk through the door. "I'm Luke, by the way. Luke Myers."

"Nice to meet you." I thought I'd better be on my best behavior, as the students all followed me toward a larger room farther down the corridor. They all kept a certain distance, as if afraid I'd slit their throats if I didn't like their paintings.

An expert had lit the room to display the art; I had to give the school credit for that. I walked up to the first piece, a watercolor painting of the Statue of Liberty.

"Subject is boring, but whoever painted this knows about light. Use this technique and do landscapes instead."

"Thank you, ma'am," a girl's voice whispered from the back. I didn't turn around but moved to the second piece. This one was an oil painting of a dark, gritty alley. "Shift focus. Less on the yellow tones, more on the blues. Good brush technique. Good depth."

"Wow." A young man high-fived another.

I walked from painting to painting, critiquing and making sure I had at least one positive thing to say about each of them. It wasn't these kids' fault they had an idiot for a teacher and a complete fool for a principal.

"Did you get it, Luke? Did she let you put it up?" a young woman to my left whispered.

"Yeah, it's right behind this wall. Out of sight of Rowe."

My curiosity rose as I turned the corner. I walked up to a canvas much bigger than the others. And stared. I stepped back to get a better overview but was unable to keep my distance for very long. I walked closer again. The colors were close to blinding in their clarity. A child stood by a window, hands pressed against the glass, and my throat clenched at the immense loneliness the painting portrayed. The glass seemed like it might shatter beneath the little girl's hands, and the curtains framing it were of the thickest, richest velvet. The dark hair of the girl glimmered in the muted light coming from behind.

"Who—" I cleared my voice. "Who painted this?" I rounded on them, scanning the young faces. Nothing of what I had seen so far was even close to this. "Who?" I asked for the third time, my voice husky.

Luke took a step toward me. "Hayden. Hayden Rowe."

CHAPTER TWO

I blinked as I regarded the painting in silence. Hayden Rowe, the rude girl that had made Gatti almost levitate from frustration. Leyla Rowe's…daughter?

"And what, pray tell, is a piece of this caliber doing here, grouped with those of students who have a lot left to learn?" I turned to Luke, the unofficial spokesperson of this group.

"I'm in my third semester here," Luke said. "During that time, I've managed to catch glimpses of Hayden's work on quite a few occasions. She's an amazing painter, but our principal, her mother, doesn't want anyone to see any of her work."

"That doesn't make the least bit of sense." I placed my hands on my hips and examined the painting of the little girl from all angles. "If the rest of her pieces are as good as this one, why haven't I ever heard of this young woman?"

"Because her mother keeps her locked in the attic." One of the girls, Goth inspired, black-haired, and with tons of smudged black eye makeup, spoke with disdain. "You saw her earlier."

"Ulli, please. Nobody has locked up Hayden." Luke shook his head. "Though, since Gatti started teaching here, who knows? He's the one who always talks about keys and guardians."

"That's because Hayden doesn't buy his credentials." Ulli stood her ground. "Personally, I think Hayden scares the shit out of that little weasel."

As much as I agreed with this Ulli's assessment of Gatti, I wasn't prepared to let these young people digress. I was standing in front of something unimaginably good, and if this Hayden had more like this, I wanted her work in my Manhattan gallery.

"How can I get in touch with Hayden Rowe?" I turned to Luke, who seemed to be the one with his head screwed on right. "Anyone have her card or her cell number?"

"Good luck with that, Ms. Landon." Another of the students, one of the gangly young men, snorted. "I doubt if Hayden bothers with either."

Granted, business cards weren't every painter's thing, but who in today's world didn't have a cell phone? "All right," I said slowly. "Where does she work? Where does she live?"

"In the south wing. She has her studio there, I think. At least that's what one of the janitors said." Luke frowned. "I've never been there. None of us have."

"I heard she used to live in this posh place right on Beacon Hill before, but she had to move here about a year ago. Not sure why." Ulli pulled half her gum out, twirled it around a paint-stained finger, and put it back in her mouth.

"Then point me in the right direction," I said, set on following this situation up right away, preferably before Leyla and Gatti realized what I was up to and threw me out. "I still don't understand why Leyla Rowe doesn't capitalize on her daughter's talent when that would attract all the attention she wants for her school." I gazed at the students, who managed to look ill at ease, all of them at the same time.

"Our principal is not advertising Hayden's talent because her daughter is retarded." Ulli shrugged. "That or insane, depending on which day of the week the subject comes up." Flinging her hands in the air, Ulli made a face at her classmates. "Hey, I'm not the one saying this about Hayden. Her mother is, when yelling at her son."

So Leyla and her son were arguing about Hayden. Perhaps

the son felt bad for how his mother treated his sister? The scenario was intriguing no matter what.

"Thank you for showing me this exhibition of yours," I said to Luke and the others, handing each of them my card. "In my opinion you showed more hospitality and decorum than I've seen from the principal and Gatti. Don't hesitate to stay in touch. Each of you has talent, but you need to develop it with other teachers to guide you rather than Frederick Gatti."

"Thank you, Ms. Landon." Luke smiled, and even Ulli looked pleased at what I had to say.

"Greer. Please. Now, can anyone of you show me the entrance to the south wing?"

"Sure. We're off to have our lunch break. We pass the south wing on our way to the cafeteria." Another of the girls, petite and with chalk-white blond hair, took a step toward me. "And I do have a business card, Ms.—Greer." She smiled shyly and handed over a very artsy-looking card. "Never too soon to start, I think."

"Now that's what I'm talking about." I tucked her card away as we all walked out of the gallery.

The students guided me through a maze of corridors, and just as I could smell that we were nearing the cafeteria, they came to a halt next to a large oak door. "Here's the south wing. Don't be surprised if she doesn't open up."

"All right. Thank you." I watched them disappear in the direction of the smell of coffee and French fries. Regarding the door with a sudden, and for me unusual, bout of trepidation, I lifted my hand and knocked.

How anticlimactic it was when nobody opened. I tried twice more, and then I moaned out loud when Leyla's voice announced her approach, accompanied by the clacking of her high heels. Thinking fast, and yes, I realize, about to trespass, I tried the door handle. To my surprise and relief, the door opened. I stepped inside and closed it behind me, praying Leyla wouldn't have the same goal as I did. She was talking to someone, perhaps Gatti, so maybe they were on their way to have lunch and bitch about me.

I was sure they had plenty to talk about regarding my rudeness in particular and what a horrible person I was in general.

I looked around the hallway, which was devoid of furniture, or mirrors for that matter. Glancing into the rooms, I saw they were all unoccupied and very sparsely furnished as well. At the far end, a winding, narrow staircase led up to the next level. I figured that since I'd come this far, it'd be ridiculous not to continue. Even if Hayden Rowe wasn't there, I might find more paintings by her.

The metal staircase led me up to an amazing room. Enormous windows let in all the light a painter could dream of. All different sizes of canvases lined the walls, facing away from any visitor. At the far end, long shelves held jars of brushes and wooden boxes of what I surmised were oils, acrylics, and watercolors. Four empty easels sat to my right, and in the center of the room, an occupied easel covered with a tarp sat, making my fingers itch.

"Why are you here?" a now-familiar alto voice said from behind me.

I turned around and finally got a good look at Hayden Rowe. Her shoulder-length dark hair wasn't just brown. It had a multitude of shades of gold and chocolate and even some copper highlights. I suspected they were all natural. Her eyes were dark, dark gray. The curvy, full lips I remembered from earlier looked impossibly soft.

Her stance was watchful, but not intimidated or nervous. I realized she was waiting for me to answer.

"Hello, Hayden. I saw one of your paintings in the gallery. I find it amazing."

"Why?" Hayden asked, sounding curious.

"Because it spoke to me. It filled me with emotions, and I wanted to learn more about the child in the painting."

"You claim that my painting had a voice?" Frowning, Hayden tilted her head. "I don't understand what you mean."

"The way you paint, the way you express yourself in your painting, makes me think of my own childhood." I don't know how I realized I had better keep my reasoning clear and simple. "I really liked it, Hayden. It's a good painting."

"Okay." She looked less confused. "You're Greer Landon."

"Yes, I am. Have you heard of me?"

"My mother has often talked about you. She wants you to come and visit the school. Good for business." She did a good impersonation of her mother with her last words, using Leyla's inflection and voice.

"I'm pretty sure I disappointed your mother today," I said, wanting to be honest with this unusual young woman. "I was almost on my way home when Luke and the others showed me the gallery. They had hung your painting of the little girl there as well."

"Without telling Mother." Hayden shrugged. "Probably Luke."

"He seems nice."

"He acts friendly."

Acts friendly? I tried to wrap my brain around what Hayden was saying. "He acts friendly"? That wasn't the same as saying that someone was a friend.

"May I see some of your other paintings, Hayden?" I thought we better get back on track.

"Sure." She seemed to hesitate. "Unless you plan to tell Mother. I don't like it when she screams."

"I won't tell a soul."

"As long as you don't tell Mother's soul."

I smiled at that, but she met my eyes with a serious, steady glance. "I promise not to involve your mother."

That reassurance relaxed her and she motioned toward the far wall of the studio. "Over there is my most recent work."

I swear my hands tingled as I strode over to the canvases. Choosing a square, rather large one, about forty inches across, I placed it on one of the empty easels and took a few steps back. And lost my breath. I had to cover my trembling lips with my hand, which shook too, as I took in the motif. Here, a long, winding picket fence started from the left and went across a field next to a gravel road. On the other side of the fence, the grass was emerald green, the trees lush in the golden sunlight. In the distance I saw a glittering sea. Then on the inside of the fence, the grass was dead, and moss and dirt covered the stones. The trees were bare, and in the center on the ground lay a doll with its hair chopped off, dressed in worn clothes, and missing an arm.

I put the painting back and grabbed another one, this one a little smaller, around thirty by forty inches. Again I placed it on an easel. Before I studied it I turned to see what Hayden was doing and found her immersed in her work over by what had to be her latest canvas.

I took another breath and turned to study the second painting. This time, unexpected for some reason, it was a portrait of an older woman. Her short, white hair framed a beautiful face where each wrinkle only seemed to add to her beauty. Dark-gray eyes, looking familiar, reflected the smile on her lips. Clearly, this woman meant something special to Hayden.

"Who is this?" I asked, too curious to even consider if my question was appropriate.

"My grandmother. Isabella Rowe."

"I like how you painted her." Unsure if I should say more than that, as Hayden didn't seem interested in any detailed critique, unlike the young people downstairs, I kept rummaging through the canvases.

I looked at three more paintings, and each of them described a wealth of emotion with unbelievable range. After viewing those six paintings, including the one in the gallery, I was drained, having gone from laughter to tears and from there over to some sort of fear and even anger. I couldn't remember feeling like this and getting so lost and wrapped up in a painting in a long time.

I made sure I placed the paintings back just as they were. For some reason that seemed important. I turned and walked toward Hayden, who was painting and not even looking at me. I made sure I stood on the other side of her canvas, as I had learned many years ago just how sensitive some painters were about anyone watching their unfinished work.

"Don't you want to see this one?" Hayden motioned toward the canvas.

"Sure. If it's all right?"

"It is." She stepped to the side a little as if to give me room.

I rounded the easel and scanned the canvas, almost bracing myself. This motif was dark. And I felt my eyes widen, as I'd been to this place. A long corridor stretched into the distance, longer than in real life, but the mirrors were the same heavy, gothic gold-framed ones I'd just left downstairs. Here in the painting, each mirror showed a face. I recognized Leyla, Gatti, and some of the students. Other faces were unknown to me, but their expressions went from contemptuous and angry to friendly and even pitying.

"Oh, Hayden. It's remarkable."

"So you like this one?" Hayden sounded matter-of-fact, but her hands squeezed the brushes so tight, her knuckles were pasty white.

"I'm not sure 'like' is the right word." I kept my gaze on her, trying to judge if she understood what I meant. "This painting brings out so many feelings in me. Anger. At your mother, to be honest. Contempt, toward Gatti. Fear of the person over there." I indicated a woman farther away in the painting. "The boy over there makes me want to chuckle." I pointed at a child in his early adolescence. "So you see, 'like' is not adequate."

Her stance relaxed. "My mother says you're the expert everyone else listens to when it comes to art. That's why she wants you to endorse her school."

"I realize that. Yes, I hold a certain position in the art world. This is true."

"Are you going to?"

"Endorse the school? I don't know. It depends on who's on the faculty. Gatti's got to go. If he stays on, I won't touch this school with a ten-foot pole."

Hayden frowned, and even if she didn't say anything, I somehow grasped that I'd used too much imagery in my explanation. "I won't endorse it if your mother keeps Gatti on the faculty. You said it yourself. After he started teaching, the students stagnated."

"Yes. He isn't a good teacher. His paintings are pretentious and don't depict what he claims they do."

"An astute observation." I gazed around the studio. At the other end of it, opposite where Hayden kept the canvases, I spotted a cot and several half-open suitcases. "You spend the night here often?"

"I spend every night here."

"What? You *live* here?" Shocked, I stared at her.

"No. I spend my days and nights here."

Sure, who in their right mind would call it *living*? It was brilliant as a studio but hardly homey. "Literally living out of your suitcases?"

"My clothes are in my suitcases. I sleep on the bed." Frowning, Hayden crossed her arms.

"Yes, of course. May I ask why?"

"My grandmother broke her hip and suffered a stroke."

I thought fast. "And you used to live with her?"

"Yes." Hayden looked quite relieved.

Guessing it would be a mistake to push her on further details, I was about to ask her if I could show some of her paintings at my Manhattan gallery when a furious voice interrupted me.

"What the hell are you doing here? Do I need to call the police and have them escort you from my school?" Leyla stood in the middle of the floor, her eyes narrowing into slits of fury. Gone was the pink-princess-cake persona from earlier.

"This is my room, Mother. Call the police if you like, but Greer can stay if she wants." Hayden stepped in between her mother and me.

"Do you think the police listen to people like you, Hayden?" Leyla snorted in a disdainful and ugly way. "You forget yourself."

"Hayden?" I walked up, standing next to Hayden, focusing my attention on her. "You don't have to put up with anyone speaking to you like that."

"You're kind, but you don't understand," Hayden said, her eyes empty. "Perhaps it is better if you leave after all."

Chapter Three

I refused to leave Hayden alone with her acidic mother. Still, if I played this wrong, Hayden could be in a world of trouble after I left. My mind raced with different possibilities, estimating the outcomes for each of them. After what seemed far too long, I had one choice left if these paintings were to find their way to a gallery.

"I have a suggestion," I said, turning to Leyla but remaining by Hayden's side. "You wish for me to endorse this school. As things stand right now, I can't do that. Not by a long shot. The teaching is poor, the students aren't where they need to be, and the management lacks insight." I made sure my voice was matter-of-fact, but I knew for Leyla these words were daggers directed at her.

"I'm listening," Leyla said through clenched teeth.

"If you make the changes I'm going to suggest, I can still endorse the school. They are nonnegotiable, though. If you don't agree to do this my way, you're on your own. We both know that will be the end of the Rowe Art School—if not right away, then in a year or two."

"So?" Tapping a pump-clad foot, Leyla showed her teeth. It would have been a smile if she didn't so clearly want to dig her fangs into my carotid.

"I come here once a week and teach a master class, and Hayden joins me as a co-teacher." A rattling noise made me glance at Hayden, who'd dropped two paintbrushes. They rolled across the floor and came to a halt in front of her mother. "Would you do that, Hayden?"

"The students can improve with the right tutoring." Hayden picked up her brushes. "I don't think my mother wants me to teach."

"Then the deal's off." I shrugged, trying for casual even if my art-loving soul moaned.

"Wait. Why do you want Hayden there?" Leyla sneered. "I'm prepared to have a trained monkey assist you if that's what it takes, but now I'm curious. Why her?"

"Have you ever bothered to examine Hayden's work?" Appalled at the searing and cruel words, not to mention the sheer stupidity of the woman before me, I did my best to stay collected.

"A long time ago. She showed me some doodling and—"

"Doodling? How old was she at the time?" I must've gaped for a fraction of a second.

"I don't know. Ten? Twelve?" Leyla waved her hand, dismissing her daughter.

I couldn't believe this woman. "And you never bothered to look again?"

"She hasn't shown me anything." Leyla glanced around the room, looking like she'd never noticed the canvases placed against the wall.

I turned to Hayden. "Is this true?"

"Yes." Hayden shifted the paintbrushes from one hand to the other and back again, over and over. She refused to gaze at Leyla. "When I was eleven years and ten months old, my mother told me never to waste her time. So I don't." She shrugged, but it wasn't very difficult to spot the guarded expression in her eyes.

"I don't want to force your hand, Hayden, but if you teach a master class once a week with me, I'll work toward exhibiting your work in my Boston gallery. I'll endorse the school too, of course, but exhibiting your art is my main goal here."

"A solo exhibit for her?" Leyla squeaked. "You're joking."

"I never joke when it comes to art. She's very good." I made sure Leyla was aware I meant every word. "It'd be a crime to not let the public see her work."

"You don't realize Hayden's issues. She was born with a mental deficiency. She can't handle being in the public eye—"

"Hayden? What do you think?" I turned my back on Leyla and focused on Hayden.

"I'll do it." Hayden placed the paintbrushes on the counter behind her.

"Excellent," I said, and pulled out my planner from my messenger bag. "Why don't we meet tomorrow and figure out which day will work for both of us?"

Hayden looked puzzled. "I don't have to work it out. I'm available every day."

"Ah. Good. Good. Let's see." Unable to hold back a smile, I browsed the pages of the upcoming weeks. "Then how about Thursday morning from eight to noon?" I glanced at Leyla, who still looked shell-shocked.

She nodded. "Fine. How much is this going to cost the school?" Folding her arms over her chest, Leyla glared at me. "And what's *really* in it for you?"

I wasn't surprised at her reasoning, as I'd known from the first time I saw her this morning that money drove this woman. In her world, that was how the world spun. Dollars spoke louder than everything else. "Only what the students use when it comes to supplies. Paints, pencils, canvases, that sort of thing. I won't charge for teaching. It'll be a privilege to work with Hayden. As for what I get out of it? I expect to see young people learn and grow. Also, I believe I'll learn tremendously from Hayden."

Hayden blinked. Had she not understood how amazing I found her work? Perhaps she was so used to having her mother snub her, it hadn't occurred to her that others might have a different viewpoint.

"I'll have my lawyers contact yours for the details," I said to Leyla and refocused on Hayden. "Do you have legal representation?"

"Of course not. My lawyers will speak for Hayden—"

"No." Hayden shook her head. "I'm going to see Isabella. She and I will contact Dominic D'Sartre."

Leyla did yet another fish-out-of-water impersonation, and I had to force myself not to cheer as Hayden asserted her independence yet again. "But, Hayden, she's old and fragile."

"If you had visited her, you'd know Isabella is recuperating." Hayden's eyes narrowed. "She is old, but the staff says she's doing much better."

"Of course they tell you that. They don't want to upset you." The sickly sweet tone was back in Leyla's voice. "I'm sure if someone like me asked them, they'd tell a different story."

Someone like her? This woman was insufferable, and the way she spoke to her daughter was atrocious. "I take it your grandmother has her own legal representation." I had to interfere before I throttled Leyla.

"Yes." Hayden glared at her mother with darkened eyes.

"Have them contact my lawyers." I handed Hayden my business card, on the back of which I'd scribbled the name of the law firm I used. She took it and cradled it against her in an odd little protective gesture. "We'll figure everything out."

Hayden relaxed marginally. "Yes." She raised her chin a few seconds later. "When do we start teaching?"

"Today's Friday. No need to waste time. Next Thursday, if our lawyers have ironed out the kinks?"

Hayden looked puzzled, and I realized my words were too cryptic again.

"Next Thursday if everything goes well." I tried an encouraging smile and could tell she understood.

Leyla, in turn, was once again smirking in an ugly I-told-you-so manner, which I wasn't going to let her get away with for long. I planned to bide my time until Hayden was ready to assume her rightful place as my greatest discovery. As a nice side effect, I'd wipe that smug expression off Leyla's powdered face, and it would be a true pleasure.

❖

I had hoped to get Hayden alone before I had to depart, but Leyla stuck around and showed no sign of leaving. This, in turn, made Hayden pull further back into her shell, and she didn't offer up any more canvases for my perusal. I took the chance to study her furtively as her mother went on and on about what a *strange* idea I'd conceived, but if that was what it took, so be it.

Leyla's voice was difficult to tune out, but I managed to reduce her chatter to a dull murmur as I studied Hayden. She was busy rearranging her paintbrushes, which occurred to me was something meditative rather than practical. With her body half turned from me, she placed the brushes in order of length, then gathered them again, only to place them in order of thickness. Next, she put them in a glass jar and arranged them until the tallest were in the back and the shortest in the front.

Her hair curled at the back of her head, folding in against her long, slender neck. I was ready to bet my new gallery in Miami on my opinion that the many highlights were natural. I couldn't imagine Hayden having the interest or patience to do anything artificial to her hair. She wore no makeup, and her high-quality clothes were immaculate. I thought of some of the girls in the class we'd be teaching, Hayden and I, and how they used their own bodies as canvases in a way, adorning them with makeup, hair coloring, tattoos, and spectacular clothes and fashion choices. Hayden seemed content to place all her skill and emotions on the canvas sitting on the easel at any given time.

"Thank you," I said, not caring that I was interrupting Leyla's monologue. "I need to get going as I have business to attend to and classes to prepare."

"Of course. Of course." Leyla nodded eagerly and tried

to place herself between Hayden and me. "This will thrill the students no end."

"Hayden," I said, and rounded on Leyla. "Here's my card with my contact information. Is there any way I can reach you?"

Hayden took the card, but her mother spoke before she had a chance to respond.

"You can call the school and ask for me," Leyla said, her voice chirping again in a way that made me have to steel myself.

"I have a cell phone." Hayden grabbed a pen and what looked like an old receipt from her desk and wrote her number.

"Thank you. May I call you either tonight or tomorrow?"

"Tomorrow." Hayden didn't offer any explanation, but her quick glance in Leyla's direction told me her mother was the reason for that.

"You have a cell phone?" Leyla stared openmouthed at Hayden in a way that was almost comical. "How did you get that?"

"Mother." Hayden sighed. "I bought it at Best Buy."

"You did. *You* did? Since when can you tolerate crowds enough to do your own shopping?" Sounding angry and hurt at the same time, Leyla took two steps closer to Hayden.

"Since I learned how to handle it and not go out during the time of day when large crowds are in transit between home and work. There is also the Internet."

"This is something your grandma has encouraged, of course." Leyla sneered.

"Yes."

Leyla pressed her pink lips together in a way that smeared her abundant lipstick outside her lip line.

"Thank you." I tucked the note with Hayden's number into my messenger bag. After a brief hesitation, I extended my hand to say good-bye, not sure if Hayden would see this act as too invasive. Hayden shook my hand, her grip firm. However, she withdrew her hand quickly, as if she'd learned to touch a stranger in a polite manner but still disliked it.

As I made my way back through the school's corridors, I was relieved that Leyla insisted on seeing me out, as I didn't want her to tear into her daughter. Relatively sure this happened on a regular basis, judging from Hayden's reaction to her mother, I didn't like it. How the hell could Hayden be creative in such a hostile, toxic environment? I didn't understand the protectiveness this woman stirred in me, as I wasn't the protective kind. My image was no secret to me—no-nonsense, hard-bargaining, sarcastic, and somewhat of a bitch.

"This plan of yours, Greer, I'm not sure…I mean, far be it for me to question your professional judgment, but Hayden isn't a trained artist. We decided to homeschool her after several failed attempts at sending her to the finest private schools in Boston. My husband taught her the first two years, and then his bat of a mother took over. Trust me, those two may have been academically qualified to teach, but they wouldn't know the right side of a brush or yellow from blue." She cackled. "Whatever she's managed to put on those canvases, it's—"

"It's all hers." I stopped inside the front door. "Leyla, you asked me here because your school desperately needs help. This means you must think my opinion matters, correct?" It didn't thrill me having to deal with this unreasonable woman, but I kept going as she nodded reluctantly. "If Hayden is self-taught, she's even more remarkable. I can't explain to you how she can be this good other than she's a genius."

Leyla shook her head. "You mean an idiot savant. That would explain it. Brilliance wasted on someone who isn't aware of her talent."

"How can you talk like that about your own daughter?" I doubted Leyla even knew what a savant was. The way her voice oozed scorn made me want to distance myself permanently from this woman, but that would mean zero chance to work with Hayden.

"There's a lot about my daughter you don't know. If you'd struggled like I have during her upbringing, you wouldn't be so quick to judge me." Leyla pursed her lips in a strange pout. "I suppose it's easy to paint me as the villain, but I've gone through hell and back for that girl."

I couldn't make myself believe her, and her long-suffering tone was a little too theatrical. If Hayden had some issue, I didn't doubt there had been hard times, but nothing excused the way Leyla treated her child now.

"I try to not judge anyone," I said and hoisted my bag. "I'm late for my next meeting. This has been most interesting, and I'll be in touch with Hayden soon."

"I'll plan a function where we'll announce our collaboration," Leyla said, now back to her glittering self, smiling brightly.

I winced, but this was the price I had to pay for having access to Hayden and her paintings. "Very well." I shook Leyla's hand and walked out the door. Torn between relief at leaving the building run by this overbearing, *pink* megalomaniac and my desire to immerse myself in more of Hayden's art, I made my way down the wide steps. There was also Hayden herself, on one hand strong and unafraid, and on the other, vulnerable and at her mother's mercy. Was the latter because she was financially dependent on her mother? Or perhaps her ailing grandmother?

Determined and with my infamous laser focus, I intended to find out.

Chapter Four

I'm dying to know if that woman is as horrible as she sounds."
India Duane, my assistant, gazed at me with bright eyes. Of
all my employees, she was the only one I considered a close
friend. India had come to work for me straight out of college
almost fifteen years ago. It took me a few months to realize she
was one of the few people I couldn't easily intimidate. If I was
irritated, she never cowered. She laughed off my mood or stood
her ground.

I learned that India was a lesbian and had a girlfriend, Erica,
a tall, blond Valkyrie of a woman who looked as if she could
break you like a twig. It didn't take the two of them long to start
trying to set me up on dates with friends of theirs. I had to make
India promise to stop matchmaking, as I was clearly a hopeless
case. All of their friends were lovely and very nice, and some I
even slept with, but I rarely saw any of them more than twice.
I blamed myself, my constant traveling, and how none of them
was into art, but the truth was…something I couldn't put my
finger on was missing.

"Well? Are you going to share what happened, or what?"
India's black pageboy hair danced around her cheeks as she
waved her hand in front of me. Her expression changed, growing
serious. "Oh, no. Something went down, didn't it?" She moved
across the office area of my gallery and sat down on the edge of
my desk, her dark-blue eyes hinting vaguely at purple.

"That's an understatement." I leaned back in my leather chair and rubbed my face. I was annoyed with myself at how preoccupied I'd been during my second appointment of the day. When I should've focused on four of my favorite artists, I'd been completely wrapped up in the images of Hayden and all her paintings. I'd sat like a drone through the meeting regarding the final stages of planning a joint exhibition at a huge fund-raising event. They were donating 25 percent of the proceeds of their art to different charities and at the same time getting exposure among the most powerful and rich people in Boston and on the entire Northeast Coast. I hoped they didn't realize most of my mind had been elsewhere.

An unnerving sound broke through my reverie; India was tapping her right foot against the metal leg of my desk. "Sorry. Leyla Rowe. I can safely say she's worse in person than over the phone. Her all-pink outfit actually hurt my eyes. She made the hair on the back of my head stand straight up, but that wasn't the worst part. I might have overlooked all of that, but, India, she's horrible. The way she treated her daughter right in front of me was contemptible."

"She has a daughter? I didn't know that. I heard she has a son, though." India pulled the pen from her hair and rolled it between her fingers. "What do you mean, how she treated her daughter?"

"Hayden, who's an amazing artist, has lived out of her suitcases in the old school gym since her grandmother became ill. I'm not sure, there's something about Hayden, perhaps she has some sort of ADHD, or similar, but her mother treats her like crap. She's never even looked at Hayden's art, for heaven's sake. India, just wait until you see her work. It'll blow you away."

India gazed at me, her mouth formed in a perfect little *O*. "Oh my God. You're smitten." Her eyes were huge and she seemed to forget to blink.

"What are you talking about?" I rapped my fingertips against the glass top of my desk.

"Whether it's with her art alone or also with Hayden herself, I'm not sure, but you're hooked." India pointed at me with her pen. "I've known you forever and never seen you look like this."

"Like this? Just to make things clear, I don't become smitten." I glowered at her. She was too close to the truth.

"Aha. Okay. I don't believe you for a second. You may not call it smitten, but we can choose another word, several in fact. Enthralled, captivated, or even mesmerized. Damn close to enamored. Take your pick." Clearly triumphant, she wiggled her ridiculous, feather-adorned pen.

Ready to snatch it out of her hand, I walked over to the luxurious kitchenette area, where I poured myself some coffee. "Remind me to take that damn thesaurus away from you." I sipped the hot beverage and made a face; it had clearly been sitting in the pot too long. Still I needed the caffeine so I didn't complain.

India came up to me, her expression contrite. "Come on, you know I'm only teasing you, Greer. Tell me more about Hayden's work. Are we going to show it?"

"If it's the last thing I do," I muttered into my coffee mug. "I've already taken the initial steps to ensure it."

"Now you've lost me." India jumped up to sit on the counter in the kitchenette. "Doesn't Hayden want an exhibition?"

India's question made me pause. Surely Hayden wanted to exhibit her art? Wasn't that what all artists desired, to be viewed, to be seen—to be paid? A small voice inside me objected. Apart from her looking pleased that Luke had sneaked her painting into the students' exhibition, I had no way of knowing what she wanted, at least not yet. "I think she does, but I have to be careful around her. She's not like any other person I've ever met."

"I see." India gave me her best wise-old-oracle face. "And how much did you have to sell your soul for to even get a chance to exhibit her art?"

"My God, you're good. I take away your thesaurus and you pull out your clairvoyance. Am I going to have to frisk you for your crystal ball?" Pouring the last of the horrible coffee into the sink, I rinsed my mug. "I'm going to teach a master class at the Rowe Art School once a week this semester." I wiped my mug on a paper towel, waiting for India's response.

"Holy cow, you're teaching? Are you crazy? You're going to work for her, the pink lady?" She shoved the pen back into her hair so hard I feared for her scalp.

"Wait, there's more. Hayden will co-teach with me." Knowing India, I might as well get the whole truth out there right away. She had these methods of extracting information from me; I'd learned that the hard way. I can sustain only so many hours of inquisition à la India. "Now I'll get to know her, and her work, better."

Her face brightening, India smiled. "Now we're talking. By the way, how old is Hayden?"

"I'm guessing mid-twenties perhaps. Hard to guess."

"Hey, we should Google her." Before I had the chance to respond, India hurried over to her desk on the other side of the glass wall. "Let's try this. Hayden Rowe, Boston. I think we have to add Leyla and the school." She pressed Enter with emphasis and started scrolling. "That's kind of weird. I don't see anything about Hayden."

"Add Isabella Rowe." Intrigued, even if this didn't feel quite right, I pulled a chair and sat down next to India.

"That's the grandma? Look! Here's something." India clicked on a link. "Wow, it looks like something from a tabloid. Hardly a reliable source."

"Let me have a look." I leaned forward. "Why would there be anything about Hayden in a tabloid?"

"God almighty. Because her granny is Isabella *Calthorpe* Rowe." India glanced up at me, looking awed. "That would explain the media posse at the time. The Calthorpes have owned most of the best real estate in Boston since they probably rowed over from Europe before the *Mayflower*."

It wasn't as big an exaggeration as India might think. The Calthorpes wielded a lot of power and came from not only old, but ancient money. They were involved with politics, culture, and industrial business, and owned two large independent newspapers. Some of the young people in this dynasty were almost as popular as the Hilton sisters in the tabloid press.

I began to read, and it didn't take me long to realize that a veritable war had been fought for years within Hayden's family. On one side, Hayden's parents, Leyla and Michael Rowe, and on the other, Isabella Calthorpe Rowe and her grandson, Oliver. At the center of the conflict: Hayden. The tabloid article stated that Hayden had some sort of autism, and her grandmother insisted that Leyla and Michael did not act in their daughter's best interest. She even suggested that their approach harmed Hayden and was emotionally abusive.

This made me stop reading for a moment, and I pictured how Hayden had clung to her brushes and also how she'd taken my words very literally. I knew little to nothing about autism, but if Hayden was diagnosed as autistic, she certainly seemed to be highly functioning. I grimaced inwardly at this thought, as it made me feel like I was describing a thing, not a person.

"When was this?" I tapped the arrow on the keyboard, making the page scroll to the date. "Really? March 8, 2001? How old can she have been then? Fourteen? Fifteen?"

"This is seriously fucked up," India said, her voice sorrowful. "I know better than to trust this type of press, and besides, I don't get it why the tabloids tear into people's private life like this. Well, yeah, I do. They're out to make money. Still, if there's any truth to this, this girl could be pretty damaged." India looked at me with caution. "But if you say she's a talented artist, that's all I need to know."

Hayden was beyond gifted, that much was obvious to me. I refused to let a rumor of a diagnosis influence me from what I'd seen of her work so far. I'd let my emotions and gut feeling steer me on several occasions during my career, and that approach had never let me down. I pictured the old gym hall, its walls filled with canvases of different sizes. Hayden said she'd stayed there for a year. I doubted she had taken all of her previous production with her to the school. This would mean she had painted what was there during that time. She clearly lived for her painting.

"Why don't you clear your own schedule and accompany me when it's time for me to give the first master class? You can meet Hayden, and her mother too, I'm sorry to say. I need you to help me plan which type of exhibition is best for her work."

India beamed. "I can join you? Oh goody!" Her computer beeped and a calendar appeared on the screen. "And you have to get ready for your next appointment. The Tokyo delegation will be here in fifteen minutes. I bet they'll be prompt." She actually shooed me toward my private area, which didn't have transparent walls.

"All right, all right. I'm going." I raised my hands, palms forward. I checked the time. I had time to quickly rinse myself off and change clothes. Being impeccable when it came to dealing with the Japanese was a courtesy they both expected and appreciated. After my morning with Leyla and Hayden, I felt like I'd run the Boston Marathon. When I stood in the shower stall, alternating between hot and cold sprays—my trademark method to sharpen the senses—my thoughts were still with Hayden. It surprised me I wasn't focusing on her art alone, which would be normal for me. Instead, I let the water gush over me, envisioning dark-gray eyes regarding me with a curious care.

❖

Later that evening, having taken the Tokyo delegation to, of all places, a sports bar, I pulled up my schedule that India had worked on during the afternoon. Apart from being an art connoisseur, India was an administrative miracle. She had freed Thursday mornings throughout the semester for four-hour master classes. Pulling out Hayden's note with her phone number, I hesitated briefly before dialing. Hayden answered after the first ring.

"Hayden Rowe."

"Good evening, Hayden. This is Greer Landon." I put the phone on speaker mode and wiped my palms on my robe.

"I know. I entered your phone numbers into my contacts." Hayden's voice was as dispassionate as I remembered it. "Your name showed up on my screen."

"Great. Excellent." Shoving my hand through my hair nervously, I forged on. "My assistant—her name is India—has gone over my schedule. I will come every Thursday morning for the duration of the semester. If that sounds all right with you, I'll have India email your mother with the contract containing the specifics tomorrow. I wanted to touch base with you first."

"Yes. It sounds all right."

Was it my imagination or did Hayden actually sound relieved? Thoughts of what might have taken place between Hayden and her mother after my visit had worried me on and off throughout the day. "Did your mother give you a hard time after I left, Hayden?" I just had to know.

"My mother always gives me a hard time. Today was no different."

"I don't mean to come off as presumptuous, but you sound… tired?" The word I really meant was weak; she sounded frail and hesitant. Perhaps it was arrogant of me to even consider myself able to decipher her voice, but I didn't think I was wrong. "Did something else happen?"

"Maestro Gatti came into my studio." Hayden took a deep breath.

This time I knew I hadn't read anything extra into her voice, as it had definitely trembled. I shoved my fists into the pockets of my robe. "What did he do?" My question came out like a growl.

"He yelled a lot." I heard Hayden walk across the wooden floor. "He…he stood too close."

Oh, my God. "Was your mother there?"

"Not at first. She came when he started shouting. Luke and Ulli came too. I think they showed up because both Maestro Gatti and my mother were yelling." Hayden sounded calmer now, as if retelling the events was helpful.

"Why were they so loud?"

Hayden sighed. "Maestro Gatti started shouting. He kept poking me above my collarbone, saying it was my fault my mother had fired him. He said I should be locked up." She cleared her voice, and some of the stress I'd noticed earlier reappeared. "I don't like him. I don't like being pushed or shoved or yelled at. I was holding my brushes…I was holding my…my brushes…" Her voice failed her and she grew quiet.

Furious now, I grabbed my cell phone and stalked up to my roof terrace. "Keep going, Hayden. I'm listening."

"I only wanted him to back off, not to stand so close." Now Hayden sounded weary. "I put my hands up and pushed—hard. Perhaps I really slammed into him? There was blood and he was screaming. Mother showed up and started shouting as well. I was holding my ears. Luke came running. Ulli too. I closed my eyes and kept pressing hard against my ears. When I looked up, everyone was gone."

"Did they come back to check on you?" I sat down in a wicker lounge chair and pulled a wool blanket over me.

"No. Mother must have listened to Maestro Gatti because I heard her turn the key in the door lock downstairs. I found blood on the handle of my brushes. He was right. I…hurt him, so they… they…they locked me up."

Her words were unfathomable. I had to put my cell phone down or I would have crushed it. That madwoman, that infuriating, pink-colored, poor excuse for a mother. I was so angry, I could hardly breathe. She'd actually locked Hayden up. What if the door was still locked? What if there was a fire? Reeling my fury in, I spoke slowly. "Please do me a favor, Hayden. Take your phone with you and walk downstairs. Check if the door's still locked." If it was, I was calling the police.

"All right."

I heard Hayden's footsteps cross the floor again. The sound of them changed as she walked down the cast-iron stairs, the metallic sound singing in the background. A rattling noise from the phone made me clutch it harder.

"Greer. It's unlocked." Hayden drew a trembling breath.

"Thank God. Listen to me, Hayden. She cannot do that. She cannot lock you in. It's against the law."

"Okay." More rustling noises, and then a deep sigh came over the phone. "The key was still in the lock on the other side. I took it out."

"Good." I pinched the bridge of my nose and told myself it was important to remain calm. "Don't give it back. Keep your phone in your pocket at all times. If something else happens that you're uncomfortable with, call me." I didn't think Hayden would actually telephone the police on her mother, but she might just dial me. "And come to think of it, why don't you lock the door from the inside from now on?"

"All right," she said again, followed by a clanking sound.

"Excellent. I'll see you on Thursday, nine a.m."

"Yes."

"Good night, Hayden."

"Good night, Greer." She was so polite, but also had more confidence in her voice. I heard Hayden begin walking upstairs again before the call disconnected.

I stood on my roof terrace, clutching my cell phone as if I were still connected to Hayden. The young woman seemed to forgo any inner filter when it came to confiding in me. I didn't get the impression she was this open with other people, not even Luke, whom she thought of as "acting friendly." Hayden was clearly very attached to her grandmother, but apart from that, did she have anybody? Was it my appreciation of her art that made her put faith in me? Or did she sense the embryonic protectiveness she seemed to stir in me? I shivered in the cool evening air and walked inside. No matter why or how, this unfamiliar connection was as unexpected as it was rare. I didn't simply take to people or find myself easily fascinated, and my own reaction was just as puzzling as Hayden's circumstances.

When I went to bed, I was far too busy drawing up plans for the master classes and working on ideas for Hayden's future showing, but a smaller part of my mind was plotting imaginary ways to get back at her mother for the stunt she'd pulled on Hayden today.

Chapter Five

The classroom was filled to the last seat. With its tall ceiling and ornamented window frames, it by far outshone the classroom I'd visited last week. Perhaps Leyla was out to impress, but I found the large room gloomy and depressing. I recognized some but saw also a few new faces, students who hadn't been present the last time. All the easels were taken. A few other kids stealthily snuck in and sat on the low storage shelves along the walls. I figured it wouldn't do any harm to have spectators.

I glanced at India, who was busy introducing herself to the students. Some of the men were giving her long looks, something I'd witnessed many times when India entered a room. Her sparkling personality combined with her dramatic colors had a pull on both men and women. The art students were no different.

I checked the time on my phone. One minute before class began and Hayden wasn't here yet. Thankfully, neither was her mother.

Five seconds before the master class was to commence, Hayden strode into the room. Dressed in a blue-gray button-down shirt and black chinos, she stopped by the podium, looking calmly at me. She carried several canvases tied together with a thin leather string under her arm. Her right hand held a set of paintbrushes in a tight grip. This reminded me of how Hayden's voice had trembled over the phone when she talked about her brushes being stained with blood. It seemed to me brushes represented a sense of safety. I couldn't imagine what having a few specks of Gatti's blood on them had done to her.

"Hello, Hayden," I said and smiled. "So nice to see you again."

"Greer." Hayden put her burden down and extended a hand. She shook mine in three rapid movements up and down and then let go very fast.

"India? Come say hello to Hayden." I waved India over. For some reason I was nervous about introducing them and had no idea why.

"Great to meet you. Greer's talked a lot about you and your work," India said and shook Hayden's hand. I noticed Hayden managed to sustain contact with India only briefly.

"I haven't heard of you or your work," Hayden said, looking serious.

India didn't seem fazed by Hayden's directness. "No wonder. I can't even draw a straight line. I'm Greer's assistant and also manage her Boston-based gallery. Just a cog among many in her vast empire."

Hayden blinked. "You regard yourself as a piece of machinery?"

"Er…" India glanced at me. "Not really. Just a figure of speech."

"I see." Nodding slowly, Hayden smiled and spoke in a way that looked totally rehearsed. "I often misunderstand commonplace analogies and metaphors. My apologies." She clutched the paintbrushes in her left hand.

"No worries." I stepped in, as I couldn't bear to see the awkwardness emanating from Hayden. How many times had she been chastised for not catching on to sayings or slang? This would perhaps look like nothing to other people, but it pained me to imagine a younger Hayden trying to figure out enigmatic adages that made no sense to her. "India runs my business here, and she's curious about the school and your art as well."

"Lovely!" Leyla's piercing, high-pitched voice sent my

skin into goose-bump mode for all the wrong reasons. I turned, forcing myself to appear polite, when all I could think about was how this woman had actually locked up her daughter only days ago. "Now, now," Leyla continued, clapping her hands as if there was a remote chance anyone in the classroom could have missed her appearance. "As you can tell, we have Ms. Landon back, and the good news is she's back for the duration of this semester. She's brought one of her staff with her…yes, your name, dear?" She motioned insistently toward India.

"India Duane." It amused me when India donned her "don't-think-I'm-impressed-with-you" face.

"How quaint." Either India's expression wasn't enough to put a dent in Leyla's demeanor, or she simply treated anyone she considered a minion in the same condescending way. "As Maestro Gatti had to leave us on short notice due to a family emergency, we're fortunate to have Ms. Landon to step in."

"Not to mention Hayden," I said, my voice silky, which didn't escape India, who smirked knowingly.

"Yes. Yes." Leyla's hands began to flutter as she straightened her collar and fluffed her golden-blond hair. Finally they settled against her midsection, which seemed to be their normal resting place. Somehow I had a vision of the small, bejeweled hands acting like cobras, able to quickly snap forward and slap a little girl's face. I didn't know why I pictured this so vividly; I had no real cause to think it'd actually happen. Then again, a woman who incarcerated her own grown daughter…

"All right," I said and broke out of my disturbing train of thought with some effort. "I recognize most of you from the last time I was here. I trust you have empty canvases to dig into?"

"Aren't you going to keep critiquing what we've done so far?" Ulli jutted her hips forward and shoved her hands down the front pockets of her tattered, stud-decorated jeans.

"I'll still do that, but today Hayden and I want to see how you use your time, what techniques you choose, what medium you prefer, and—of course—your motif."

"So we should paint something out of thin air?" Luke frowned at his canvas.

"No. I've brought ten reference pictures and some objects from which you can find inspiration and guidance." I turned to India. "Would you tape the posters to the whiteboard over there, please?"

"Sure." India took the large folder sitting next to me and waved to Hayden to assist her. I should have known my sneaky assistant would find a way to get Hayden alone, sort of.

"You have fifteen minutes to plan and one hour to finish. Use your technique for speed painting. Don't overthink."

"As you're adamant about Hayden's presence," Leyla said slowly, sounding far too pleased with herself, "why doesn't she put up an easel and paint along with the students—lead by example, as it were?" She gave that sweet smile I've come to recognize and loathe.

I wasn't sure how I knew a trap lurked behind Leyla's words, other than her accompanying Cheshire grin. "Hayden? Is that something you would want to do? Speed paint and show how it's done?" I walked up to Hayden, who was taping a photo of a rainforest to the whiteboard. "It's up to you."

"That's an incorrect assumption." Hayden frowned. "When it comes to art, there are plenty of ways to do it the wrong way, but also many to do it right. My way is right for me. It may be wrong for the students."

"It'd be great to actually see you in action, Hayden," Luke said, grinning. "I've seen a couple of your paintings, and you rock."

"I assure you, I do not. Rocking would destabilize my grip on the brushes."

Luke opened his mouth to say something but clearly changed his mind and tried again. "Eh, I meant…I meant you're really good."

"Thank you." Hayden nodded. Turning to me, she smiled

again. Or rather, she presented that stretching of her lips, which made me consider if it was something she'd learned to do, as it didn't affect the rest of her features. Still, it was oddly endearing. "I will paint."

"As long as you're sure." I turned to address the class again when Hayden continued.

"I'll be sure when Mother leaves the classroom."

"What?" Leyla sputtered. "I have a right to oversee what goes on in my own school." She gestured emphatically.

"If you stay, I'll go back to my studio. Unless I'm mistaken, this will mean Greer leaves too." Hayden looked at me questioningly and I nodded slowly. If it wasn't obvious before, I had sided with Hayden and committed to the terms of teaching once and for all.

Leyla was an annoying, quite horrible person in my eyes, but she was no fool. She glared at us but then laughed, a shrill, silvery sound meant to come across as amicable, no doubt. Sort of like saying, "Oh, that rascal daughter of mine," which, of course, nobody bought. She waved girlishly and left, the clacking from her tall heels hard and unforgiving, like the spray of hail from a shotgun.

It was easier to breathe, and I thought I actually heard several people sigh in relief. Hayden hurried out the door and quickly returned with an extra easel and an empty canvas. To my surprise, I now looked forward to the master class not only because of her, but also because of these young people who looked at me as if I had all the answers. Instead of finding their trust daunting, I motioned for them to commence.

"I'll be walking among you. Don't be nervous if I stop to comment or ask questions. I'm not interested in failing anyone in this class. Quite the contrary."

"Gatti used to yell and make us feel like idiots when he got mad." Ulli pursed her lips as she grabbed a wide brush. She dipped it into a jar of clear water and began to place a gray wash of color over the upper part of her canvas. "Are we allowed to talk, by the way? We've seen some weird-ass rules about that before."

"As long as you're not disturbing someone who wants to be quiet, I don't see a problem with that."

"Music?" Luke asked.

"Perhaps not this first time. You can discuss that among yourselves. It has to be unanimous if you want music." I strolled among the canvases and saw some of the students hadn't started yet. They were perusing the reference photos, and one girl looked pale and concerned.

"How can I help you? Tell me what you're thinking." I stood next to her. "What's your name?"

"Mio." She had at least twenty blond braids sticking out at different angles around her head, and now she chewed the tip of one of them. "I don't paint much scenery. I'll just end up painting something dorky if I do that."

"Why not try something from the cityscape photos? Use the forms and shapes for inspiration. It's not about copying. It's about interpreting. Catch the mood, the light, the essence, and the feelings you experience at any given time."

Mio sucked on the braid and let it go with a plopping sound. "All right. Got it. I think."

"I'll check back with you."

She hummed something incomprehensible and returned to her easel with determined steps. I took the opportunity to walk over to Hayden. She worked quickly, her eyes mere slits and her lower lip in a firm grip between her teeth. I rounded the easel and stood for a few minutes, watching her motif take form. She clearly used the rain-forest photo as inspiration for her background, with a long, straight road from another of the photos disappearing among the trees. Dark forms loomed behind the shrubbery, and as I found myself mesmerized by the darkness of the painting, she added brightly colored birds in the foreground. The contrast was staggering.

"That's downright eerie," India said next to me. "You weren't kidding. She's scary good."

Hayden didn't scare me, but her painting instilled dread in me as I now saw some of the beautiful birds were lying dead and broken on the ground. I wanted to ask her why the beauty in the painting was dying, but I couldn't do that in front of the students. If Hayden kept talking openly with me, it needed to take place in a confidential setting, not in full view of virtual strangers. It was rather ironic, since Hayden had known these young people much longer than she'd known me.

I spent the next hour walking among the students, slowly getting to know them a little, even if I would have to pin name tags on them eventually. Luke, Ulli, and Mio were easy to remember, and one by one I'd memorize the rest.

"Fuck!" Ulli threw a brush onto the floor and tugged at one of her piercings.

"What's up?" I rounded her canvas and studied it closely.

"It's almost done, but here…" Ulli pointed with disgust at the right upper corner. "It's looking muddy."

She was right; she'd tried to add too much detail when trying to paint lace against her dancer's arms.

"Hayden, we need you here."

Hayden looked up from her painting with a dazed expression, which cleared when she joined us.

"Can you help Ulli find a way to clear up the lace fabric she's after here?" I pointed.

"Yes." Hayden examined Ulli's brushes. Finding an unused, old, and spiky-looking one, she glanced at Ulli. "May I use this one?"

"Sure." Sending me a curious glance, probably wondering why Hayden would even ask, Ulli shrugged.

Hayden gripped the brush with something close to reverence. "Do you wish for the lace fabric to hint at maroon?"

"Yeah, and it's supposed to be broken. Tattered, kind of." Ulli stepped closer, looking intently at Hayden.

"You have the skin tone done correctly, as this woman is dancing in the moonlight. This will make the maroon lace also take on a colder hue. We can use what you've already applied and add the highlights to hint at the lace. You don't need to paint every single thread of it…just hint." Hayden dipped the spiky brush in white and mixed it with some ochre and gray. "Watch." She moved the brush slowly to show Ulli, creating the highlights with such a light hand I actually believed I detected each individual thread of the lace.

"Whoa. You're freaking awesome." Ulli patted Hayden's shoulder.

Hayden went rigid and nearly dropped the brush. My heart began to race at how such a friendly touch affected Hayden. She looked like she wanted to run but remained with us, clutching the brush with whitening fingertips.

"Yikes, sorry. Didn't mean to startle you." Ulli looked as alarmed as Hayden did.

"Tactile approach creates a nervous reflex. It's an automatic response."

I guessed this gut reaction of Hayden's was difficult to deal with. She harnessed her onslaught of nerves, but it cost her, judging from the beads of perspiration on her forehead and upper lip.

"You should see me when my boyfriend pulls his stupid pranks and scares the crap out of me. One time I screamed so loud, the neighbor called the police."

Looking intrigued by this piece of information, Hayden turned her entire focus on Ulli. "Did the police incarcerate your boyfriend?"

I held my breath, wondering if this talk about the police had stirred memories from the other evening when Leyla had locked Hayden's door.

"No, no. I told them he was just being his usual moronic self. He can be a total di—idiot," Ulli said, stopping a potentially crude word after glancing at me, "but I love him anyway." She crinkled her nose.

"Unconditional love." Hayden turned back to the painting and continued laying down the highlight. "I've read about that concept."

I found it difficult to swallow. What did that statement mean? I filed it away for future reference as I followed the graceful movements of Hayden's hand while she made the thinnest lace appear like magic.

"See?" Hayden said to Ulli. "Try it on the shoulder where the light hits. Just very lightly."

"Like this?" Ulli did her best to mimic Hayden's brushstrokes.

"Barely touch the canvas. The brush needs to be dried off before you dip into the colors. Yes, much better." Hayden nodded approvingly.

"Damn, she's freaking awesome," I heard Luke whisper behind me, and only then had I realized that the whole class was following Hayden's first teaching experience.

"Good job, Hayden—and Ulli. Excellent lesson for all of us." I smiled toward Hayden, who merely nodded and returned to her canvas. I didn't follow her, as I feared this might make her self-conscious. She threw herself into working on her own canvas, and her shoulders relaxed and sank.

I worried about how tense she'd been while being the center of all the attention, but when I passed her a few minutes later, I saw a faint hint of something I'd never seen before. Hayden was working on her speed painting, and for a fleeting moment I could have sworn she gave the tiniest genuine smile.

CHAPTER SIX

I walked among the finished speed paintings. The students had gone on their break before their next class, and India had returned to the office. As I perused the result of their first master class, I was aware of Hayden as she stood cleaning her brushes under the faucet in the corner.

"Tell me," I said, stopping at Mio's canvas, "what's your first impression?"

Hayden didn't answer right away but finished with the brushes before turning her attention to me. "You have to be more specific. First impression about what?"

Realizing my question lacked precision, I waved Hayden over. "Sorry. Let's start with Mio, here. What do you think about her painting?"

Hayden pulled her upper lip in between her teeth and gripped her brushes tightly. "I see a lot of pain."

I blinked and returned my gaze to Mio's piece. The background, an urban setting washed with stark moonlight, set a stark background for the main motif—an ethereal elfin or fairy that clung to a wilted bouquet of flowers. Yes, Hayden was correct. A definite pain was present.

"And loneliness," I said. "That little creature is all alone in the dark alley."

"Yes. Impending danger." Hayden nodded.

"I'd say Mio managed to grab our attention and fulfilled her assignment well." I made a note on my tablet and moved to Ulli's canvas. "Ah, our lace-covered dancer. She did do a pretty good job of implementing your technique."

"She did." Hayden frowned and leaned closer to the painting. "She's careless in how she lays down the background. Perhaps she's in a hurry to start painting the main motif."

I had to agree. While the figure with the tattered lace drew my attention, the rest appeared sloppy and a missed opportunity to entice the viewer. I made yet another set of notes.

Luke had painted with bold, vivacious strokes. Unlike most of the others, he'd used oils and also added shredded paper for more texture. This practice gave life to his landscape and beautiful insects.

"And this?" I pointed at Luke's work.

"He shows impeccable technique, but…" Hayden stepped closer and then backed up several steps. "Ah. I was mistaken. You need to view it from here."

I walked over to her and regarded Luke's canvas. At first I didn't realize what she referred to, but after a few moments, I noticed the astute way Luke had constructed his speed painting. The insects were there and could be seen as part of the scenery, but they also described the outline of a beautiful man's face. "Very clever."

Hayden nodded. "So much hidden, yet available under the surface." She spoke thoughtfully and tapped her lower lip with the back end of a brush.

I used her exact words as I wrote down my notes regarding Luke's work. We walked among all the paintings, some quite good, some rather bad, and a few hinting at the promise of future brilliance. When we reached Hayden's painting, she remained quiet.

"I'm not going to critique you like you're one of the students. Your work inspires them and shows them what to strive for." I smiled in encouragement as I sensed tension growing within her.

"Would you share your thoughts anyway?" Hayden asked in a low voice. She shifted her brushes back and forth, sorting them from largest to smallest without looking at them.

"Sure." Her painting drew me in, making me want to revive the poor little birds on the ground. The shadowy figures in the background instilled worry and fear. What inside Hayden had she transferred into the painting? Residual anxiety from being locked up? Resentment toward her mother?

I realized Hayden was waiting for my response and that perhaps my delay made her nervous, judging from the way she traced the wood pattern in the handle of her brushes. Clearing my throat twice, I relayed my gut reaction to her work but withheld my speculations about her potential motives. "You have a true gift of expressing yourself like this, Hayden," I said as a finish.

Hayden's shoulders lowered as she exhaled. Had she been that anxious? Now she looked relaxed, and the brushes stilled between her fingers.

"I'm going to lunch." I seized the moment. "Would you like to join me?"

At first I thought she'd readily accept, but Hayden grew tense again and frowned. "Where are you having your lunch?"

"I figured that little Italian restaurant down the street from here. I've been there before and the food is amaz—"

"No." Hayden turned her back and tucked her brushes into their casing. "Should I leave the canvas here or take it with me?"

"Leave it for now, please. Hey, if you don't like Italian food—"

"I do."

"Why don't you want—oh, you have other plans?"

"No."

"Then why?" I kept my tone nonjudgmental as I carefully stepped closer to Hayden.

"I—I don't handle crowds well. It is lunch hour. Lots of people." She'd saved one brush to hold on to, and her coping technique made tenderness erupt in my chest.

"What if I call ahead and ask the maître d' to arrange for a booth away from the main area?" I observed her features for signs of stress. I knew that some cases of autism, if she indeed had this condition, made it hard to process increased levels of sound and other impressions. Too much stimulation for the senses could overwhelm the individual because their brain had difficulty processing it all at once.

"You've been there before?" Hayden looked hesitant, stippling the inside of her left palm with the strands of her brush.

"Yes. It's a popular restaurant, but it's also well managed and it's not a buffet, so you don't have to fear wrestling someone over the different dishes."

"I would never wrestle with anyone for food. I'd let them have it if they were that hungry." Hayden obviously found such behavior appalling.

"I was exaggerating," I said, berating myself for confusing her when I knew better. "So, would you trust me to take you out to lunch?"

Hayden tilted her head, her dark hair falling to her shoulders in rich waves. "All right. Yes. All right." She held on so hard to her brush that I feared she might break it.

"Good." I dialed the restaurant, having found it in my list of favorite places to dine. The maître d' was more than accommodating, and I reached for my coat as I disconnected the call. "They have a booth for us."

Hayden regarded me with something that looked like terror-filled delight. She grabbed a jacket from a hook by the door and pulled it on. Then she pushed her hands into the pockets, paintbrush and all. As I passed her to leave the room, she turned back, and for a moment I thought she'd changed her mind. Instead she took a few more brushes and tucked them in her right pocket. She shoved the brush casings into her box of art supplies. Crossing the floor, she walked with long strides toward me.

"All set?" I almost guided her by touching her back but stopped myself, as I knew how she would receive such a touch.

Outside, the weather was nice and quite warm in the sun. Spring was on its way. Tiny mouse-ear leaves had sprung from the branches of the maples. People had started to fill planters with pansies and other flowers, which presented a colorful backdrop to the old brick buildings.

The sidewalk wasn't entirely congested with pedestrians, which made me sigh in relief. Not sure how Hayden handled being jostled by stressed-out business people, I suspected she found it nerve-racking. Even I wasn't feeling the love whenever I tried to navigate among a bunch of rude and careless people. No doubt I'd been guilty of hurrying along sidewalks a few times in my life, but I never shoved people aside to get ahead.

The crowd became denser when we neared the block hosting several restaurants. Hayden walked closer to me, her eyes darting back and forth between the faces of the oncoming people.

"It's all right. We're almost there."

"Good."

Glancing down, I saw her right hand working around her brushes, a now-familiar sign of increasing tension. "Listen, why don't you walk on the other side of me?"

"Yes." Hayden rushed to my right.

"Better?"

"Yes." Hayden's breathing slowed.

I tried to imagine being this sensitive, to feel so exposed and vulnerable. No matter what, she was damn courageous to brave the surroundings like this.

The Grande Gusto sat tucked in between a bookstore and a boutique. From my many previous visits, I knew the restaurant combined rustic ambiance with a contemporary Tuscan elegance. Avoiding red-and-white-checkered tablecloths and runny candles in old wine bottles, they'd opted for cream-colored linen, dark wood, and brass light fixtures. I love the versatility of Italian cuisine and knew this place wasn't all pizza or pasta.

As we approached the entrance, much to my dismay, a line of people waiting to get a seat had formed along the wall. I'd lined up here before, but today that wasn't an option. Glad I'd called ahead, I squared my shoulders and had to remind myself not to put a protective arm around Hayden's shoulders. I remembered her reaction to Ulli's friendly touch.

"Hey, ladies, there's a line here." A man dressed in a three-piece suit raised his voice and waved from the back of the queue as I motioned for Hayden to enter.

"We have reservations." I bared my teeth at the guy, daring him to object. He didn't, but a woman in front of him put her hands on her hips.

"They don't take reservations. Not during lunch time." She frowned. "We've waited twenty minutes already."

"We—we should go. I should go." Hayden was pale now and kept her hands pressed into her pockets. "This was a bad idea." Her eyes, huge and dark, showed she was about to turn and run. Breathing in staccato bursts, she started to take a step back.

"Cut it out, lady. Can't you see that girl needs to get inside?" A middle-aged African-American man shook his head. "Just go. You'll be fine."

Got to love Boston, I thought as I ushered the now-trembling Hayden through the door. She didn't even notice my hand against the small of her back.

The maître d' guided us to a horseshoe-shaped booth in the inner corner, away from windows and prying eyes. Hayden more or less threw herself in as far as she could get and sat there, panting and clutching her brushes in her pocket.

"Hey, we made it. Take your time to find your bearings."

Hayden blinked rapidly. "I already have my bearings. I know exactly where I am."

"Of course. I meant, regain your calm so you can enjoy the food." I worried I sounded too condescending, but Hayden seemed to take my words at face value and nodded.

A waiter showed up with our menus and poured some ice water.

I studied Hayden furtively when she opened the leather-bound menu and started looking at it. I soon realized she was reading through the entire thing, and when the waiter appeared to take our orders and began to list the daily specials, I interrupted and told him we needed more time.

Closing the menu several minutes later, Hayden looked calm again. She wiggled out of her coat and didn't look like she needed to clutch her brushes anymore.

"So, what are you having?" I motioned at the menu.

"Minestrone soup. Carpaccio. Stuffed portobello mushrooms." She nodded with emphasis. "I like starters. Small dishes."

I smiled in a way that felt soft and brilliant and completely different from that teeth-baring growl I'd offered the pesky woman outside for scaring Hayden. "Wonderful. I'll have some soup as well and their famous antipasti platter."

Hayden nodded again. "That sounds good also."

I got the waiter's attention and placed both our orders after seeing Hayden go rigid at his presence. Was it because he was a stranger? Or was it the setting? Hayden had never seemed shy or apprehensive with me, so that suggested it was more the situation. Or perhaps the chemistry between us benefitted Hayden's equilibrium? I sipped my water. "I'm so glad the first master class started out well."

"It was rewarding. I found it interesting to watch the students work without Maestro Gatti. He's not a good teacher. He…" She looked up against the ceiling, as if searching for words. "He did not allow them their own thoughts or ideas. He didn't want them to be themselves but to mold them." She regarded me cautiously.

"You're correct. I know Gatti from before, as you might have understood. He tried to pass himself off as an Italian maestro and fancied himself as the new Leonardo da Vinci. I wasn't alone in bursting his bubble, but I helped." I shrugged. "I guess I can be pretty scathing when I'm angry."

"I never showed him my work. My grandmother always tells

me to be careful who I show my paintings to. She says my heart is in them and I should be cautious. I don't always understand what she means, but she is right about Maestro Gatti. He's not trustworthy."

Certainly not with anything containing Hayden's heart, I thought grimly as I envisioned Gatti slashing at the beautiful paintings with his contempt—mainly because he had enough expertise to see they were amazing and to hate Hayden…My mind slowed to a halt. Could that be one of the reasons he'd been so horribly venomous toward her? Had he in fact seen some of her pieces and recognized her talent? Thinking about it, I found it logical but decided not to share this idea with Hayden. It would distress her, I just knew it, and I wanted her to relax and enjoy the food.

After eating our soup in silence, Hayden dug into her carpaccio with enthusiasm. She might not be so capable of expressing her emotions verbally, but I found nothing obscure about the way she enjoyed her food. She hummed around the first bite, looking so beautiful when she did, I lost my breath. I guessed her beauty wasn't of the type that turned heads for being overtly sexy or sensuous. Instead she possessed a quiet loveliness that grew with each moment, and it certainly pulled me in.

The expression "moth to a flame" came to mind, and I tried to backpedal. My presence in Hayden's life was that of a mentor, perhaps a future business associate. No matter how the muted light in the remote booth ignited golden highlights in her hair or her full lips closed around her fork in such a way it made me think of kisses, I had to focus on what was best for Hayden. I was great at business and sucked at relationships. That was the bottom line. I could *not* regard this woman in a romantic or, God forbid, sexual context. Her life was challenging as it was.

Hayden picked this moment to look up at me quizzically. "Is something wrong with your antipasti?" She pointed at it with her fork.

"Oh. Oh! I'm sure it's fine. I got lost there for a bit."

"But you're here. You've been here the whole time." Hayden frowned.

"Yes. You're right." I speared a piece of salami and added a large green olive to my fork. Chewing on them, I could tell they were delicious, but I really didn't care. I couldn't look away from Hayden, and I understood I was in trouble. I needed to snap out of this unwelcome bout of attraction and enter damage-control mode.

CHAPTER SEVEN

Hayden declined my offer of coffee. She seemed content to sit in the booth, studying people as they came and went in the restaurant. Her dark-gray eyes glittered as something caught her attention. She tilted her head as she fumbled behind her. I was about to ask her what she was looking at when she pulled out a pencil from the inner pocket of her jacket. Another pocket held a small pad, and Hayden flipped it open and began sketching. She kept glancing at something, or someone, behind me.

I scooted closer around the semicircular booth and watched Hayden draw a portrait. I didn't hide my interest, as it didn't seem to bother her. Casting a furtive glance at whoever had captured Hayden's attention, I saw a woman in her eighties sitting next to a man who looked slightly older. She put butter on some bread and handed it to him. He regarded it as if he didn't quite understand what to do with it. The woman cupped his hand with such love and raised it to his mouth. The man took a bite, and the sheer joy on his face made my breath catch. The woman smiled at the man, perhaps her husband, and her expression was so beautiful, yet bittersweet.

I shifted my gaze to Hayden's sketchpad, and I suppose I shouldn't have been so surprised, but I did find it astonishing how she'd captured the woman with what seemed just a few strokes of her pencil. What struck me were the woman's wistful expression and the aging beauty of her finely wrinkled face. Hayden drew her with such…such *love*, I realized, and this was in part what kept my throat from working as it should. I tried to swallow in spite of the lump lodged there, and it took me a few tries before I managed to speak.

"An amazing portrait, Hayden," I said, my vocal cords obeying with obvious reluctance.

"She has an interesting face," Hayden said, sounding distracted. "She looks the same age as my nana."

"You must miss your grandmother." I rested my head in my hand as I reveled in the pleasure of observing her work and listening to her alto voice.

"No."

"No?" Taken aback, I tried again. "I mean, do you miss living with her?"

"Yes." Hayden gave me a "what a stupid question" look before she returned her attention to her sketchpad.

I fell silent, not knowing what to say next. I witnessed the tender portrait of the woman develop, done with a sensitivity that contrasted starkly to Hayden's matter-of-fact words.

"My nana will never live in her house again," Hayden said, startling me.

"What? No?" This fact had to be devastating for both of them. "I'm sorry."

"It's not your fault. Her doctors say she needs a level of care impossible to administer in her home. It's old and would need major reconstruction."

It was clear Hayden was repeating verbatim what the health-care professionals had told her. Her voice was, not indifferent exactly, but rather laconic. I found myself considering how a woman of such a controlled demeanor displayed such clear and obvious emotions in her work. Hayden's eyes met mine; they'd literally darkened to black. Of course. This was where her feelings could be glimpsed: behind the lenses of her eyes. Just because she struggled to articulate them didn't mean they weren't pouring out in other ways.

"What sad news. Is it possible for you to live in your grandmother's house on your own?"

Hayden didn't blink or shift her attention, but the way she gripped her pencil showed this subject distressed her.

"I'm sorry," I said, trying to smooth things over. "It's none of my—"

"I want to, but I can't." Hayden placed the pencil on the table, patted it with gentle fingertips, and closed the sketchpad. She didn't reach for any of her brushes but clasped her hands on the table. "My nana's house is a bungalow. One floor. I cannot live like that. Not alone." Her words lacked intonation, but sadness radiated off her.

"Are you uncomfortable being on the first floor?" I wanted to ask if she was afraid of the dark, but the question sounded too patronizing.

"Yes. Alone. At night. I don't handle darkness well. I panic easily and believe I see faces in the windows. My mother lets me stay at the school as this is my only option." Hayden now sounded forlorn, as if her circumstances weren't merely less desirable, but also confusing to her. Frowning, Hayden seemed to wrack her brain for words. "She said I could have my old room back at her house, but it's impossible for me to paint there." Hayden's fingers twisted around each other in what looked like a human Celtic knot.

"Which is the same as saying it's impossible for you to live there."

"Yes. I haven't stayed with her since I was fourteen."

Remembering the article about the custody battle, I decided never to mention that India and I had Googled her ourselves. Not to make myself look better in her eyes, but not to hurt her. I understood so much more now. "You can't stay in the home you shared with your grandmother because of how it's built. What about a condo above the first floor somewhere? Surely there are better alternatives for you than the school?"

Hayden's lips grew tenser. "Condos are filled with strangers. I may meet them in the hallways or the elevator. They're also badly lit. I couldn't paint there." She cleared her voice. "It's better now that I have the key. I don't have to be afraid of all the sounds when it's dark."

"Your mother…" I was unable to go on. I didn't want to poison the moments with Hayden by bringing up her mother constantly. I gripped the edge of the table hard with one hand and fisted the other on my lap.

"My mother sees me as a burden."

"That's wrong on so many levels it's crazy." I was rather impressed with how calm I sounded when I really wanted to slam my fist into the table. "I don't pretend to know anything about your childhood or your family dynamic." I dislodged my hand that was gripping the table and placed it, relaxed and palm up, on the tablecloth. I knew she wouldn't take it, but I hoped the gesture would convey I meant what I said. "I'm sure you have good reasons for thinking the way you do, but I can't fathom anyone not liking you."

A series of expressions dashed across Hayden's face as she processed my words. I had come to realize how her mind worked to some degree, and now I saw how she mulled everything over.

"Do you like me?" Hayden folded calm hands on the table before her.

"I do. Very much."

"You don't know me."

"If you mean it's not logical, you're probably right. I'm going with my gut feeling here." I shrugged and knew I wasn't explaining well, using too much imagery.

"Our emotions are processed in our brains," Hayden said. "Do you mean you trust your stomach more?" She wasn't being facetious; her eyes gleamed with obvious interest.

"Surely you've heard the saying before. Gut reaction?

Gut feelings?" I struggled to clarify. "I think it comes from the strange sensation I can get in my stomach when I feel something strongly. Good as well as bad."

Considering this explanation, Hayden nodded once. "I see. I have experienced this when I have a dentist appointment. It makes me think of parasites invading my body."

I was impressed, even if I wouldn't compare my liking Hayden to a parasitic infestation. Still, this was the first time I'd witnessed Hayden work her way through a metaphor—and somehow it was special. Perhaps I was reading too much into it, but the connection between us felt genuine.

"I tend to think of this tickling as butterflies. Sure beats the idea of parasites."

"You prefer insects?"

"At least the imagery of butterflies." I grinned now, sensing the lightheartedness emanating from Hayden.

"They are more aesthetically pleasing. Their wings allow for excellent color studies. It's one of my goals, to achieve the gradients found only in nature."

"I'd love to learn about that and the rest of your goals," I said. "The way you paint tells me you have a very special gift. I'm still trying to grasp the fact that you're an autodidact. You're an enigma when it comes to your work." And she was an even bigger mystery regarding how she lived her life and managed on a daily basis. Especially when life sent her hurtling into the unknown, like her grandmother's stroke had.

I blinked in surprise when it dawned on me that Hayden was now studying me intently. Swallowing, I envisioned her gaze as a light touch on my face and neck. She seemed to memorize my form, and I began to feel self-conscious. I had to prevent my hands from smoothing down my hair or straightening my shirt.

"You are a puzzle also. It's what my nana says when she tries to understand someone. She calls her friend Mrs. Coya a riddle comparable to one of Fermat's mathematical theorems." And there it was, Hayden's rare, faint little smile. It transformed her face, gave it an iridescent sort of life, so appropriate somehow. And it unnerved me, for some reason, making me clench my jaws. "I have spent enough time playing cards with Nana and Mrs. Coya to understand the analogy. This woman changes personality several times during a single visit."

"Oh, my. Really? Sounds exhausting." Chuckling, I forcibly relaxed my jaws and reached for my coffee.

"No, merely interesting. Well, perhaps tiring for her."

Laughing out loud now, I checked my watch. "I have to get back to the gallery soon." I wondered if I sounded as regretful as I felt. I didn't want to leave Hayden just yet—not when we were having this lighthearted conversation and she'd lowered her guard even further. This in itself was puzzling, as I got the impression from Luke and the other students that they considered Hayden somewhat of a recluse. Was I reading too much into her opening up to me? Was it because she realized I understood art? Or something instinctive and personal? I told myself to not get carried away. I was starting to scratch the surface with Hayden, and if I became pushy, she might withdraw.

"We need to leave." Hayden stood and held her jacket in front of her. She glanced around the restaurant. It was half-full by now, and the tables closest to the door were empty.

"I'm ready." I rose and pulled on my coat. Then I started walking, making sure Hayden was right behind me, but I still reached the door before she did. I had placed my hand on the handle and turned to wait for her to put on her jacket, when I saw she had stopped at the table where the elderly couple still sat. Hayden took out her sketchpad and browsed through it. She tugged at one of the pages and dislodged it from the pad. Handing it to the woman, she nodded and said something I was too far away to hear. I walked up to them, concerned at what might happen.

"Oh, look, darling. This nice girl drew a portrait of me." The old lady patted the man's hand and showed him the sketch.

"That's an amazing likeness...and done with such sensitivity. Are you sure you want to give it away—for free?" She eyed Hayden, probably seasoned enough to realize some starving artists would do anything to sell a picture or a painting at times.

"Yes."

"Then, thank you very much. What's your name, my dear?"

"Hayden Rowe."

"Hayden. An unusually beautiful name. Would you sign it for us, please?"

Hayden tilted her head for a moment but then nodded. "Yes." She produced one of her pencils, but I stepped in.

"Hold on. I have something better," I said and opened my messenger bag. I gave Hayden a thin marker. "Here. Make it permanent."

She regarded the pen with obvious suspicion. After signing the portrait, she attempted to give the marker back, but I motioned for her to keep it. "I just know it'll come in handy a lot in the future." I smiled at the couple. "And I would take care of the sketch, if I were you."

"I will. Thank you again." The woman looked a little confused.

"Here's my card, ma'am," I said and handed her a business card. "I own some galleries. If I can persuade her, Hayden might show her paintings in them one day. You're welcome to stay in touch."

"Greer Landon." Her expression pensive, the woman tapped the card with an immaculate pink nail. "I thought I recognized you. I believe we're neighbors. I'm Penelope Moore and this is my husband Edward."

"What a coincidence." I nodded at the old man, who gave me an uncertain smile back. Now when she mentioned it, I had a faint vision of a woman in a pastel-colored gardening outfit. Less elegant, but with the same clear blue gaze under straight, pale eyebrows. "Are you in the house closest to the park?"

"We are." Mrs. Moore looked relaxed. "If it's ever convenient, please call on us anytime. We're usually at home. Today was…a special occasion."

"Thank you." Hayden's prompt answer surprised me. "I want to paint you. Oils. Twenty-by-thirty canvas. It should be a garden setting in the sun. Perhaps it'll be too cold for you at this time of year?"

I swear my jaw came as close to dropping as it ever had. I looked back and forth between Hayden and Penelope Moore, not sure what would come of this.

"What do you mean, 'too cold,' dear?" Mrs. Moore asked, raising an eyebrow.

"You're old and potentially fragile. You might get pneumonia," Hayden said.

Seeing the risk of Mrs. Moore being irreparably offended at being called old and frail, I was about to intervene. Hayden might not understand such a reaction.

"That's…considerate of you." Mrs. Moore smiled and ran gentle fingertips along the edges of the sketch. "At my age it can be a concern. Would it be possible for you to paint in our conservatory on a sunny day? The light there should be just as good as in the garden."

Tilting her head in the way I've come to recognize as Hayden giving something serious thought, she then nodded. "Yes."

"Delightful. Here's *my* card." Mrs. Moore gave us one each from her purse, and I glanced at mine. Classy in off-white and black, printed on thick, expensive card stock, it said "Penelope Moore, Author," followed by an email address and phone number. "Ms. Greer knows where I live, and as I said, just stop by anytime."

"I will." Hayden shoved her hand toward Mrs. Moore, who took it. Hayden didn't give the brittle-looking hand her usual steady one up-and-down shake, but held it lightly for a moment. "Thank you."

"You are most welcome, dear." Mrs. Moore placed a hand

on her husband's arm. "Eddie and I look forward to seeing you again."

Once we'd said good-bye and left the restaurant, we stood silently on the sidewalk. Hayden was lost in thought and so was I, trying to figure out what had just happened. Hayden had zoomed in on Penelope Moore, and clearly she was not afraid of approaching a potential subject. As a matter of fact, now she seemed shell-shocked, or at least a bit shaken. I had the feeling she was planning her portrait, and it appeared I was right when Hayden turned to me and actually grabbed my upper arm.

"When can we visit Mrs. Moore?"

My arm tingled beneath her touch against the coat sleeve. Taking a chance I patted her hand. "You heard the lady. You're welcome anytime." Her skin, soft and warm, made me want to hold onto her hand for real. I didn't push but kept my hand in a whisper-light pat against hers.

"I—I can't go alone. You have to come too." Now something close to panic stirred in the depths of Hayden's eyes.

"All right, all right." Who was I kidding? The opportunity to spend more time with Hayden and watch her work was golden. I must have grinned like an idiot, but I couldn't stop myself. Not only did she want me there, but for whatever reason, she also accepted my touch, however brief. Reluctantly I let go of her hand. "I'll walk you back to the school." I hated to hurry her along, but my schedule was pretty tight, as India had been forced to shuffle appointments around to fit in the master classes. Gazing at Hayden, I hated to see the light go out of her eyes. "Today's Thursday," I said quickly. "Why don't I come and get you this weekend whenever you're not visiting your grandmother? I can show you my home and we can drop in for a quick visit with the Moores."

"Yes. And yes." Hayden relaxed visibly. "Pick me up on Sunday. I always spend Saturdays with Nana."

"Great. One p.m. okay?"

"Yes."

We walked back to the school in silence. The sidewalks weren't crowded at all; the sun flooded everything in sight. While walking next to Hayden, I knew that, for me, spring was definitely here.

Chapter Eight

My Friday quickly went downhill. I'd spent Thursday evening in such a good mood after the master class at Rowe's Art School and the lunch with Hayden. As a backlash to this high, nightmares woke me up every hour during the night. They weren't the type of dreams you can retell afterward; rather they were filled with imageless dark emotions of dread and fear. I tend to have such dreams when I'm stressing, which made me reflect. Was I worked up about Hayden and her situation, even if my spending time with her was rewarding?

As soon as I stepped into the gallery and made my way to the office area, India met me, hands on hips.

"You've *got* to string that man up. Toes first. Over an open fire." She tugged at her hair and pivoted, stalking back to her desk.

"Don't tell me. Andreas Holmer." I put my messenger bag down on the floor next to her visitor's chair where I sat with a thud. "This might just be his third strike."

"I wish!" India glared at me. "You were so sure you'd gotten through to him, but he keeps blowing me off and demanding to talk to you. He really doesn't get what position I hold here, does he?"

"Clearly not. What happened this time?" I pressed beneath my tightening jaw with both thumbs. Tension always hit me right there and made me clench my teeth.

"His showing is in two weeks, and we needed to ship the last two pieces to the Chicago gallery like yesterday. He hasn't even *started* painting either of them yet." India rapped her fingertips, boasting turquoise nails, against her desk.

"What?" I sat up straight, lowering my hands. "Please tell me you're joking." I, of course, realized she wasn't. Her furious expression was all too real.

"As I said, he needs a serious talking-to. Or stringing up. Preferably both."

Andreas Holmer was one of my most gifted painters, very edgy and with a style all his own. He mixed genres and media in ways that made him difficult to categorize. Almost as a balancing act, his persona was as cliché-filled as you could possibly dream up. Perhaps Andreas thought his brilliance as a painter compensated for his temper tantrums, blatant disregard for the business side of his work, and general bad manners.

India had been on the receiving end of this disruptive behavior on more than one occasion, and now I saw that she'd had it. If her furious expression wasn't evidence enough, the faint tremors in her hands, combined with the Extra Strength Tylenol bottle sitting in plain view, were. Like mine, India's stress manifested itself in her facial muscles, and hers led to headaches while mine to shoulder pain.

"You don't have to talk to him again. I'll tell him what the deal is here and either he shapes up or he's out. You know me. I always have a backup plan."

"I do. Thank you." Rolling her shoulders and doing a dog-shaking-water sort of move to relax, India tucked the Tylenol into her top drawer. "Just for your information, I taped the last phone call with him. I told him so, and he still called me horrible things and went off the deep end."

"Glad you told me. Hang on to that tape. We might need it." I didn't look forward to tackling Andreas, but it was part of my job.

Fifteen minutes later I was circling my desk like a shark,

and a quick glance at my reflection in the window revealed I'd actually bared my teeth like one. Andreas was ranting away over the speakerphone, spewing his bile, mainly about India, criticizing everyone but himself, pretty much. Glad I'd closed my door, I rounded on him. I'd had enough.

"Shut up," I said calmly.

"And she is totally incapable of underst—what?"

"Your turn to be quiet and listen." Again, I pressed the pads of my thumbs against my jaw for a few moments. "You are not honoring your contract with me when it comes to the Chicago showing. Had this been the first time, I might've overlooked it. In fact, I have, twice before. This is your third and last chance, Andreas."

"I'm an artist! I cannot be expected to perform on a schedule." Andreas sounded as appalled as if I'd asked him to paint tourists at Disney World.

Somehow the whiny sound of his voice made me think of Frederick Gatti. Shaking the notion, as Andreas was no talentless con man at all, I shushed him again. "You may not be able to work like this," I said, conceding to his point. "However, that's how my chain of galleries operates. I need to partner with artists who know how to keep a realistic deadline. Remember, I asked *you* when you would be able to complete the twelve pieces. *You* set the date. Now you're two paintings short, and I'm facing three options here."

"What—what do you mean?" Clearly a lot calmer, Andreas came across as very young.

"Either you show only ten paintings but share the limelight with another painter, or you deliver the paintings in no less than four days, *or* we cancel completely and don't renew your contract."

The silence from his end was telling. I'd been stern with him before, but I'd never issued an ultimatum like this.

"Andreas?"

"Um, I'm, eh, I'm here. I'm thinking. I mean, I…it's

impossible. I can't...I know I can't manage two pieces in four days. It's a ridiculous assumption."

I realized what he meant but couldn't resist deliberately misunderstanding him. "You're calling my decision-making process ridiculous, Andreas?"

"No! No, no. Ha-ha." Coughing, he then swallowed loudly. "Do you have anyone suitable lined up that might be okay? I mean, someone who kind of fits?" He was smart enough not to say anything like "someone good enough."

I thought fast, and my sudden inspiration, which didn't surprise me as much as it should have, made me sit down abruptly in my chair. "I do. A new talent who matches yours very well, but whose style is very different from yours. You won't get mixed up."

"Ah. Have I heard of him?"

I snickered soundlessly. "Her. And no. You haven't."

"Really? Hmm. Where can I find her website?"

"Don't think she has one." Or at least that was my assumption. Perhaps she did? I shook my head. No, we would've found it when India Googled her.

"Old-school, huh?"

His words made me laugh as I thought of where Hayden currently lived. "You have no idea."

"Okay, then. We're good?" Andreas was starting to sound like his old cocky self.

"For now, yes. Depending on how your showing goes and what mutually satisfying agreement we can reach afterward. That's when we'll know if further collaboration is doable. If not, we're done."

"All right. I get it. I'll talk to Peter. He's been on my case too."

Not sure if Andreas expected me to feel bad for him since his agent and I were ganging up on him to finally man up and be an adult, I merely hummed.

"While we're on the topic of being on your case, there's one more thing." I paused, and when I continued, I used the tone I knew induced chills in the recipient. "If you're ever disrespectful to India again, or anyone else on my staff, I'll nullify your contract. And before you say anything, have your agent explain the fine print to you. Are we clear on this?"

"Yeah, yeah."

I didn't care for his flippant tone. "Are we clear?" I asked again, this time with a barely audible voice.

"Yes. Yes, we're clear."

"Good."

After I disconnected the call, I walked out to India, who looked at me expectantly.

"First," I said, "our bad boy knows what I expect of him now—and what happens if he talks to you like he did again. If it occurs, it won't be pretty."

"Wow." India lit up but then looked concerned again. "Please tell me he's got something up his sleeve."

"No. He doesn't."

"So twelve paintings have become ten. Considering the size of his canvases, it's a lot more than it sounds like." India pushed her fingers into her hair.

I agreed. We had just expanded the square footage of our Chicago gallery, and the part of it that was meant for exhibitions would look strange if we didn't fill it like planned.

"I made him choose, just to see what he'd do. Believe it or not, somewhere behind his image of entitled artist, there's somewhat of a realist. The idea of canceling and losing his contract immediately sobered him, so to speak." I grinned and sat down on the edge of her desk.

"So?" India rested her chin in her hand. "Do share your wisdom, please. I can use some of it so as not to strangle him when I see him next time."

"He agreed to share the showing with another artist."

"Really?" India gawked at me. "Mr. God's-gift-to-the-art-world is ready to share?"

"He is."

"With whom? Do we have anyone who can toss a few paintings in? They need to be new ones and—" India broke off and sighed. "And you've already picked someone. You're always several steps ahead, which drives me nuts, or would, if I didn't learn so darn much. So, who is it—oh, *oh*!" India caught on quickly, I could tell. "Hayden?"

"I'll at least ask her. It might be a great way for her to experience what having a showing is all about without having to do it alone. This way, if the reception of her art is less enthusiastic than I hope, we'll find out and can work with her on it and not burn any bridges to the critics."

India mulled this idea over. I could envision her weighing the pros and cons. I was aware that none of my other artists, who were all established in their own right, were ready or willing to share a showing with Andreas Holmer. His reputation for being full of himself and hard to work with had spread, it seemed. I hoped to shake this less than desirable trait out of him, as his talent was undeniable, but the outcome of such an attempt was, of course, still up in the air. Besides, I had the notion Hayden might just be the type who could fearlessly challenge someone like Andreas.

"Hello? Wakey, wakey. Greer?" India waved in front of my face. "Where did you go?"

"Sorry. I was considering how to bring this up with Hayden. I suppose the sooner the better. I'm picking her up on Sunday. That'll do."

"You're seeing her already on Sunday?" India's eyes began to sparkle, and she leaned toward me. "First lunch, which you've given me zero juicy details about, I might add. Then Sunday brunch or something?"

"Wrong. She's not going to visit me. One of my neighbors invited her to her house. Penelope Moore." I stood but pivoted at India's gasp.

"Penelope Moore? *That* Penelope Moore. The author?"

"I believe she's a writer, yes. You've clearly heard of her." I took two steps back as India flung her hands in the air.

"Heard of her? I know you've got precious little time to read, but if there's anything you should read, it's her books. She's an amazing fantasy author. Critics compare her to Tolkien and all the greats of the early fantasy era. J.K. Rowling has been compared to *her*."

"She's lived on my street for as long as I can remember." I'd inherited my house from my grandfather after visiting him every week for most of my life. The last year of his life, I'd sold my condo and stayed with him. He had around-the-clock care, but I'd spent as much time with him as I could. I'd never been away from my business as much as I was during that time, but it was important to me. "All this time I had no idea who she was."

"I've read all her *Ylanthia* novels. There are twelve of them, at least four hundred pages each. Love thick books." India looked starstruck. "I need to take a stroll past her house next time I'm at your place. All casual like."

"Don't be ridiculous," I said and laughed. "I'll introduce you when there's a right time for it. On Sunday, we plan to drop in on Penelope and her husband, Hayden and I." I told India what had taken place at the lunch restaurant.

"Oh, boy. That's amazing. Hayden's full of surprises. I normally play the devil's advocate when you put forward some of your more unorthodox ideas, but this time, about Chicago I mean, you're very clever to do it this way. I hope mama Leyla doesn't throw a paintbrush in the gears."

"What do you mean? Hayden's an adult. If she doesn't want to do it, fine, but I'll be damned if—what?" I glowered at India, who was shaking her head with a sorrowful expression on her face.

"What if Hayden isn't in charge of her own affairs? I mean, she clearly has some problems handling certain situations. What if someone in her family has some sort of guardianship over her? God forbid, if that's the case, what if it's Leyla Rowe?"

"Shit." I hadn't even thought of that. Hayden hadn't said anything about it, and why would she? It's not something you'd just blurt out to a stranger. "Hello, I'm not in charge of my own life. My mother calls all the shots." My rampaging mind reeled. To be honest, I didn't think Hayden had been declared incompetent. Still, if I intended to do business with her, I needed to find out once and for all.

I decided to wait until after Sunday. This wasn't something you asked over the phone, and I didn't want to ruin the Sunday outing for Hayden by bringing up something potentially hurtful. Turning to India, I sighed. "I'll make sure."

"Good. For what it's worth, I don't believe it." India stood and approached me. "What are you doing tonight?"

"I have a date with my hot tub, and then I'll watch my favorite shows I recorded during the week. I'm certainly not in the mood to socialize. Got to deal with some work tomorrow, but tonight, my sights are set on chocolate, the couch, and my sixty-inch plasma TV."

"And here I hoped I could persuade you to go to a party with us. We can both bring a 'plus one,' and Erica is taking a guy from her work as hers. He's new to the Boston area, so she's doing it as a favor."

"I'm sorry. Sweet of you to ask, but you better think of someone else. I can't imagine anything I want less, I'm afraid." I smiled wryly, knowing India wasn't offended.

"All right. My yoga coach is never hard to convince." She grinned in a way that said she'd been prepared for my bowing out.

I gently touched her shoulder. "Thanks. And have fun."

"Oh, I will." India pointed at her computer. "But no rest for the wicked. Tons of stuff to do before I can even plan what to wear to the party."

"I better get back to it as well." I sauntered to my office and found myself thinking about Hayden and her work. Of the paintings I'd seen, several would fit in the Chicago gallery.

I needed to see more, to choose from a wider selection, but remembering the multitude of paintings sitting in the old gym hall, I was certain we'd find the right ones. I prayed India's and my sense of Hayden being in charge of her affairs and her life was correct. If Leyla was the one ultimately calling the shots, we were pretty much screwed.

CHAPTER NINE

As it turned out, Hayden had one major issue with cars. Not that she was afraid of riding in them or had to go through some sort of ritual to get in. It was worse than that. Hayden insisted on driving.

"You have a driver's license?" I blurted out before I edited myself.

Hayden merely nodded. "Yes." She opened the trunk and placed a bag, an easel, and a large canvas there. Dressed in jeans and a windbreaker over what looked like a white T-shirt, she looked lovely and casual.

"I—I wasn't aware of that." I looked at my baby, my Mercedes SUV. I honestly loved this car and turned to Hayden to tell her it was out of the question. The words froze on the tip of my tongue at the sight of her sparkling eyes. Her full lips were slightly parted, and she regarded my car with a dreamy expression. "I have to ask, are you an experienced driver?"

"I have only driven once a week during the last year, but before then I drove almost every day."

"You own a car?"

"No."

"Then how?" This was confusing.

"I drive Nana's car. She has a white Lincoln Town Car from 2006. I used to chauffeur her where she needed to go, and when she was hospitalized, she told me to keep using it." Hayden leaned forward and peered into the front seat. "You keep it tidy."

Not sure why Hayden sounded equal parts surprised and pleased, or if I should be insulted she pointed it out at all, I said, "Thank you." I tried to think of how to refuse her without hurting her feelings but came up with zero. It began to dawn on me I was setting a daunting precedent for the future if I couldn't say no to her regarding something this small. "All right. On one condition."

Hayden was already in the driver's seat, adjusting it. So far I didn't see any sign of paintbrushes. "Yes?"

"You have to listen to my directions and still maneuver safely." I had no way of knowing anything about her multi-tasking ability.

Hayden looked surprised. "How else would I be able to drive there? I don't know where you live."

"Good." Dreading this experience, I sat down in the passenger seat, realizing this was the first time I'd ever sat there. Buckling up, I said a small prayer to whatever deity was ready to listen.

Hayden started the car and checked all the mirrors, adjusting them meticulously. With soft hands and practiced ease, she pulled into traffic. I don't know what I'd expected, but any misgivings on my part were clearly unnecessary—and I had to admit, prejudiced. I guided Hayden toward Beacon Hill and to the street where I'd spent a good deal of my childhood, teens, and all of my adult life the last twelve years. We didn't speak much in the car, other than my giving her directions, since I didn't want to distract her. She seemed fine with the moments of silence, which was such a big difference from the times I drove somewhere with India in the car. She either chatted nonstop or sang with the radio.

Large maple trees, just starting to sprout leaves, lined the street. As it was a Sunday, some of my neighbors were out in their front yards getting them ready for spring and summer. I had a gardener who took care of the yard for me, as I had no time for such things and knew next to nothing about it. Still, it was cozy seeing people tend to their homes in the sun.

"You can turn in there." I pointed at my driveway. "That's my house."

Hayden did as I said and parked the car. Stepping out, I noticed Hayden had managed to center the car perfectly. I wasn't surprised.

"Here we are then. My home. Used to be my grandfather's."

"Your paternal or maternal grandfather?" Hayden asked and looked up the old brownstone house with its three floors and rooftop area.

"My mother's father."

"He died?"

"Yes. Twelve years ago."

"Were you sad?"

"Very." Curious at the short and choppily asked questions, as I didn't remember Hayden asking very many before, I studied her carefully. Was she pondering what might happen to her grandmother's house whenever she passed away? Or how she'd mourn?

"Want to go inside? I'll give you a tour." I motioned toward the heavy double oak door.

"Yes."

Hayden walked up the flagstone walkway, and after I unlocked the door and switched off the alarm, she stood in my foyer and pivoted slowly. I knew it was an impressive sight with the massive marble staircase and tall ceilings.

"Here. Let me take your jacket."

She let the jacket slip off, looking absentminded as she took everything in.

"I had it restored to its original state." I motioned at the stairs. "My grandfather had a lift installed the last two years of his life. It ran along the railing."

"Was he ill?"

"Like your grandmother, he suffered a stroke. His left side was affected and he couldn't manage the stairs." This information piqued Hayden's interest and she scrutinized them.

"He lived in his home despite his condition?" Hayden walked closer and stopped with a hand on the bannister. "I've wished so many times I could care for Nana." She pushed her hand down into her jeans pocket and moved around something I figured was a small type of brush.

"Looks like her stroke hit harder than my grandfather's did," I said, gently placing my hand on Hayden's. It twitched underneath mine, and she gazed at our hands as if she'd discovered a mystical entity sitting on the polished wood. I moved my hand before she became too uncomfortable. "Want to tour the bottom floor first?"

"Yes."

We walked into the main reception room, the area I mainly used whenever I was entertaining guests. I had kept my grandfather's beautiful oriental rugs but had removed his carpet and redone the hardwood floors. The walls were off-white to display parts of my personal art collection.

Hayden stopped so abruptly, I nearly walked right into her. Her eyes, wide and bright, took in the room and, mainly, the artwork. She walked slowly across the floor to the large Salvaggi above the couch. Kicking off her shoes, she climbed onto the cushions and stood close to the painting. She didn't touch it but moved her hands in patterns as she examined it, as if she was following the painter's brushstrokes. The motif, a Tuscan vineyard illuminated by a setting sun, was romantic but also one of my grandfather's favorites. I had bought it for him after I brokered my first art deal at twenty-three.

Hayden jumped down but ignored her shoes as she regarded the painting from across the room.

"My granddad loved this. He was often in Italy as a young man. During World War Two, he was deployed to Sicily, and afterward, he stayed and hiked all through this devastated but beautiful country. He met his wife there, a British nurse. They spent their honeymoon in Tuscany before they returned to Boston. They went back every few years throughout their lives."

"And the painter?"

"This is by a young man, Milo Salvaggi. It's sad he didn't survive to experience his fame. He got cancer two years after painting this." It had broken my heart to learn of Milo's rapidly progressing illness. He'd been destined for greatness but never lived to see what success his body of work up till then had reached.

"He was very good. Do you have more by him?"

"No. I was tempted to buy more, as all his pieces were amazing, but I didn't think it was fair. His work should be divided up and shared. Be viewed in museums, which it is. I sometimes loan this one to a museum or a gallery. It's rather funny, but I miss it when it's gone."

"That's not funny. On the contrary, since it makes you sad." Frowning, Hayden looked at me with concern. "I wasn't aware you could miss an inanimate object. I miss Nana every day, but she's a person."

"Perhaps..." I stopped to think. "Perhaps this painting represents a little bit what I felt for my grandfather, and also the sadness about the artist dying so young." I studied Hayden, who looked back and forth between the piece of art and me.

"I see." Her expression made me think she actually did.

"If you were away from your paintings and brushes for longer than a few days, you'd miss them and what painting makes you feel and experience, right?"

Hayden paled. "I've already experienced that. Many times, when I was younger."

I could've kicked myself. Of course she had. I just had to go and psychoanalyze her, didn't I? "I'm sorry, Hayden."

"Why? You weren't responsible." She looked honestly nonplussed at my apology. Her color had returned already and she was curiously exploring the room. We viewed some of my other pieces of art, but she didn't react to any of them with the same passionate examination as she'd done with Milo's Tuscan vineyard.

The kitchen coaxed out her faint smile. She stood in the center of the floor between the kitchen island and the breakfast nook and pivoted slowly. "I like it." She pointed at the bay window. "You have a window seat. Nana has one too."

So this part of the house felt homey to her. This pleased me no end. I loved it too, even if I rarely cooked. Again, I saw myself sitting as a little girl at the table, eating waffles. Granddad used to make them, dressed in his apron with a big lobster on the front. "I sat on that window seat and read for hours." I smiled at the old memories. "Mainly books about young girls and horses when I was twelve to fourteen. Did you go through a horse phase too?"

"No." Hayden shook her head. "I sometimes attempted to draw horses and other animals in my room. I spent a lot of time there. My nana says if she hadn't gotten custody of me, I would still be there." Her dark-gray eyes grew almost black. "After I went to live with Nana and Gramps, I could go wherever I wanted, and paint anything."

So Leyla's idea about locking Hayden up and away from people was an old habit. Or method. Was she so ashamed of having a daughter with a psycho-psychiatric condition? I just didn't get it. Granted, I had no way of knowing what Hayden had been like at that age and younger, but that still didn't excuse breaking the law and locking someone in their room. "I'm relieved too. I can't imagine what it might've been like for you if you hadn't been allowed to develop your art. There's only so much you can do from inside a room."

"I sketched what was on TV when I lived at my mother's. It was...difficult to find the right perspective, the correct textures. When I came to stay with Nana, I touched everything in her house and outside. I smelled it. I tasted it too."

"Everything?" I wondered if she meant it literally.

"No. A lot. When I put grass and dirt in my mouth, my Nana stopped me and said smelling it was enough. I agreed."

"Good thing you did." I smiled at her, but inside I was appalled—not at the dirt-tasting, but at the implication of *why* the very young Hayden had done this. Had she not been outdoors at all before? Surely that wasn't the case? I couldn't bring myself to ask. Hayden would tell me the truth, but I wasn't prepared to hear it. Not yet. I might react in a way that would land me in prison.

"Oh, my. Where are my manners?" Eager to change the topic, I hurried to the fridge. "Can I get you anything to drink?"

"Mineral water." Hayden had turned to look at a small piece of artwork, when she stopped herself. "Thank you."

"You're welcome." I pulled out two bottles and filled our glasses after adding some ice. "Here you are."

We kept strolling through the house, Hayden commenting and asking questions every now and then. The second floor held the four bedrooms and en suites, which didn't seem to spike her curiosity. She looked at the artwork and only stopped with interest when we reached my bedroom. Scanning the room I'd decorated in light blue, gold-beige, and white, since I loved the New England style, she nodded as if approving. Those colors combined with dark wood furniture gave my eyes the rest they needed after a day of looking at colorful pieces of art.

"Serene," Hayden murmured, sounding dazed. "Like the beach. Sky over sand and water. Serene."

"Hayden?" Concerned at her tone, I reacted without thinking, putting my arm loosely around her waist.

Hayden went rigid but didn't withdraw. She turned within my light grasp, her eyes huge. "Greer?"

"You all right? You sounded a little out of it."

"Out of what?"

"You sounded a bit overcome."

"I'm not. I'm fine." Her polite toothy smile appeared as an afterthought. "Thank you for asking."

Her learned politeness would have been discouraging if it wasn't for the fact she was still accepting my arms halfway around her.

"Good," I said lightly and let go. "Now, I've saved the best for you." I pointed upward. "Come on." I nearly took her by the hand but thought better of it. I didn't want to scare her off by being too forward. My inner words gave me pause and nearly made me trip on the first step on the stairs leading to my rooftop garden. *Being too forward?* With Hayden? I gave myself a mental kick at even having such thoughts. So unprofessional.

Hayden's reaction to my favorite place in the house—in the world, really—was worth everything. Her mouth fell open, and she simply stood among all the evergreen plants and the ones just starting to come up. The comfortable deck chairs, the fire pit, and the hot tub—nothing escaped her laser attention. I still waited for her to discover the best thing from her point of view. The moment she spotted it, I knew I'd done the right thing by bringing her here.

"A studio?" Hayden whispered with reverence, her voice sounding fragile. "You have a *studio*?"

"I do. Granddad built this for me when I was a teenager, thinking my painting might be good enough. It wasn't, even if my eye for art is. I use it as storage during the winter for the deckchairs and so on. It's empty, and my house cleaner just gave it a once-over. Want to take a look?"

She gave me her familiar "stupid question" look. "Yes."

I opened the door for her, and we stepped into the small, but airy and bright studio. Designed like a 175-square-foot greenhouse, it had walls and a roof made of wood-framed glass. Granddad had made sure you could open half of the windowpanes, to avoid being virtually cooked in there in the summer. I'd even celebrated some fun teenage sleepovers up here, as my birthday is in July.

"You like it?" I had to ask as her now-blank face startled me.

"It's a real studio. Better than the gym hall. Better than the conservatory at Nana's. It's up here, away from everything…like the sky!" Hayden wrapped her arms around herself and squeezed. Her eyes glistened with tears, and I think my next crazy idea began to take form right then. How could I deny her the chance to paint in a place nobody else used? I had to find a way for Hayden to do all her new work here. It was clear to me, judging from the look on her radiant face, that whatever she created here would be something new and amazing.

CHAPTER TEN

It took me a while to tear Hayden away from her new favorite place—my rooftop studio. She explored every windowpane, every board, and if I hadn't interrupted her, I was pretty sure she would have dropped to her knees and examined the floor as well, tile by tile.

"Did anyone paint here besides you?" Hayden walked backward out of the studio.

"No. Only I did, until I realized I wasn't very good. We tried growing a few plants here at one point. Tomatoes. Cucumbers."

"Until you realized you weren't a good horticulturist either?"

I burst out laughing. Hayden had asked from such an innocent and logical assumption. "Exactly." It was true. I didn't have a green thumb by any means.

"It should be used," Hayden said dreamily as we walked downstairs.

"I think so too. I'll get back to you about this. I promise."

"Good."

"Now's a good time to head over to the Moores'. You all set?"

"I need my shoes." Hayden walked into my living room and put on her loafers. I hadn't even noticed she wasn't wearing them as we walked outside on the rooftop. No doubt, Hayden's changing facial expressions enthralled me too much.

"I'm ready." Hayden stood by the door, the excitement back on her face.

"Want to get your stuff from my car?"

"Yes."

Hayden seemed set on carrying everything herself but relented when I offered to carry the canvas.

"Mrs. Moore might not be able to sit for you very long today, but you can set a schedule that fits both of you."

"Any day but Thursday and Saturday. Thursdays I teach with you, and Saturdays I visit Nana." Hayden looked at me seriously.

"That gives you five days to fiddle with."

"Yes."

The Moores' house was bigger than mine and located on a corner lot facing the park area. It was clear Penelope Moore enjoyed gardening. Tulips were already in blossom, as were several cherry trees. This gave the house a charming fairy-tale setting. Even I, who despised cuteness in art and design, had to admit that. I rang the doorbell, and it only took a few moments for a young woman to appear at the door. Dressed in jeans and a green golf shirt, she smiled politely. "Yes, can I help you?"

"Mrs. Moore asked us to come by anytime." Hayden spoke up before I had a chance. "This is a convenient time for us. Is she home? She said she and her husband Edward are always home."

"She is. Let me get her for you." The woman looked curiously at Hayden before opening the door fully. "Please come in and wait."

The Moores' impressive foyer was also cozy. Antiques and art-deco pieces reflected the owners' eclectic taste. White marble floors and stairs made it bright and airy.

Determined steps alerted us of Mrs. Moore's approach. Hayden gripped some brushes and held them in front of her like a shield.

Penelope Moore walked up to us, extending her hand. She wore navy-blue slacks and a light-gray blouse, the latter badly wrinkled in a few places as if from being bunched up. "Ms. Rowe. May I call you Hayden?"

"It's my name, so yes." Hayden relaxed.

"Excellent. Please call me Penelope. I'm so glad you realized I meant what I said about dropping in. Greer." Penelope turned to me and shook my hand. "This is long overdue. I've seen you around the neighborhood since you were a little girl."

"Thank you, Penelope. I agree." I stepped closer to Hayden. "Hayden's really set on starting her work on your portrait."

Penelope glanced back and forth between Hayden and me, her clear eyes proving she didn't miss much. She smiled gently and nodded. "Actually, your timing couldn't be better. Tina and I just helped Edward into bed for his nap. He gets tired so quickly these days. Especially after the visit to the restaurant. That's why we seldom go out. It takes him a full week to bounce back afterward. Sometimes longer."

"Who is Tina? Your daughter?" Hayden asked.

"No, dear. We never had any children, Edward and I. Tina is one of his caregivers. We have around-the-clock help." Penelope motioned for us to follow her. She led the way through a living room decorated in a more modern style, but still with fantastic art and antiques everywhere. At the far end of the living room, a French double door led to the conservatory. Here exotic plants grew and blossomed in a multitude of colors. I heard Hayden whimper and guessed it was from the onslaught of beauty.

"Will this do, Hayden?" Penelope asked.

"Yes." Hayden unfolded a portable easel as she gazed around, her eyes focused. "I want you over there, on one of the wrought-iron chairs. You might need a cushion so you don't get sore."

I covered my eyes for a moment. Hayden was direct and expected everyone to take her words at face value. I hoped Penelope wouldn't be too stunned when she understood Hayden was concerned she may get a sore butt from the unforgiving chair.

"Very considerate. I'm sure you're right." Penelope turned to leave but stopped as Tina entered the conservatory.

"Excuse me, Penelope. I checked on Edward and he's fast asleep already. Is there anything I can bring you out here? Perhaps some coffee?"

"Lovely idea, Tina," Penelope said. She introduced us and then asked Tina to fetch cushions and coffee for all of us. Clearly, Tina functioned as more than Edward's nurse. I guessed she also helped Penelope with the daily chores.

Tina returned balancing a tray on one hand and carrying red cushions under the other arm.

"Goodness, child," Penelope said and moved as if to take the tray, but I beat her to it.

"Allow me." I placed the tray on the round wrought-iron table and liberated her from the cushions. Tina shot me a broad smile in return. I placed the cushions on three of the chairs and glanced at Hayden, whose eyes had narrowed and gone close to black. Confused, I walked over to her. "Want me to help you set up?"

"Yes." Glaring at Tina, Hayden pushed her bag into my hands. "Put my colors in order over there." She pointed at a table normally used for work on the pots and plants.

"Yes, ma'am." I began sorting her oils, looking at her sideways. What did she have against Tina?

"Please. I forgot to say please." Hayden shook her head. "Nana tells me all the time."

"Ah. Never mind that. You just focus on the portrait. I'll be over here with my coffee." I don't know what I was thinking, or if I thought at all, but I kissed Hayden's cheek. I did it as reassurance as well as with affection, and then it dawned on me and I waited for Hayden's inevitable evasive reaction.

But no. Hayden stopped in mid-movement and seemed to hold her breath as she turned to look at me. She let go of her brushes—luckily they fell onto the table and not the brick floor—and raised her hand to her cheek. Touching the spot I kissed, she stared at me with huge eyes, now bright and wondrous. My heart boomed. I'd been so certain I'd overstepped Hayden's boundaries once and for all, but instead she looked like I'd given her an unexpected gift.

The scraping of a chair being dragged against the bricks made me jump. Hayden blinked and refocused her attention on Penelope, who took her seat.

"Perhaps you want me to wear something fancier than this?" Penelope looked down at her outfit, plucking at the hem of her blouse.

"No." Hayden was busy sketching using a pencil. "You're perfect like that."

"Why, thank you, dear." Penelope's eyes softened. She relaxed where she sat and didn't ask any more questions.

I nursed my excellent cup of coffee and watched Hayden work. She drew the outline of Penelope and the surrounding flowers and plants. A faint grid suggested she wouldn't leave out the fact that we were in the conservatory. I remembered Hayden had wanted to paint Penelope in an outdoor setting, but it seemed true to her nature to keep it real. The old structure was lovely, its old charm undeniable.

"Will we disturb you if we talk?" Penelope asked.

"No." Sounding distracted, Hayden glanced at me and then back at Penelope. "As long as I'm not expected to answer."

"You're not." Penelope turned her attention to me. "It made me glad to see you move into the neighborhood. Geoffrey often spoke of you and kept us apprised of your success when you started out in the art business."

"He did? Did you attend any of his music events?" Memories of Geoffrey Landon, my grandfather, flooded my senses. He had been famous for his music soirees. Small evening gatherings with friends and neighbors, one piano or a string instrument—his all-time-favorite was the cello—and he would be one big grin. I didn't partake as much as he'd liked, but on occasion I did. I was particularly glad I had been present for the few private performances of Vivian Harding, one of the world's most celebrated mezzo-sopranos. She had later gone blind, which might have ended her illustrious career, but it didn't. India, who had her ear to the ground regarding everything to do with famous LGBT people, kept me updated on Vivian's continued success and personal happiness.

"I did, until Edward couldn't participate anymore. It was he who had the interest in classical music, but now he doesn't respond to it anymore." Penelope sighed. Then she lit up. "But you can never guess what he did respond to and hasn't let go of lately."

I had to admit, I had no clue.

"The drawing Hayden made of me at the restaurant!" Penelope beamed. "I had it framed for him, and he has it on his nightstand. He keeps touching it and looks at me and says, 'But, darling, it's you.'"

"It's a fantastic sketch," I said. "I guess you never know what's going to resonate with people. What happened to Mr. Moore?"

"Just call him Edward, dear." Penelope waved her hand. "He has rather advanced Alzheimer's, I'm afraid. He recognizes me most of the time, but on his bad days, he calls me 'Mother.' On his worst days, he calls me horrible things. I think he forgets he's married to a wrinkly old woman and wonders where his young Penelope went." Her eyes filled with unspeakable sorrow, and I glimpsed the hell it could be to witness a loved one fade away and disappear little by little.

"Is he on any of the new medications?"

"Yes, for quite some time. Our doctor says they're not working as well for him as they did initially." Pressing her fingertips against her lips, as if to keep them from trembling, Penelope gently cleared her throat. "I'm sorry. I'm sure you didn't come here to listen to this."

"On the contrary," Hayden broke in, indicating she'd

heard every word. "I don't mind listening to your story. My grandmother is in a facility, and I wish I could learn from you how you are able to care for your husband at home. I've been told it's impossible for me to do so for Nana." Hayden stopped working for a moment. "Greer cared for her grandfather until he died. We have an understanding and interest you can rely on."

"When you put it that way." Penelope looked stunned. "Thank you. I'm reluctant to share what our daily life is like with friends and family. They hate seeing Edward like this since it muddles their image of him as strong, vibrant, even arrogant and proud. Going from being the focal figure of every gathering and enjoying it immensely to becoming this husk of a man…It's hard for the ones who loved the old Edward. Our friends adored our parties, and we were always honored guests at theirs since Edward loved socializing. He had a way of making every single person feel seen and validated and, God forbid, never bored. I was the introvert, the author who lived more in my head than outside of it."

"And now it's all changed for you?" I spoke gently.

"Now? Now Edward looks at them uncertainly, like a bashful child, and on occasion he'll lash out when he's frustrated for not recognizing them."

"My granddad became frustrated when he had his second stroke and couldn't even use the lift. He was confined to his bedroom if I wasn't there, as he refused to let the staff help him downstairs. He didn't trust them. I think he was a little paranoid, so sure they were out to get him. It was hard to see him struggle like that." I blinked at the burning sensation behind my eyelids.

Hayden had started painting again, still laying down background by blocking in colors. "Nana gets angry and tosses things. She tries to speak and I understand most of what she says, but the staff doesn't, and she pushes the dinner tray off the table and just yells. The staff says she's hard to deal with. I don't understand this. I understand *her* but not them. They're supposed to be experts." Hayden gripped her brush hard. She took an unused one and swept it under her chin. "I wish I was able to care for her. They say I don't possess the skills because of my own condition."

"Condition?" Penelope asked.

I held my breath, as I had never asked Hayden about herself regarding this subject. I was worried how she'd react to Penelope's question.

"When I was two years old, my parents learned I'm autistic. At ten, other doctors tested me and confirmed the diagnosis but said also that I'm high functioning. Two years later, they concluded that it's Asperger's syndrome."

"All I see is a lovely young woman who's immensely talented." Penelope smiled at Hayden, her eyes warm. "That said, I don't mean to belittle any struggles you might go through, or potential intolerance."

"I prefer to be treated like a person. I know my limitations. I don't function well in crowds. Loudness of any kind induces symptoms. My mother's presence does too. My nana used to tell me to avoid negative stress. This last year it's been impossible."

The mere thought of Leyla made me clench my jaws. "So this is perfect in more ways than one. We all understand some things about each other that few in the outside world do." I wanted the other two to relax and trust in this understanding from experience. "We don't have to explain in great detail to know we're understood."

"You're absolutely right." Penelope leaned against the backrest and tipped her head back, closing her eyes as the sun flickered through the leaves.

"Straighten up." Hayden frowned. "Please." She shot me a glance.

I smiled at her barely remembered politeness.

"Whoops." Penelope raised her head. "Forgot."

"Penelope?" Tina said from the living room threshold. "Excuse me, but you have a phone call."

"Unless it's an emergency or my sister, please take a message."

"Will do." Tina gave me a broad smile. "May I offer you something else, Ms. Landon? Anything at all?"

Now her flirtation was obvious. Some people's gaydar ran on the highest setting. Not a bad thing at all, but as I wasn't even remotely interested in the cute and perky caregiver, it annoyed me that my own was slow on the uptake.

As it turned out, whatever setting my intuition had at the moment, looking at Hayden showed it worked fine when it mattered. She glowered at Tina, and her full lips compressed to thin lines. She was clearly unimpressed, and had I not known better I'd say she looked jealous.

"No, thank you. I'm good," I said, answering Tina. Cringing, I wanted to tell Hayden that if this was indeed jealousy on her part, it was totally uncalled for, as Tina couldn't compare to her for a fraction of a second. Of course I'd never put it like that out loud, as that would be admitting to the world that I was attracted to and *really* cared about Hayden. I had to keep this professional. Loyal friendship at the most.

A sharp crack made us all jump. Tina blinked and left the doorway. I looked at the broken brush in Hayden's hands and stood hastily. Rushing over to her, I took her hands in mine. "Did you hurt yourself?" Those brushes are made of hard, sturdy wood. For Hayden to snap one would take quite some force.

"I'm not…injured." Pale, but not looking upset, Hayden let go of the broken brush and gripped my hands firmly. She looked into my eyes, broke eye contact for a moment, and then met my gaze again. She repeated this action a few times before giving up. She turned to grab a new brush but stopped in mid-motion. Her lower lip trembled as she inspected the broken brush on the floor between us.

I bent and picked it up. "You know, there's nothing we can't fix. In this case, with some glue."

"And in other cases?" Hayden whispered.

"We can always find some medium to fix whatever's broken. No matter what." My promise was more than I could keep, but she needed reassurance. I knew this even if she was unaware.

"All right." Turning to dip a new brush in some ochre, Hayden seemed to be done with the topic. At least for now.

I reeled, though, mainly for having confessed my true feelings to myself. I'm very good at denying my emotions to myself if necessary—it's easier that way, but I couldn't hide from the way I cared about Hayden. I didn't want to dissect them. Not yet. I'd taken such a leap for myself; acknowledging my feelings held a personal element with traces of romance. This wasn't just huge; it was monumental and scary as hell. What was I to do with such emotions when it came to a woman like Hayden? I could, of course, do what my nature dictated and ignore them. Why this turned out to be impossible, I had a vague notion. No matter what, I would need to keep things professional and still make Hayden understand that no woman like Tina—or anyone else, for that matter—was a threat. Was Hayden jealous, or did she just dislike the caregiver for some unknown reason?

I sat down again, sipping my now-cold coffee. Hayden focused on her work again, and Penelope seemed far away in her thoughts. I didn't feel like talking either, so I passed the time studying the woman who'd consumed most of my thoughts these last weeks. Considering the questions I wanted to ask her, I wasn't sure which to bring up first—the exhibition opportunity in Chicago or moving in to stay with me and use my empty studio. Then there was the issue of her legal status.

If Leyla called the shots or if Hayden declined either of my offers, I wasn't fooling myself—it would hit me hard.

CHAPTER ELEVEN

Penelope sat for Hayden for more than an hour before Tina reappeared. We kept conversation to a minimum, and it was a comfortable silence, something I valued, as my days usually consisted of meetings and negotiations, which meant talk-talk-talk.

"Penelope? Edward is awake and is asking for you." The young caregiver looked apologetic. I glanced at Hayden, who ignored the interruption.

"Thank you, Tina." Penelope nodded and stood, looking stiff as she rolled her shoulders. "How's your work coming along, Hayden? You've worked with such focus, I'm very curious."

"You can take a look." Hayden gestured to the canvas.

Penelope and I stepped closer, and I found myself staring at the painting. Hayden had managed to sketch, lay down background, and paint a great deal of Penelope's face and hair. She'd barely hinted at the flowers and plants so far, but the details of Penelope's face, her dreamy-yet-strong expression, drew me in as if it was indeed filled with the older woman's life force. How Hayden had been able to paint every detail with this meticulous care, I had no idea, even if I had followed every brushstroke. Penelope's hair gleamed in the sun, her eyes radiated such brightness, yet shadows lurked when I looked closer.

"That's how you see me, child?" Penelope whispered. "You

have a talent…no, more than that. You have a *gift*. The way you tell the story of my presence, of the now I live in, is amazing."

"May I leave the easel and the painting here until I can continue?" Hayden looked as if Penelope's praise hadn't touched her at all, but I could tell from the way she stood there, no brushes in her hands at the moment, her face so relaxed and that enigmatic little smile in place, that she was content.

"Certainly, Hayden. Do you have anything to cover it with?"

"Yes."

"Good. Tina and I need to tend to Edward." Penelope pressed both hands into the small of her back with a wry smile. "It's quite the workout. Keeps me fit in my old age."

"You've been very hospitable, Penelope. Thank you." I extended my hand to her, but Penelope took me by the shoulders and kissed my cheek. Not a polite air kiss, but a real one.

"You're most welcome. And you two can pop in anytime. Don't wait too long. I loved having you here."

"We'll be back in a few days." I thought I could promise this, as I knew Hayden was itching to work on the portrait.

"All days but Thursdays and Saturdays," Hayden said again. She wiped her hands on a rag, which she folded into a neat square and placed on the ledge of the easel. Her hands were still stained, but I figured she could wash up later at my house.

Penelope repeated the gesture again, kissing Hayden's cheek. I held my breath, but Hayden merely grew a bit rigid. We began walking toward the foyer when a voice bellowing from upstairs made us jump.

"Penny! Penny!" A male voice that had to be Edward's roared. "Damn woman, where are you? Who locked me up in here?"

"Oh, my. Got to dash." Penelope hurried up the stairs, and I heard Tina try to calm the agitated old man.

As we let ourselves out through the front door, Hayden's furrowed brow showed her concern.

"What are you thinking?" I asked.

"Why did Mr. Moore—Edward—assume Penelope locked him up? Doesn't he realize she's just trying to keep him safe?"

"I think he's too affected by the Alzheimer's to understand. He's forgotten big portions of his life and tries still to make sense of it all."

"Nana often acts out too."

"That's different. Your grandmother is still herself, even if her speech is impaired and her body affected. She still has her memories of her life and of you. When she demonstrates frustration, it's because she mourns that her life didn't turn out the way she'd counted on and hoped."

"And I can't do anything to help her. I tried to talk to her doctors, but even if I'm listed as her next of kin and she signed the medical power of attorney to me, they claim I can't manage her care at home. Nana always said I knew her and her wishes better than anyone. I should be able to make things better for her, but I'm failing." Hayden's jaw worked after she stopped talking. Her eyes filled with tears and she stopped just outside Penelope's gate.

"You're not failing anyone." I spoke with all the conviction I could muster. Her expression gutted me, and I swore to keep that expression off her face in the future if possible. She had also answered one of my yet unspoken questions. No one could give medical power of attorney to someone who'd been declared legally incompetent. "I have a few suggestions for you to think over, and I hope you'll find them as exciting as I do. It might be something you can share with your nana next Saturday. Something she'll enjoy hearing."

Wiping at her eyes, Hayden cleared her throat. "What?"

"You like my rooftop studio, right?" I placed a gentle hand at the small of Hayden's back, ushering her toward my house.

"Yes."

"If you were staying in one of my guest rooms, you'd be

able to use it whenever you wanted." There. I'd voiced my idea out loud. I was aching as every single muscle group in my body tensed while anticipating her answer.

"Yes."

"Eh…yes, you understand, or yes, you want to move in with me?" Damn, I blushed at my choice of words.

"Yes. I want to move in with you. For how long?"

Forever. I nearly said it out loud but stopped before I made a complete fool of myself. "For as long as you want."

"All right. I'd like that."

"Your mother will blow a fuse." I liked the idea of Leyla imploding, but it wasn't fun to imagine Hayden caught in the crossfire.

"I doubt if her anger will affect the fuse boxes. She's not telekinetic. Just loud." Hayden wasn't joking.

"If you insist," I said, and smiled to ease the mood. "So you want to stay with me even if it sends you on a collision course with your mother?"

"Yes. And the second?"

"What? Oh, yes. The second thing. Would you want to show two of your paintings in Chicago in twelve days?"

"Which ones?"

Good question. Hayden hadn't declined, but perhaps that depended on which paintings she would want to show. "The one with the girl and the white picket fence, and any other painting you choose." This was a gamble, I realized, but it would show me which of her paintings Hayden valued the most.

"I'll pick four and you will choose from them. I'm not good at putting together a gallery showing. This is your area of expertise." Hayden walked up the flagstone path to my door. "I'll take some of my paintings from Nana's house to the gym hall." She looked determined and apprehensive. Perhaps she was reluctant to let more work be in her mother's presence.

"Why not ship them directly here? You have only a few suitcases with personal stuff at the gym hall. You could pick a day, and I'll come and get you and your things over here." Everything was moving so fast now, I felt dizzy.

"How about tomorrow? I can manage. I have Nana's car."

After Hayden cleaned her hands in my mudroom, we moved to the living room, where she sat on the far end of the couch. I sat down on the other end of it. "Works for me. I'm at the gallery until six p.m. I'll text you after I drive home."

"I'll be ready with my suitcases and the picket-fence painting." Hayden sounded breathless now. "Am I going to have a room of my own again…and a real bed? It's been so long."

I ached for her and the way she looked, so forlorn and hopeful at the same time. I scooted closer to her. "You're going to have a room, a bed, a closet, a bathroom, and most important, I imagine, a studio."

"And you." Hayden looked at me with wide eyes. "You'll be there too."

If she hadn't said "and you" in such a breathless manner, or looked at me with stormy eyes, I might have been able to stick to my noble intentions. Or perhaps that's a damn lie, because all I knew was how gorgeous and alluring she was and how I adored everything about her. Lacing my fingers through Hayden's hair, I slid them along her jawline and reveled in her silky complexion. "Yes, you have me," I murmured, and kissed her full lips. God, yes, she sure had me.

So soft, her lips grew even more pliant as I pressed my mouth to hers. The kiss was better than any other I could remember. Hayden parted her lips and pressed them more firmly against mine, showing me the kiss was welcome. Most important, she wasn't freaking out.

"This okay?" I murmured, my lips still on hers. "Mmm?"

"Yes." Hayden was out of breath, as was I, and she leaned against me.

As much as I wanted to pull her into a closer embrace, I was well aware this was a big step for both of us. No, huge. I had no idea what type of relationships Hayden might have had before she moved to the school. I doubted her nana had been the type to shield her from life. Hayden appeared innocent in some ways, but though she was different from most women her age, regardless of sexual orientation, she wasn't necessarily inexperienced. No matter what, I had to use caution, as our future relationship mattered to me more than I could say. It wasn't for the art and our professional collaboration, or at least that was a very small part of what I felt. I had come so far in my self-awareness I knew I was falling for her. If I wasn't careful, I could end up hurting Hayden badly, and that would shred my heart.

Pulling back a fraction of an inch, I cupped Hayden's cheeks and smoothed my thumbs across her cheekbones. Her features were delicate but with sharp planes and angles, giving her a strong charisma. She wasn't a classic beauty, but nobody could meet her silver-gray eyes, now more of a dark slate, and not be spellbound. Her long, thick eyelashes and her straight, dark eyebrows framed them beautifully.

Hayden's full lips moved, and she leaned forward as if trying to capture my lips. I kissed her back, a quick peck with closed lips, then smiled. In this very moment I was so damn happy—an unusual feeling for me, which felt as alien as it was wonderful.

"You're so lovely, and the way you kiss is bound to go to my head," I said, and moved my thumbs up and smoothed along her eyebrows. "You're amazing."

"I want to kiss you again," Hayden said, holding on to my shirt with strong fists, pulling me closer.

"There's nothing I'd rather do, but we need to be careful, Hayden."

"Why?"

"If we move too fast, we could both get hurt. I'd absolutely loathe hurting you, darling." The term of endearment came out before I realized what I meant to say.

"I don't want to hurt you either, but I might." Hayden's eyes lost their glitter.

"That goes for me too, but if we both acknowledge it's not

intentional, we should be able to talk it through." Heeding my own words, I had to ask her the most basic question or I might set myself up for immeasurable heartache down the road. "Hayden, you must recognize I'm a lesbian. Do you identify yourself as one too, or…?" I prayed she would confirm this point.

"Yes. Nobody else has asked me up front, but judging from my reaction to the female form, yes, I am," Hayden answered promptly. "For artwork, the male form is just as interesting and beautiful, but as a potential mate, I learned several years ago it's not for me." She leaned her cheek into my hand and gazed at me with longing. "I think the term is correct. I respond sexually to you."

"Oh, God, you do try my self-control." I chuckled and decided that any more intimate questions had to wait. I was already on fire and it was too much too soon—I didn't want to mix these breathtaking emotions with what I hoped and wished for her professionally. Something told me I was facing quite the challenge if Hayden was attracted to me and decided to act on her feelings.

"You're holding back. It's your protective side. I'm not as fragile as you think." Hayden smiled now but had stopped trying to get closer.

"Perhaps. Just indulge me. Look at it this way: it shows I truly care." I hoped she could understand what I meant. I wasn't trying to act superior or as if I knew best. Or maybe that last part wasn't entirely true. I assumed I had more life experience than Hayden did, which was true when it came to years. When it came to variety, Hayden had lived through things I couldn't even imagine, so it was a matter of perception.

"You're beautiful," Hayden murmured. She was still leaning into me, but in a relaxed manner now. "Your face tells a story, and your symmetrical features create the type of beauty painters have recognized for centuries."

Her romantic words, uttered with such typical honesty, stirred a new set of rampaging emotions in me. I kissed her forehead and then her lips. When I raised my head, I found Hayden had managed to drag me closer. I relented and just sat there with her, unable to remember when I'd last held someone like this. I've never been comfortable with cuddling for any long period of time, but with Hayden, the nearness felt natural.

Images of a furious Leyla set on destroying things for Hayden crept into my mind. Determined to stop her from interfering, I nuzzled the top of Hayden's hair, inhaling her clean scent as I pushed away the dark thoughts that threatened to ruin the moment. Soon enough I had to drive her back to the school, but I told myself it was just for one night.

Tomorrow, Hayden would come and stay with me.

CHAPTER TWELVE

I've always loved Mondays. They signified returning to work and diving into the business of my four galleries, and, if I could discover new talent, Mondays set the tone for the rest of the week. On this particular one, I was distracted and wasn't focusing on my paperwork. Instead, I itemized any potential hang-up Hayden might run into and worked on solutions for each one. India always claimed I was a "glass half-empty" kind of woman, and perhaps it was my pessimism that caused this endless list of what-ifs.

I glanced at my cell phone, debating whether to call Hayden. Having refrained from dialing her since last night, I gave in. I just needed to hear her voice.

"Greer," Hayden answered by way of greeting.

"Hello, there, Hayden. I'm just calling to see how you're doing."

"I've packed paintings, suitcases, and my art supplies. Will my easels fit in your SUV? I don't have enough space in the Lincoln." Hayden sounded as matter-of-fact as usual and not upset, which was a relief.

"I think so. My backseat folds down." Tipping back in my office chair, I smiled. "I'm so glad you think this is a good idea."

"I'll like the studio and the bed."

"I'll like having you with me." I hadn't planned to say something so personal over the phone, as I was uncertain how Hayden would interpret it. I knew she found it hard to express how she felt and that she thought I was too cryptic sometimes. "I guess I simply enjoy being around you." My warming cheeks made me cringe. I never blushed, normally.

"I want to be with you also."

I actually pressed a hand to the center of my chest. Hayden's words could mean so many different things, and despite being so straightforward, she could certainly say things that could have very different meanings. For now, I had to take everything at face value. If I started to read things into her words, I'd end up confusing both of us. "Great," I said. "I thought we could have dinner up on the rooftop patio tonight unless it starts to rain. I have gas heaters up there."

"We could see the stars." Hayden sounded as if she was smiling, and I didn't think I imagined it.

"Absolutely. See you at six, then. Call me if you need something. Anything, okay?"

"Okay. Bye." Hayden disconnected the call and I sat without moving for several minutes. So far so good. I told myself I was worrying unnecessarily. I'd simply drive over to the school, help Hayden fill my car up with paintings and easels, and then drive home. Hayden would follow in her Lincoln and everything would be *fine*.

The rest of my afternoon was more pleasant. I had a shipment of five paintings by a talented woman I'd discovered the last time I was in Paris. India and I unwrapped them carefully and spent an hour going over them, analyzing them in detail. I then made a point of wrapping up the rest of my more tedious tasks so I wouldn't leave Hayden waiting.

At 5:10 p.m. my phone rang and I answered without checking the display, distracted by a contractual mistake. I was expecting a call from one of my lawyers and was taken aback when I discovered it was Hayden. Not the calm, assertive woman from earlier in the day, but a Hayden with a hollow voice.

"Greer, you must come. Right now."

The contract I'd been working on disappeared from my

mind instantly. "What's wrong, Hayden?" I was already pulling on my jacket and slinging the messenger bag over my shoulder. "I'm on my way."

"Good. Hurry."

The call disconnected, and I shoved the cell phone into my inner pocket as I rushed through the outer office. "India?" I called out. "I'm leaving for today."

"Already?" India poked her head up from behind her screen. "Hey, you all right? What's up?"

I hadn't told India about the spontaneous plan Hayden and I had come up with. I didn't think she'd object, but she was protective of me, and I wasn't ready to add her "but-what-ifs" to my own list. "Oh, just an appointment I'd forgotten," I lied. "See you tomorrow."

I could tell India wasn't convinced, but perhaps something about my demeanor made her realize raising questions wasn't a good idea.

I drove to the school, cursing rush-hour traffic. Checking the time, I had to harness myself, as I was seriously stressing out. My heart jerked spasmodically as my idiotic mind created all kinds of horrific scenarios in which Leyla was causing Hayden grief. Yes, there were situations that could set Hayden off, I knew that, but her hollow, almost-dead voice didn't bode well. Hayden reacted differently when something triggered her fears. This had sounded…so bad.

As it was late afternoon, the parking lot at the school was half empty. I parked as close as I could to the main entrance and took the stairs two at a time. Pushing the door open, I hurried inside and headed for Hayden's gym hall. As I approached, I heard loud voices, both male and female, echo through the corridors. They were coming from the faculty office area. I shouldered through the half-open door and just stood there, taking in the scene.

Hayden was standing ramrod straight over by the window, clutching a whole set of brushes. Her dark-gray eyes looked like wells in her chalk-white face. Next to her, with his arm around her, stood a young man, his face radiating fury. His physical resemblance to Hayden was uncanny.

Leyla was facing Hayden and the young man, speaking furiously, and she hadn't seen me yet. Behind her, seemingly holding her back, stood a tall, lanky man with a shock of gray hair and bushy, black eyebrows.

"You're not going anywhere," Leyla said. "You don't know this woman, and you've no idea what her true motive is for keeping you under her roof."

"Then why don't we ask her," the young man said calmly, even as his ice-gray eyes shot daggers at Leyla. "I believe she's arrived in the nick of time." He looked at me with something I could only interpret as sorrow. "Welcome to the poshest dysfunctional family in Boston."

"Hayden," I said, and crossed the floor in long strides. "Are you all right? What's going on?" I cautiously wrapped my arm around her back and the young man let go of her shoulders, but he didn't leave her other side. Hayden seemed rigid but turned out to be trembling, fine, invisible tremors that I easily detected as I pulled her closer.

"Hayden doesn't like to be touched by strangers," the older man said, frowning. "I suggest you let go of her, for your own good."

"Greer isn't a stranger." Hayden spoke firmly, but the way she pressed against me proved how upset she was. I caressed her side under her jacket, out of sight of the others.

"Of course I'm not. We're good friends." I raised a deliberate eyebrow at the man. "You have me at a disadvantage, as I'm sure Leyla has spoken of me. You are?"

"Michael Rowe. Hayden's father."

"I'm Oliver, her older brother." The young man extended his hand. "Glad you could come over right away. Hayden's been holding the fort against these two all day, but I was worried they were wearing her down."

I shook his hand, studying his face closely. He seemed to be on Hayden's side, but I knew better than to pass judgment after only a brief encounter. "Nice to meet you. Call me Greer, please."

"Oliver!" Leyla gasped. "You don't know what you're talking about. You haven't seen how Hayden idolizes this woman—"

"Correct me if I'm wrong, Mother, but isn't this the same Greer Landon whose praises you've sung for the last year or so? The one you wanted to come and endorse your school so you could start raking in the big bucks? The way you spoke of Greer made her sound like the next Messiah, for heaven's sake. Now she's discovered Hayden's talent, not to mention the fact Hayden's living in a fucking gym hall, and she's offering her a better living arrangement and a chance to sell some paintings."

"You're so naïve, Oliver, that it's ridiculous," Leyla spat. "The mere fact that Hayden's taken with this woman should send up warning flags to you, like it does to your father and me. Hayden doesn't like people. Throughout the years, has she had a single normal friendship, not counting your grandmother?"

"You know next to nothing of my life, Mother." Hayden spoke quietly and squeezed her brushes hard enough to whiten her knuckles. "I've had friends, several, and you don't know because I was certain you would wreck it for me. Nana suggested I keep that part of my life to myself."

"Trust the old bat to say something like that." Leyla turned and hid her face against her husband's chest. "You've got to do something, Michael. How are we ever going to have the slightest glimpse into Hayden's life if she leaves here? I'm not happy your mother's ill, you know that, but the one good thing that came from that was us getting Hayden back."

"God. Reality check, Leyla," Oliver said, sounding disgusted enough to forgo calling her "Mother." "You didn't get Hayden back, as you put it. Hayden didn't have anywhere else to stay. This was her last option, which is shameful, really."

Michael glowered at his son. "Did Hayden call you today? Is that why you deigned to visit for the first time in six months?"

"Yes, she called to ask if I could help her move. Besides,

I see Hayden every couple of weeks. Did you think I'd pass up actually being able to help her for once?" Oliver took a step closer to his parents, and I wondered if they were going to come to blows. "You just don't get her. That's the whole basis for this far-too-typical scene." He turned to me. "I'm sorry you had to witness this altercation, but if Hayden's going to stay with you, it's good for you to know what her situation used to be like before she lived with Nana."

"I've figured some of it out, but I agree." I turned to Leyla, who was sobbing against Michael now. "I'm missing something here. What could possibly be wrong for Hayden about our arrangement?" I half knew the answer: they didn't want to lose the control they had over her, but there had to be more to it.

"You're going to fill her head with dreams, and we'll be the ones picking up the pieces when everything falls apart." Michael sounded genuinely sorrowful. "You've made her think she can be a true artist, able to sell paintings and make a living from it. When her condition throws a wrench in the wheels, she'll come crashing down. Then you'll wash your hands of her when there's no more money to be made." His voice sank to a growl. "I know your kind."

I was floored. I couldn't care less what they thought of me. I'd met many protective parents over the years, worried I'd exploit their talented son or daughter for my own gain alone. So far, I'd been able to put all such worried minds to rest. No, what had me aching inside was how they regarded their daughter.

"Her 'condition'?" I know I sounded shocked, because I was. "Hayden's not ill. She has Asperger's, which is a syndrome, not a disease. We'll find ways to make this work for her. I think her work, her art, will speak for itself. I'm not sure if either of you, at least Leyla, who claims to have an eye for art, has even bothered to look at any of her paintings." I turned to Oliver. "Have you?"

"Not lately." He smiled apologetically. "I'm not artistic at all. I can't draw a stickman to save my life. I do know Hayden can draw and paint, but I'm not able to judge if she's good or great."

"But I am." Whipping my head around to glare at Leyla, I continued in a low, menacing voice. "And you know I am. That's why you wanted me here to begin with. Endorse the school, then teach master classes. My ultimatum just expanded. If you stand in Hayden's way, I withdraw both."

Leyla held out her hands, looking pleadingly at me. "That's just it. She doesn't know what she wants. You fill her head with this and she thinks that's what she wants. You say she can walk on the moon, and she'd buy a space suit tomorrow. For some reason she's latched onto you and—"

This had gone on far enough. When her mother started comparing Hayden to a brainless leech or something, I couldn't be around her or her husband anymore. "Oliver," I said, "Hayden's prepared canvases, some boxes, and her suitcases. Can you help us carry them down to the cars?"

"Sure thing." He ushered us out of the room. The sound of Leyla's wailing sobs echoed behind us. Was she truly upset or was this yet another method of manipulation?

"It's going to be fine, Hayden," I said and kept my arm loosely around her. She wasn't shaking as badly, but she felt cold. Still pale, she stopped just outside the door to the staircase leading up to the gym hall.

"I can't." Hayden shook her head. "I can't walk through the door anymore."

"Is this everything, sis?" Oliver poked his head out. "You managed to drag all this down the stairs all by yourself?"

"Yes."

"Okay. I'll start with the boxes. Those are the heaviest." He hoisted a cardboard box and then put it down again. "Wait. We can't run back and forth with all this. Let me get one of the carts from the cafeteria."

"Clever thinking." Relieved not to have to drag this out by

running a gauntlet with Hayden's things, I began moving the canvases through the door. Hayden took them from me and put them along the wall, careful not to cross the threshold.

"You don't believe anything your parents say, I hope," I said casually. "They have a very old-fashioned view of what Asperger's and autism is, from what I just heard."

"So Nana says." Hayden sighed. "Do you believe I don't know my own mind?"

"No, I don't believe that at all. Let me know if something doesn't feel right, okay?" I wasn't just talking about her art and the professional part of our relationship, but I didn't want to bring such details up when we could be overheard.

"Okay. I'm a terrible liar, Nana says."

"Excellent." I, on the other hand was good at lying, but I vowed to be as truthful as possible to Hayden. She deserved nothing less.

Glancing at the canvases leaning against the walls, I had a thought. "Do you still have the key to this door, Hayden?" I envisioned a wrath-filled, vindictive Leyla going up to Hayden's old domain and either slashing or stealing art pieces, claiming them somehow. Until we could arrange for movers to pick them up for safe storage, we should lock the door. Perhaps that wasn't enough, there could be a master key on Leyla's keychain, but it was worth a shot.

"You think we should lock up the rest of my work." Hayden's mind seemed to follow mine.

"Yes. I don't know why it didn't dawn on me before now, but I suppose I didn't consider just how…adamant your mother is."

"All right." Hayden locked the door and tucked the large key into her small backpack. "If there is another key to this door, nobody has used it as far as I know."

"Let's hope not. I'll arrange for movers tomorrow."

"Does that mean I have to be here?"

"I think so, but you won't have to do it alone. I'll be here too, and perhaps Oliver as well. We'll ask him."

Oliver returned with a large stainless-steel cart that could hold all the boxes for the first trip to my car and Hayden's suitcases and the ten canvases during the second one. Relieved to be out of the imposing building, I tried to put the thought of having to return on Thursday out of my mind.

"Do you have a car, Oliver?" I asked as Hayden got in behind the wheel of her car.

"Yes, I'm parked over there." He pointed at a red Audi. "Why don't I follow you guys and help you get the boxes where they need to go? Then I'm off on a hot date, so you have to unpack yourselves." He winked at me, and I wondered if this hot date of his was real or if he wanted Hayden to settle in as independently as possible. This young man impressed me more and more, and I already liked him.

"I'm really grateful you were here today. Your mother clearly has some sort of hang-up."

He shrugged. "Mother saw the custody battle with Nana as the ultimate defeat, and I've heard her express her wish to get back what was hers many times. I don't think she realizes Hayden's her own person, an adult who's clearly able to lead her own life. To Mother, Hayden's still that problem child she felt the doctors blamed her for. She took Hayden to dozens of pediatricians, trying to find out what was wrong with her. Looking back, I think she was simply trying to find a doctor that would clearly state that this problem with Hayden wasn't her fault. Back then, some docs still talked about autism and Asperger's as having something to do with the mother rejecting the child."

"As hard for her as this must have been, it wasn't Hayden's fault."

"That's putting it mildly." Oliver smiled toward his sister, who was busy double-checking the rearview mirrors.

"I have a question for you. Are you free sometime tomorrow afternoon? I just realized we need to store the rest of Hayden's pieces, and I'm sending some people over here to pack them up. I'll join her, but with the scene your parents caused today…"

"I can be here after four p.m. No problem." Oliver nodded solemnly and hurried over to his car.

I turned to Hayden, who was ready behind her wheel. Making a circular motion with my finger, I then tapped the window. She looked blankly at me and frowned.

"Roll down your window." I grinned, suddenly so relieved and happy after all the turmoil.

Hayden opened the door. "I can't roll any windows down. There's a button for this purpose."

"My mistake. Should I perhaps say 'unbutton the window'?"

Hayden's mouth created a perfect circle and then, there it was, her smile, the real one. "More like 'button down the window' I think," she said, and snorted.

Floored. There was no other word for it. Hayden's broad smile and the short laugh had me turning into a puddle. It was as if I was reaching her little by little, and I had no clue what I was doing or what might be working or not. Just that it did. And what it did to me was miraculous. The analogy of the puddle was accurate. Something inside me was melting, and I hadn't known just how frozen it had been.

Not until I met Hayden.

CHAPTER THIRTEEN

Hayden stood in the center of the studio—I already thought of it as hers, which startled me still. I, who trusted very few people on a personal level, had taken in a young woman who I feared would be strenuous to live with. I chastised my inner demon, as I also knew if anyone caused problems it would probably be me. Hayden only wanted to paint and live where she felt safe and cared for. I could imagine what the impressive but impersonal and poorly equipped gym hall had done to her. She hadn't been safe there, of that I was certain. Being locked up by a controlling mother was just one indicator that something much worse could've taken place. What if a stranger had snuck into the school during the day, hid out in a broom closet or wherever, and attacked her when everyone else had gone home? I bet that hadn't even crossed Leyla's mind.

Now Hayden was placing her three easels meticulously. She kept moving them around, an inch farther to the left, turning them a few degrees. The setting sun wasn't in the right place to really do this, but she was glowing, and I thought she needed to just wind down where she felt the safest.

"Where do you want these?" I asked and put down the last of the canvases. "Over there?" I pointed toward the northern corner, which was the darkest part of the studio.

"Yes." Hayden moved the last easel half an inch. She snapped her head up and gave me her shy smile. "Please."

"Okay. That's about it. Oliver put your suitcases in your room. He said he'd meet us tomorrow, but he had to rush to meet his date."

"Oliver always has a girlfriend. Very seldom the same one as the last time. Nana never remembers their names. I do."

"It was great of him to show up and be supportive of you and your decision to move." I sat down on one of the stools my grandfather had bought for me when I used to paint.

"Yes. He visits as often as he can, but he has his own life to live."

"I bet that's what your nana says." I had to smile at how clearly she was reciting someone older.

"Yes."

"Let me know when you're ready to go down to the kitchen. I thought I'd cook something. Don't expect me to be anything like those master chefs on TV, though." I wasn't too bad in the kitchen, but I rarely cooked for more than one person and felt out of practice.

"Why would I think that? You haven't demonstrated any culinary prowess this far."

"True." Grinning, I stood. "Why don't I go check out what's available? You come down when you're ready."

"Okay." Sounding absentminded, Hayden was untying the protective cover around her canvases, placing two unfinished ones on the closest easels. On the third, she placed a blank canvas. With a reverent expression, she placed paintbrushes in jars next to each work area. I realized I hadn't moved at all and pulled myself together. If I became this sidetracked just from watching her work, my workflow might stagnate.

The fridge provided me with salmon, vegetables, lettuce, and tomatoes. I started my rice cooker and measured water and brown rice. This was easy enough. I had an indoor grill next to the gas burners, which heated up in no time. I put my wok on the stove, where I intended to stir-fry my vegetables.

"I can help." Hayden made me jump where she just emerged to my left. "I don't like cooking, but I'm good at cutting."

"Excellent. Here. Thin slices."

"How thin? Exactly?" She was frowning at the cutting board, knife, and bowl of freshly rinsed vegetables.

"Oh, I'm not sure. An eighth of an inch or so."

"Okay." The wrinkle between her eyebrows was still in place, this time from focusing, Hayden placed the carrots in a row to her left, sorted by size, shortest to longest. The onions followed, placed the same way. She pulled the stems off the mushrooms, carefully inspecting each one. It took her but half a minute to sort even those in the same manner.

I had turned down the heat of the wok, thinking it would take her quite a while to slice everything. I had a mandolin, but no way would I let her use it until I knew she was familiar with the super-sharp tool. It'd be disastrous if anything happened to those gifted hands and fingers.

A fast drumming sound broke me out of my reverie and I stared in disbelief at Hayden, who was slicing the vegetables like a pro. She'd clearly taken notice when the chefs on TV demonstrated the correct way to use a knife. She went through the carrots and onions, put them in a bowl, and pushed it toward me. "You're starting with these, right?"

"Um. Yes." I cranked up the heat and tossed in the slices. After brushing oil on the pieces of salmon, I put them on the grill. This would go quickly. I looked at the cooker, hoping the rice wouldn't take too long to get ready. As it turned out, it seemed we were going to time it perfectly. I found myself humming, which didn't seem to bother Hayden in the least. She was slicing the last and smallest mushroom and gave me that bowl as well.

"There."

"You're good with sharp objects, obviously." I admit I was curious.

"Thanks to Nana, I can do basic things in the kitchen, but

she never lets me cook alone. Not after the time when I lost track of time while I was waiting for the sauce to get ready. I started sketching on napkins and forgot about the food on the stove. The smoke set off the smoke detector, and the firemen came. They said I could've burned down the entire kitchen."

"Oh, my. So, would you say that was a fair assessment of your grandmother—not allowing you to be in charge alone in the kitchen?" I thought so, but wanted to hear what Hayden's take was.

"Yes. I get to assist, but you're responsible." Suddenly looking concerned, Hayden straightened. "Does that work for you?"

"Yes, it does. This way we can cook together, but I know my kitchen won't one day be just a fond memory."

"Why would it be—oh. Oh!" Smiling now, Hayden tilted her head. "You're joking."

"Just teasing you a bit." I watched the vegetables and judged it was time for the mushrooms. After adding some spices and stir-fry sauce, I pulled the wok aside to wait for the rice and the salmon to get ready. "Want to eat in the breakfast nook?"

"If it's all right to have other meals than just breakfast there, yes, sure."

"Of course it's okay, why wouldn't it—" I stopped talking as Hayden slapped a hand over her mouth, but not before I spotted her broad smile. "Ah, come on, you're pulling my leg."

"I don't. I haven't touched your leg. I haven't even been near it." Hayden gazed at my legs, looking like she contemplated what pulling one of them might accomplish.

"Just a silly saying that means you're joking."

"Exactly. That's what I said."

I filled two plates for us and carried them to the table. "Silly me." Chuckling, I turned and pointed at the top drawer behind Hayden. "Knives and forks there. You'll find glasses in the cabinet above. What do you want to drink?"

"Mineral water."

So she really liked mineral water. Good to know. I made a mental note to stock up on some tomorrow, as I had only a few bottles left. When we sat down to eat, I noticed the perfect placement of the utensils and the glasses, before I looked up and my eyes met Hayden's. She took my breath away. The soft light from the lamps cast highlights in her dark hair, and her long, thick lashes played with shadows in her eyes. My heart contracted painfully, and I gestured at the food while trying to sound casual.

"Please," I said, close to gasping for air, "dig in."

Hayden ate as if she hadn't seen food since yesterday. Our dinner tasted fine, but it could've been from McDonald's for all I cared. I couldn't take my eyes off Hayden, and only when I was in danger of stabbing my fork through my hand instead of the salmon did I glance at my plate.

When Hayden finished her meal, she looked at me with a worried frown marring her forehead. "We have to discuss the financial agreement."

"What?" I blinked and was brought back from my dazed frame of mind with a thud. "What financial agreement?"

"I can't live here for free. You'll have extra expenses because I'm here. I need to know how much so I can transfer money to you online."

That was directness for you. I didn't know whether to be slightly offended or admire her way of bringing things up head-on. "I hadn't even thought that far." The only thing important to me was to arrange for a safe and inspiring environment for Hayden. A very tiny, insistent voice in the back of my mind suggested that it wasn't exactly painful to rest my eyes on this wondrous woman either.

"I'm not a charity case." Hayden's eyes darkened further with each passing second.

I agreed quickly. "Not in a million years."

"I have a trust fund set up by my paternal grandfather when I was born. It became mine to do with as I please when I turned twenty-one. I paid rent at the school."

"You—you what? You paid rent for the gym hall?" This was yet another strike against Leyla. "What, pray tell, was it used for before you *rented* it?"

"Nothing. Some storage." Looking uncomfortable, Hayden seemed to pick up on my anger. As it wasn't directed at her, I reeled it in and focused on what she was saying.

"All right. You want to pay your way, which is totally fine with me, but I can't charge you rent as I have no mortgage on this house. It was paid in full long before I inherited it. You can pay a smaller portion of the electricity and gas if you like."

"Good."

"And I assume I don't have to worry about keeping you in paint and canvases?" I winked at her, trying to lighten the mood. My jaws tightened and signaled I was heading for full-blown spasticity. I massaged them with my fingertips.

"No." Hayden tilted her head, regarding the actions of my fingers. "Are you in pain?"

"Just a bit tight. Happens sometimes." I waved my fingers dismissively. Jittery, all of a sudden, I stood and began clearing the table. After filling the dishwasher, I found Hayden had wiped all the surfaces and washed the wok. She'd been well brought up by her grandmother, I guessed. "I have some calls to make and papers to read," I said, reluctant to leave her.

"I'll unpack my things." Hayden started walking upstairs.

I stood at the foot of the stairs until her lithe form was out of sight. Heading for my study, I closed the door behind me, as I had to call India and didn't want Hayden to overhear accidentally.

India picked up on the second ring. "Where did you run off to? You looked about to commit murder or something."

"You have to ask?" I sat down and kept massaging the left side of my jaw.

"Oh, God. Leyla Rowe."

"The very same. She found out Hayden's plans and cornered her. It was ugly."

"What plans?" India asked, sounding cautious.

"She's moved out of the school."

"She has? Oh, that's brilliant! She really shouldn't stay at that monstrosity of a building—wait. Wait. Greer, you didn't? She's staying with you, isn't she?" India raised her voice. "Erica! Erica, I have Greer on the phone and you have to hear this."

Groaning, I knew I was done for. If India was a force of nature, Erica Kramer was a category-five hurricane. She was soft-spoken until someone got her ire up, which usually happened if anyone came on to her girlfriend or insulted any of her friends. Right now, I wasn't sure how Erica would react to my news.

"What's up? Why are you yelling?" I heard Erica say in the background.

"You're on speakerphone, Greer. Honey, this girl I told you about, Hayden? She's moved in with Greer."

"Really?" Erica sounded surprised but not upset. Good.

"Let me clarify that," I said, slumping into my leather desk chair. "She's going to stay here, yes, but we're not *living* together. I mean, like a couple. Just so you know."

"I've seen the way you look at her and listened to how you talk about her. It's a whole new you," India was insisting, and I could easily picture how she gestured to emphasize her words, completely mindless of the fact I couldn't see her.

"Regardless of how I look at any given time, the fact is, Hayden is staying here to be able to live in a decent place and work without having to fear being locked up by a crazed mother."

"Locked up?"

Damn. I'd forgotten I never told India about that. It had seemed so private, but if she was to understand why Hayden was moving out of the school and living here with me, I had to tell her. My voice tight, I explained what had happened after the first time I met Hayden. The short, stunned silence from the other end told me what I wanted to know.

"And she has nobody else, does she?" Erica asked.

"She has a brother who seems great, but his circumstances don't seem to allow for a painting sister who requires space to work and who's wary of the dark when she's on the ground level. Here, her room is on the second floor and the studio is on the rooftop."

"Oh, right. I rarely think of that part of your house. I mean, I've seen it as a greenhouse, really." India sounded calmer. "I'm still worried though, Greer. Hayden is all taken care of, it seems, but what about you?"

"What do you mean, what about me?" I frowned at the phone, an expression that was just as ineffective as her imagined gesturing.

"You care for her. And by that I mean you care-*care* for her. This woman could break your heart, Greer."

"And here you've been trying to set me up with every single gay woman in Boston for the last fifteen years. There's no pleasing you, is there, India?" I chuckled, but a lump in my throat nearly made me start coughing.

"You've taken that in stride because you weren't really into any of them, not really. This woman, with all her challenges, not to mention the weird family...I'm just worried you're heading for a world of pain. I'm not saying she's not wonderful and great, because she is. She's probably the most honest person you could ever have in your life, as I think she's totally without pretense."

"She's very honest. We just negotiated our financial agreement—she insisted. I wouldn't allow her to pay rent, but she'll help with the utility bills. I honestly didn't even stop to think about whether she may or may not have any money. I just figured she'd have something, as she drives her grandmother's car and orders her paints and supplies."

"She drives? Wow. That's surprising. Well, I guess we all have our prejudices." India sounded impressed. "Goes to show you what I know."

"There's nothing wrong with her intellect," I said. "She mainly has problems with certain social interactions. That, and the first fourteen years of her life, when she lived with her parents. I'm starting to realize her grandmother might just have saved her life by getting custody before the Rowes destroyed her soul. The things she lets slip sometimes…" I didn't share any of them as they were deeply personal to Hayden, thus special to me too.

"God. What some people do to their kids." Erica sighed. "So, what's your game plan, Greer?"

"First, rescue the rest of Hayden's paintings from the school before her mother finds it in her heart to slash them or hold them hostage. Second, prepare Hayden for the showing in Chicago. I think we need to visit her grandmother and explain what's going on. That should be reassuring for Hayden as well."

"Sounds good. I'll help you arrange for our favorite art movers tomorrow. The guy who runs that team has a soft spot for me. Ow. Stop pinching, Erica. He knows I'm a lesbian and very taken. Don't be silly." India giggled, but sounded serious as she continued. "Just let us know if you need help with other things, Greer. I mean, outside of work. Perhaps you don't see it the way I do, but after watching you put your profession before everything else for so long, this is so new…and I can't help but worry. So, what I mean to say is I'm glad you called."

"Please, don't tell me you're crying, India?" I begged her. "Erica, is she?"

"Not really. Or not yet, I should say. Misty-eyed at the most." Erica's gentle smile was easy to detect in her tone. "You know India. She's all heart."

"A tigress with a very huge heart," I said. "But thank you, both of you. It's good to know where my true friends are."

"And we'll be Hayden's friends too, whether she wants us to be or not, in the process." India sounded determined, and I hoped Hayden would respond well to this proclamation once she found out.

"Thanks. I'm going to work on some of the contracts I ran out on when Hayden called. See you at work tomorrow, India. The two of you might come by in a few days just for coffee or something? It'll be a good start for Hayden to get to know the people in my life."

"Sure thing, boss." India paused. "Be careful, though."

"I will."

We hung up, and I wondered if it was too late to promise such a thing. Taking Hayden in, with all my good intentions, wasn't going to be easy. My heart was hanging in the balance and perhaps India was right. I was in danger of getting hurt. Then I thought of Hayden, clutching her brushes as her mother drenched her in insults and emotional blackmail. No matter what potential hurt I might be risking, getting Hayden away from that toxic environment and helping her do what she lived for was worth it.

Having booted up the computer, I pulled up the contracts and started going through them. I often used work as a Band-Aid when something was wrong in my life, but this time it was hard to focus. It took me almost two hours to correct the issues at hand.

Walking upstairs, I listened for any sounds from Hayden's room, but it was so quiet, I was afraid she wasn't there. Calling myself a fool, I tiptoed to her door, which was half open. Peering inside, I saw she had her bedside lamp on. She'd fallen asleep on top of her bedspread, dressed in a tank top and pajama shorts. The room was air-conditioned, and, worried she'd be cold, I fetched a fleece blanket from my room and gently spread it over her. Watching her for a few moments, I took in the way her hair spread across the pillow. I spotted something protruding from under it, and, of course, Hayden had three paintbrushes tucked away where she could reach them. At least she wasn't clutching them now. This had to mean she felt safe under my roof, I prayed.

Heading to my en-suite bathroom with a much-longed-for shower in mind, I thought an early night in bed would be a good idea, considering tomorrow would be challenging in all sorts of ways. As the hot water sprayed me, I closed my eyes and recalled India and Erica's reassurances. My life had changed drastically in the last two weeks. Those two weeks felt more like two months. How was it even possible? Did this really happen or had I stumbled in some damn rabbit hole on my way to the art school that day?

I dried myself off and dressed similarly to Hayden. I thought of the light kiss we'd shared and the way Hayden had allowed me to hold her. Too much. Too soon. I needed to pull back and let her find her bearings and keep painting. Anything else from my end would be selfish. As much as my body craved the closeness we'd experienced, I should put her first and not distract her with something confusing like a budding relationship on top of everything else.

My heart clenched painfully, but I told myself it would get easier with time once I found the tools to be around Hayden without wanting her like this. A glance in the mirror nearly unhinged me. My eyes were dark and glazed over with tears. And I never cry. Ever.

Blinking against the burning sensation, I made myself think of what pleasure it would bring me to witness Hayden grow and succeed with her painting. Then and only then, I might revisit these emotions.

CHAPTER FOURTEEN

Hayden's room was empty the next morning. I called downstairs, thinking she might be up early having breakfast, but the house was silent. Of course. How silly of me. I tied the belt of my robe and walked up to the roof. The sun was just up, painting the sky purple and pink. The studio door was half ajar, and inside, Hayden stood, already busy painting. Still only dressed in her nightwear, her skin glowed in the morning light.

She glanced at me for a moment but didn't greet me until I stepped through the door. "Good morning, Greer." She used a wide brush, laying down colors reminiscent of the sky outside.

"Good morning. Sleep well your first night here?" Despite my best intentions on keeping us on a professional level, the sight of her stole my breath away.

"Yes. The bed is comfortable and I felt safe."

Well, that summed it up. "I'm glad on both accounts. What if I make us some breakfast and bring it up here?"

"Yes." She turned her head over her shoulder. "Thank you."

"Eggs, bacon—or?"

"Eggs, bacon, fried tomatoes, and orange juice. No coffee."

I did ask. "Coming up. How do you want your eggs?"

"Scrambled."

"Got it. Tomorrow you cook breakfast for me and I watch."

Hayden stopped what she was doing. "All right. That's fair."

I hummed on my way to the kitchen, pulling out what I needed for our meal. I wasn't a splendid cook by any means, but my scrambled eggs were famous with India and Erica. The thought of my friends and the conversation we'd had yesterday made me somber. I went through the motions of cooking, but my mind wrestled with the same questions I'd thought of as I tossed and turned last night. Was I being fair to Hayden by withdrawing after initiating physical closeness? How the hell was I going to handle this?

I tossed two light blankets over my shoulder and carried the large tray upstairs, crossed the still-cool deck, and shouldered through the door to the studio. Placing the tray on the table in the corner, I closed the door as I started shivering in my thin robe. A glance at Hayden proved she was probably too far into her work to feel the cool wind.

"Mmm. Smells good." She walked over and sat down on one of the stools.

I gave her one of the blankets. "I don't know about you, but I'm cold."

"Thank you." Hayden felt her thigh. "Looks like I'm cold too. I didn't notice before."

"I guessed as much." With the door closed, the sun warmed the studio fairly quickly, and I picked up a piece of bacon with my fingertips. Chewing it, I cast a glance at the new painting. "You're painting the view from here?"

"Yes."

"It's stunning. I'm sure your work will be too." I watched Hayden eat with what I'd noticed was her usual good appetite. "I seem to make breakfast to your liking."

"Especially the eggs. As good as Nana's."

"High praise. Thank you." I had to smile at the contented, blissful expression on Hayden's face as she scooped up the last bite on her plate. She sipped her orange juice and eyed my coffee mug. "Do you regret not having coffee?" I asked. "You can have a sip of mine if you like. I take it with a bit of milk."

"It's not polite."

"To have milk?" I blinked.

"No. To drink from someone else's mug."

"But I offered. That's different."

Hayden tilted her head. "Next time," she said. "I know coffee won't taste good once I've had something citrusy first. The tastes clash."

"True." I usually saved my orange juice for last for that very reason. "I'm going into the office in an hour or so. Are you going to stay home and paint, or—"

"Yes." Hayden frowned, her fingers fluttering at the edge of the blanket. "Unless you don't want me here when you're not home."

This made me jump. Had I somehow managed to give the idea I didn't trust her? Or was this her parents' doing? Moving my stool closer to hers, I took her hand gently in mine. "Listen. You can come and go here just as you please. I was just going to make sure I didn't forget to give you the keys and show you the alarm system."

"Oh." Hayden's eyes glistened in the sunlight. "I'm good with numbers. And I promise not to cook."

"Then we agree. I have staff that shows up here at regular intervals, and I'll show you that schedule."

"Okay." Hayden bent forward and kissed my cheek.

I drew a deep breath but forgot how to exhale. Her satin lips brushed so shyly against my skin, but it was the very first caress she'd initiated like this, and it made my decision from last night heartbreakingly impossible. I clearly had no self-control when it came to her. Cupping her cheek, I ran my thumb along her cheekbone. "What was that for?"

"I wanted to."

Of course. Any answer Hayden was ready to give would hold the truth as she saw it. She kissed me because she wanted to. Scattered thoughts of the implications of this act buzzed at the outer perimeter of my mind. Not wanting her to think I didn't appreciate her caress, I pressed my lips to her forehead. "I'm sorry. I have to get into the shower. I'll use the intercom when I'm ready to leave." I pointed to the small box just inside the door. "From that you can reach the kitchen and my study."

"Okay." Hayden walked over to the intercom and read the small list next to the buttons. Nodding, she returned to the table and lifted the tray. "My turn."

Charmed at how eager she was to do her bit, I thanked her. "This will give me a few more minutes in the shower."

Somehow my words made Hayden lower her gaze, and her earlobes turned a faint shade of pink.

I normally showered quickly in the morning and couldn't wait to get to the office. Now I took more time and used a body scrub that helped me wake up from my dazed feeling. I could still feel Hayden's innocent kiss, but I had to focus on so many other things. Storing Hayden's paintings in a safe facility took precedence today. This reminded me I had to break the news to her that we had to go back to the school during office hours. I doubted Leyla would help us out by keeping the place open longer. We should probably be grateful if Hayden's paintings were still there, unharmed.

Hayden was waiting for me in the kitchen when I came downstairs. I had taken the time to write down the alarm codes and handed the paper to her, along with the house keys. Pointing at the sheet, I explained. "This set of numbers is the code for when you leave the house and nobody else is home. The second set is for when you, or both of us, are at home. The lock to the front door opens with either this key or a fingerprint, which I'll help you install later."

"Okay." Hayden looked at the numbers and I saw her lips move. She then tore the note in miniscule pieces. "Done."

"Impressive." I smiled gently at her. "Now. I'll call you after lunch sometime when India has arranged for some movers we work with to fetch your paintings from the school. I'm sorry, but you have to be there."

Swallowing hard, Hayden nodded. "Will you come too?"

"Of course I will. I won't let you deal with your parents alone unless you want to. You could call Oliver and ask if he can be there too. I'm pretty sure I can't keep India and her girlfriend Erica away either. We'll be a whole gang." Hoping she'd feel the strength in our numbers, I cupped the back of her neck and leaned in to kiss her cheek. Hayden moved at the same time and turned her head, capturing my lips with hers. I froze. I was so unprepared, as this was not the type of kiss I'd instigated. I knew I was being silly, but, hell, if we were going to kiss on the lips, I needed to brace myself! Now she had caught me off guard and my defenses were malfunctioning.

I angled my head, unable to resist her. Exploring her full lips, I trembled with the effort not to deepen the kiss. Hayden seemed content with the sweet caresses of our lips brushing together. She murmured something against my lips, but it took me a while to register it as I was drowning in my own feelings. Dazed, I pulled back enough to speak. "W-what?"

"I said, thank you." Hayden smiled.

I realized that's what I'd heard whispered against my mouth as we kissed. "What for?" I wasn't following her reasoning.

"For this. These feelings. For the bed. For the studio." Hayden pulled at the hem of her tank top. "For you."

"Oh, Hayden." I knew then and there, I should just let go of all the self-imposed rules I'd come up with last night. There was no way in hell I'd ever be able to resist her. All she had to do was look at me like this, say things like that, and I was ready to hold her forever and never let her go. This wasn't just a matter of physical attraction or some protectiveness-turned-affection. It was far more than that, and even if I knew I could crash and burn, I also knew I'd still not be capable of refusing her. If this was selfish of me, so be it. As long as Hayden wanted me in whatever capacity, she had me.

❖

It was quite the group meeting up outside Rowe's Art School. Hayden and I, India and Erica, Oliver and three art movers, all of them women. I kept a furtive eye on Hayden, as did Oliver, I could tell, but so far she looked calm and together. This was important for more than one reason, as she and I were due back in two days to teach another master class. At least she knew she didn't have to set foot in the gym hall again.

"All set? Let's go." I took the lead as I realized everyone seemed to expect it. I didn't mind. Part of me was hoping we wouldn't run into Leyla, but I had to confess, another part of me wanted to have a proper showdown. This was wishful thinking from a purely selfish point of view. In reality, I'd do anything to make this as easy as possible for Hayden.

Hayden gave me the key and I unlocked the door to the staircase leading to the gym. It was reassuring that it was indeed still locked, but my heart pounded as I walked up the stairs. India had offered to keep Hayden company while we were taking stock of the canvases upstairs.

I stood in the middle of the floor, gazing around me, trying to picture what the room had looked like when I was there last. Hayden's personal things were gone, as were her easels and supplies, but as far as I could tell, the canvases were undisturbed. I walked over to the closest ones that I'd seen before and pulled one of them out from the wall. All the canvases were facing the wall, and as I scanned the first painting, I saw nothing untoward. Then a bright yellow square in the upper corner caught my attention. A Post-It note, which I was certain hadn't been there earlier. "Estimated value, 150 dollars. Too gothic."

Furious, I tore the note off. This was Leyla's handiwork. Showing it to Erica, I hissed, "Let's go over every single painting and remove these. I know there'll be more. Do *not* tell Hayden about this." I glanced at Oliver, who'd already turned two more canvases and removed the Post-Its. He gave them to me, and on each one, an insulting "price tag" combined with a malicious review showed just what a cornered person can do to her own child. It could of course be her father, but I didn't think so.

Eventually I stood there with forty-seven yellow slips of paper, having read each one while pure hatred for Hayden's mother simmered in the center of my chest. She'd priced Hayden's paintings between twenty-five and two hundred dollars. Her comments ranged from "naïve" to "pretentious" to the worst one of them all: "pitiful."

I shoved the notes into a zipped compartment in my messenger bag, intent on filing them for future reference, as I had a feeling they would come in handy at one point. I'd lock them up in my safe at work, which would ensure Hayden wouldn't come upon them by accident.

I'd called down to Hayden and India right after we entered the gym, reassuring them the paintings were all there. Now the movers were packing them and carrying the boxes down the winding staircase.

"I can't imagine how you lived up there," I heard India say to Hayden. "Honestly, this building is kind of creepy."

"The light was good. It allowed me to paint, but I didn't enjoy living there." Hayden spoke shyly but seemed relaxed around India, whose kindness no doubt was as palpable as usual.

"No kidding. Much better at Greer's place, huh?"

Oh, she was fishing for information. I knew India, and now she was out to get some juicy details from Hayden, who *didn't* know her.

"Yes, the bed is very comfortable. And Greer served me breakfast."

Great. Now Hayden made it sound as if I'd served her breakfast in bed. I only had a few steps left when India responded.

"She did, eh? Well, the two of you are getting really close."

"Yes."

"India." I only had to say her name in my no-nonsense tone, and she grinned sheepishly at me.

"Oh, hi. Done already?"

"The movers are fast. They'll be finished in an hour or so. Erica and Oliver are speeding things up."

"What's going on here?" Leyla's voice hissed from behind me. Of course. Too good to be true. No such thing as flying under the radar in this place.

"We're fetching my paintings, Mother." Hayden spoke calmly. "It will be another hour."

"I haven't authorized this intrusion. I'm going to have to ask you to leave the premises—"

"No. I have paid rent until the last of this month. I have every right to be here and bring my—my friends. It was you who insisted on a legal contract, after all, Mother." Hayden's dark eyes clearly showed her inner turmoil, but she kept her voice steady. "Or have you forgotten?"

"Of course I haven't. You—you never bring anyone around. I was merely taken aback. It's so easy to have people take advantage of someone like you, a person who's not accustomed to...socializing. You say these are your friends. What will it take for you to understand that blood is thicker than water?"

"I fail to see what these fluids have to do with the fact that I'm getting my artwork into storage. You have never taken an interest in my work before. Why now?" Hayden pulled out three brushes and squeezed them.

"Oh, but I have. I have examined all of the paintings you have here."

"You went into the gym hall when I wasn't there? You were trespassing?" Hayden gasped.

"I did nothing of the sort. I own this building."

I'd had enough. Soon, Leyla was going to mention the malicious notes she'd left on Hayden's paintings, and that wasn't going to happen. "You may not walk into a tenant's home without proper cause. Certainly not to peruse their belongings. If you did that, I'll have to let my lawyers examine the rental contract and see what actions Hayden might take."

Backing up, Leyla looked like she was ready to throttle me.

When she first met me, she was close to kissing my feet, and now she must've regretted ever contacting me in the first place.

"Fine. Do what you wish with your doodling. I have a school to run." Leyla began to walk down the corridor, the many mirrors multiplying her light-blue-skirt-suit-clad body. She stopped and pivoted, her eyes ablaze. "I expect you to fulfill *your* contract, Greer, and show up for the master class every Thursday until my students graduate."

"But of course. We'll both be here," I said sweetly. "Wouldn't miss it for the world." I strode over to Hayden and ran the back of my curled fingers along her cheek. "You okay?"

"Yes." Gazing back and forth at India and me, she smiled with tremulous lips. "I'm with friends. That's very okay."

India's expression had gone from stunned fury at Leyla's outrageous claims to warm softness as she regarded Hayden. "I'd say you have some pretty close and loyal friends here. I'm honored to be counted as one of them."

I could've kissed India for those words. She'd been so concerned for my well-being last night, and now she seemed to understand why I had to act so fast.

When all the paintings were loaded onto the truck, we walked to our respective cars. Hayden was walking ahead of us, talking to Oliver, when India and Erica ambushed me.

"You gave her breakfast in bed. That's not taking it slow and easy, exactly," India said, studying me closely.

"I didn't. We had breakfast in the studio."

"Uh-huh. Sure. She said—"

"She said she liked the bed. And that I brought her breakfast. I heard."

"Oh. So you two didn't—"

"India, for God's sake! What kind of person do you take me for? A predator unable to control myself?" I snapped, then regretted it immediately. "Sorry. Sorry. I know what you mean. And no. Of course not." And I could tell I blushed. I did have problems with my self-control around Hayden. Perhaps India had picked up on that somehow?

"Hey. She's yanking your chain, Greer. Relax." Erica placed a large, reassuring hand on my shoulder. "Hayden's happy and relieved. You're…well, you seem happy too, if not relieved, or very relaxed, actually. But you two will figure it out. She's awesome. I like her a lot."

I drew a deep breath and grinned like a fool. "She is. And thank you again for being here. It made it infinitely easier for both of us."

"Pity I wasn't there when Her Highness came by." Erica rolled her shoulders like a prizefighter. "Oh, well. Maybe next time."

Laughing now, I saw Hayden turn around and meet my gaze. It had turned out to be a pretty good day after all, and she must think so too, since she wore a big smile, her real one.

CHAPTER FIFTEEN

Four days later, on Saturday morning, I was in my study, sorting through paperwork. I could hear Hayden moving in her room, getting ready to visit her grandmother.

The last few days had been the downtime we needed after the tumultuous start to the week. Hayden had spent most of it in the studio, except for when we taught the second master class. I dreaded running into her mother, but as it turned out, Leyla had been otherwise engaged on Thursday. The relief on Hayden's face when we found out mirrored what I felt. I wasn't in the mood to be part of another ugly scene anytime soon.

I thought of another new element in Hayden's living in my home. Each night at bedtime, and every morning after breakfast, Hayden would kiss my cheek. No more, no less, just a very sweet, lingering kiss on the cheek. I'd come to terms with my own desire for her but wasn't going to be selfish. As much as I wanted to go further—God knows I ached for her—I only returned the caress, ran my fingers through her hair, and kissed her cheek back. Sometimes I'd hug her gently, but she usually grew a little rigid and seemed to prefer kisses. I thought of the snuggling we'd done that Sunday she came to visit. Perhaps it was because we'd been together all day and she'd been painting that she'd been able to relax into an embrace. During the weekdays, I was gone most of the day.

"Greer."

I looked up and saw Hayden lingering in the doorway. "Yes?" She was wearing her usual sleep attire.

"Today's Saturday."

"Yes?" I put down the papers in my hand and turned the black leather chair, waving her over. "You're going to see your grandmother, right?"

"Yes. I want you to come."

This was unexpected, but I didn't hesitate. "Sure. What time?"

"Eleven. We leave at ten twenty. I've calculated the distance from here."

"Excellent." I checked my watch. "Guess we need to get ready then."

"Yes." Hayden didn't move despite agreeing.

I stood and walked up to her, putting my hands on her shoulders. "Are you worried about anything?"

"Nana doesn't like very many people since her stroke. She can be rude."

"Oh, Hayden, I know that. I won't mind."

"She can't help it." Looking relieved, Hayden walked into my arms, hiding her face in my neck. "I still want you to like her."

I wrapped my arms around her, not too tight, but enough to hold her close. "Prickly women are my favorites." Inhaling her scent, I pressed my lips to the top of her head. She was still relaxed and so soft in my arms that I tried not to quiver. Her arms came around my waist, and the way she held me made me think she wasn't merely clinging for comfort. It was as if she really wanted to hold me back, and I dared to kiss her temple. "You're my ultimate favorite," I said. "Just so you know."

"Okay." Hayden tipped her head back to look at me. Her lips were slightly parted, which was an invitation I didn't have the strength to resist. I kissed her briefly. Hayden sighed against my mouth, and the small puff of air made me shiver. "I want you to meet my Nana. I've never taken anyone with me to visit her."

This meant Hayden's grandmother would realize I held a special place in her life. Would she be perceptive enough to pick up on how I felt about her granddaughter? And if so, how would she react? Afraid of having to battle yet another Rowe family member, and this time one Hayden loved and listened to, I forced a smile to my lips and pulled back. "Better hit the showers, or we'll be late."

Looking aghast, whether it was at the thought of being late or actually striking at the shower, Hayden took a step back, pivoted, and rushed out of my study. Chuckling, despite my trepidations regarding this visit, I walked into my room and began running my own shower. As I removed my robe and stood there just in my shorts and tank top, Hayden opened the door.

"You can't wear perfume. There's a rule at the clinic against that."

I stared at her, as she was clearly wearing only a towel wrapped around her. "All right," I murmured, and cleared my throat. "I'll remember that."

"Good." She turned to leave and then turned back, looking stricken. "I forgot to knock. I'm sorry."

"Yes, you did, but it's all right. I forgive you. I'll try to remember to lock the bathroom door so we're not totally embarrassed some other time."

"I'm not embarrassed, but I know others can be." Hayden tiptoed forward and ran her fingertips along my cheek—much like I'd done with her several times. "Bye." Pivoting, she was out the door just as fast as before.

I stood there for a good ten seconds, my mind whirling. Hayden in a towel, Hayden instigating kisses, and Hayden wanting me to meet the woman she loved most in the world. I felt as if I were treading water but still sinking. Nearly forgetting to undress first, I fled into the shower, turning it to scalding hot and then as cold as I could tolerate. It always perked me up and sharpened my senses. I was going to need it.

❖

The rehabilitation clinic was more like a fancy hotel. Clearly, this was how the wealthiest could afford to recuperate, even if illness struck relentlessly, no matter their social status.

Hayden walked close to any of the walls whenever possible, and as this was a busy day for visitors, several people were in every new corridor we entered. I kept even steps with her, hoping it would help, but judging by the way she clutched at the brushes in her pocket, I wasn't sure it did.

Isabella Calthorpe Rowe resided in a double suite consisting of a bedroom, a living room, and a large bathroom. The only things betraying that this wasn't a hotel were the railings in the ceiling, to which the lift was attached, and the bed, which was a faintly disguised hospital bed.

"Nana." Hayden walked over to the small, fragile-looking woman sitting in a recliner by the window in the living room. "You're up."

"Of course I'm up. It's past eleven." The woman's speech was slurry and slow, but she wasn't as hard to understand as I'd feared. I remembered Hayden telling me the staff often found it difficult to comprehend what she said. How much time did they take to listen to the old woman?

"I meant you were more tired last time I was here." Hayden seemed unfazed by Isabella's brusque tone. Perhaps it was because the old woman took Hayden's hand and held it in an unsteady grip.

"I'm better today." Isabella turned her head and looked curiously at me, where I remained in the doorway. "And who's this?"

"Greer. Remember I told you she likes my paintings? I live with her now."

Groaning inwardly, I realized I had to introduce myself.

"Hello, Mrs. Rowe. I'm Greer Landon, a friend of Hayden's. I offered one of my guest rooms to her, and also I happen to have an unused studio where she can paint."

"And you did this because?" Isabella scrutinized me unabashedly.

"I think I happened upon Hayden at the right time." I wasn't sure how much Hayden had told Isabella of what had taken place lately. Perhaps Isabella was too frail to take the worst details.

"From her angle or yours?" Isabella started to cough. She wheezed, a worrisome sound, but Hayden calmly waited for the attack to abate.

"Both." I had to be honest or Isabella would see right through me. If I started to sound like some wishy-washy philanthropist, I'd never get her approval, and for Hayden's sake, I needed to do so. If I alienated Isabella, Hayden would get caught in the middle, which was the last thing I wanted.

"Oliver helped me move. He'll visit you soon, he said. He has a new girlfriend. Again." Hayden was unusually chatty and seemed oblivious to the undercurrents between Isabella and me.

"When doesn't he?" Isabella shook her head. "Be a darling and fetch me a new pitcher of juice from the staff, please, Hayden?"

"Okay." Hayden got up and left the room.

"Sit down." Isabella flicked her hand at the chair next to her.

I did as told. "You sent her out to learn my true objective." I thought we better put our cards on the table.

"Astute observation." Isabella regarded me with sharp, slate-gray eyes. Her hair was short and styled professionally in a modern hairdo. She was dressed in tan slacks and a dark-brown silk shirt. Had it not been for the drooping left corner of her mouth and her unmoving left arm, I wouldn't have guessed she was anything other than what she seemed, a sharp old woman, born to old money. "So, do tell me. What do you want with my granddaughter?"

"I want to show her paintings and help her launch her career."

Isabella regarded me closely. "And what's in it for you?"

"I might make money from selling and buying artwork, but bringing forward new talent is what I live for. It would be a crime if people never saw your granddaughter's paintings. She's a true genius. I believe she deserves this chance, and this is my only motive." Taking a deep breath I spoke with emphasis. "As for the living arrangement…I couldn't in good conscience leave her in a gym, Mrs. Rowe."

Isabella's facial muscles twitched a few times, and then a lopsided grin spread over her face. "You're very direct. Something I…appreciate. I suppose I'm used to Hayden's way of expressing herself after all these years. I find I'm not patient if someone goes on and on." She closed her eyes briefly. "I'm too tired, to be honest."

"Understandable." I knew better than to pat her hand or do anything else common to "comforting" the sick and elderly. No doubt, this woman would slap my fingers if I tried. "I've grown very fond of Hayden, and for what it's worth, I only have what she wants in mind."

"So, not 'what's best for her'?" Isabella scrutinized my face.

"She knows what's best for her. I had to try and she accepted the offer." Images of Hayden in that gym, of the cot she slept on, and of the expression of elation and sense of freedom on her face at my suggestion made it hard to breathe and swallow. I had to make Isabella understand that I understood Hayden and her former circumstances. Not only that, but also how I firmly believed in Hayden's intelligence and abilities. I spoke with a firm voice. "Hayden's her own person and very capable of doing her own bidding."

"What am I bidding for, Greer?" Hayden asked, entering with a crystal pitcher filled with orange juice.

"Just another saying," I said, and moved to another chair so she could sit closest to her grandmother. "It means, make your own decisions."

"It seems Greer has come into your life when you needed

her the most, my girl." Isabella took Hayden's hand. Hayden in turn raised the wrinkly, blue-veined hand to her lips and kissed it tenderly. "As I understand it, you're going to need Dominic's help with some contracts. You have his information in your phone, right?"

"I do."

"Good." Closing her eyes, Isabella drew a deep, unsteady breath. "I miss my roses. Can you swing by the house one day and check on the garden? I know old Mr. Larson is still taking care of everything, but I always tended to my roses myself."

"Until you fell off the ladder when tying some of them up." Hayden shook her head. "And I wasn't there. I feel responsible."

"You keep saying that, and it's not true." Slurring worse now, Isabella trembled. "I shouldn't have brought it up."

"Wait a minute," I said, my heart aching for both of them. "Why don't we come back tomorrow, and, if you're feeling well enough, we'll all drive out to your house so you can check on the garden?"

Two faces, so alike even if at least sixty years separated them, turned to stare at me. Hayden's eyes glowed and she smiled broadly. Isabella looked more shocked.

"I'm too much to handle. The wheelchair—"

"It folds up. And Greer has an SUV. A Mercedes. I've driven it." Hayden clung to her grandmother's hand with both of hers now. "Say yes, Nana. You haven't been home since this happened."

Isabella's eyes softened, and she freed her hand and ran it through Hayden's hair. "All right, my girl. I'll be ready after my nap tomorrow. Two p.m.?" She directed that question to me.

"Sounds good to me. We'll be here. Now, please excuse me. I'm going to find the guest restroom." This would give them some time alone, I thought.

When I returned ten minutes later, Hayden had helped her grandmother to the dining table, as it was nearing lunchtime.

Isabella insisted we leave, as we were getting together the next day and she'd need her rest to have the energy.

I suspected Isabella wasn't comfortable eating in front of me, still a stranger, since I knew Hayden usually stayed much longer. I feared Hayden would be disappointed at the early dismissal, but she was so excited about the idea of taking Isabella home, even for an hour or so, she didn't seem to notice.

She kissed her grandmother good-bye. There was something special about this old woman, a strong, quite-demanding presence that really spoke to me. I felt I'd known her much longer than the hour we'd visited.

"What a great idea, Greer." Hayden sat down in the driver's seat of the Lincoln and started the car. I buckled up and then cupped her neck gently under her hair.

"I'm glad I thought of it. You would've had a hard time doing it on your own."

"I've been here with Oliver." Hayden frowned as she pulled out of the parking lot. "Yet we never thought of it."

"Then I'm glad I did." I let go of her neck and instead took her hand. She glanced quickly at me but then squeezed my hand and held on to it. I used my thumb to caress her lightly as she drove us home.

At the house, Hayden walked up to the studio without a word, and I thought I could guess why. So many emotions—about her grandmother, about tomorrow, and, I thought without conceit, about what was going on between us. If I had no words yet for how I felt, for what Hayden's presence did to me, how could I expect her to be able to?

Like everyone else, she experienced the full spectrum of emotions but had very few words for them. I'd heard her say "I like" and similar phrases, but never anything more specific. When she talked about her fear of living in a bungalow-style house, all she said was "I can't." She never spoke of fear per se. When she told Penelope and me about her problems with crowds, she put it in terms of not functioning well. The paintings held all of Hayden's feelings. Looking at them with her history in mind, I could see the joys, fears, and trauma as clearly as if I'd read her diary.

I decided to leave her up there to do what she needed to, while I took care of some more never-ending paperwork. Walking upstairs, I stopped just as I reached the second level and heard the drumming of Hayden's flat pumps as she hurried toward me from above.

"Hayden?" I frowned.

"I forgot again." Hayden flung her arms around me. "I forgot to say thank you."

"Oh, darling," I said, nearly biting my tongue at the term of endearment. "You don't have to. The happiness on your face was enough for me." I hugged her close.

Hayden pulled back enough to scan my face. "Yes?"

"Yes."

And then she kissed me. Not a soft brushing of the lips or a quick, hard smooch, but a long, slow movement of her lips against mine. It was still rather chaste, no tongues involved, but so sweet and with a definite tinge of passion that was anything but chaste.

Breaking the kiss, she smiled widely at me and then was gone again, rushing up to her studio. And for the very first time, I heard Hayden humming. Paperwork forgotten for a long while, I followed her just so I could keep listening.

Chapter Sixteen

I stood in the well-maintained garden belonging to Isabella Rowe and had to admit it nearly beat my roof. Birds chirped like someone paid them to, and the faint sound of a lawn mower could be heard to the south of us. It was a sure sign spring was heading toward summer. Cherry trees blossomed and some had even lost a few of their petals, which looked like tiny feathers on the ground.

Flagstone paths wound themselves around the backyard. The person in charge of designing it had made it into several "rooms" with four different areas for socializing or relaxing.

The roses were budding as Isabella had predicted, and behind me, I heard Hayden rolling her grandmother's wheelchair through the patio doors. I turned and smiled. "It's wonderful out here." The look on Isabella's face made me choke up. Her eyes were bright, if a bit teary, and she turned her head back and forth as if trying to take in the whole garden at once.

"Drive me around the paths, my girl. I want to see everything."

"Okay." Hayden pushed the wheelchair slowly along the trails, stopping every time Isabella raised her good hand. The frail, slender hand caressed new leaves, fingered buds, and nipped at a withered stalk every now and then. It was clear she knew this garden intimately. This was Isabella's domain, her favorite place, and she'd lost it. My heart clenched at the idea of having something happen to you that took away everything you loved.

I glanced at Hayden, who bent over her grandmother's shoulder and responded to something inaudible. Isabella hadn't lost everything. Hayden's devotion to her nana was unmistakable, and apparently, Oliver came to visit her, if not as often. How did it feel for this proud, strong old woman not to have the same connection with her son? Did she hate Leyla passionately, or had she resigned herself to the fact they never would see eye to eye? Perhaps winning the custody battle all those years ago was enough.

I sat down on one of the white wrought-iron chairs and just enjoyed the warm sun. Taking off my sunglasses, I closed my eyes and tipped my head back. I never sunbathed, normally, but I couldn't resist letting the rays hit my face. Multicolored fractals erupted on the inside of my eyelids. Smiling to myself, I crossed my legs and let my mind drift.

"Are you asleep, Greer?" Hayden spoke so close to my ear, I jumped and uncrossed my legs too fast. Reaching for armrests where there weren't any, I would've fallen off the chair if Hayden hadn't steadied me.

"Try not to kill the poor woman," Isabella said and gave a husky chuckle. Her eyes shone, and it was as if being home rejuvenated her. "I can't help you hide the body."

"I'm not trying to kill Greer!" Looking shocked at such a thought, Hayden gaped. "And it's illegal to hide bodies. You know that."

"Sorry, my girl. I couldn't resist teasing you. I know I shouldn't."

"You were joking." Relieved, Hayden smiled too and didn't seem to notice she was still holding me by the shoulders.

"I think I'm okay now," I said, and patted one of her hands.

"Good. I'll go get our basket." Hayden hurried in through the patio doors.

"What basket?" Isabella asked.

"We brought some pastries and something to drink, as the weather's so lovely. We thought we could enjoy them here, if you're not too cold." I rose and stopped short of placing my hands on the wheelchair handles. "Mind if I put you against the table, Mrs. Rowe?"

"For heaven's sake, call me Isabella. And no, I don't mind."

I carefully adjusted the wheelchair, mindful of Isabella's feet. I'd once been in a wheelchair for two weeks as a teenager after spraining both ankles in a skiing accident. I remembered vividly when my friends had taken turns pushing me around high school, constantly misjudging how much my feet protruded at the front.

Hayden came out carrying the basket and three blankets. She placed one around Isabella's back and the others on the seats of the chairs. I unpacked the basket, placing Danishes, croissants, and a thermos of coffee on the table. We also brought small cartons of orange juice and coffee creamer.

Isabella smiled. "Marvelous. Are those from Café Vanille?" She eyed the bags closely.

"Hayden said they're your favorites, so, yes." I placed the plate with pastries well within reach of Isabella. "Coffee? Juice?"

"Both, please." Reaching for a Danish, Isabella nodded her thanks. "This is such a surprise. I should've thought of it myself."

We ate in silence for a while, and I felt more content and relaxed than I'd been in years. It gave me a lot of pleasure doing this for Isabella and Hayden. Even if it was temporary, they could sit in their garden and enjoy it like they used to.

Once we were full, Hayden packed the basket back up. I made sure she put the leftover pastries in a bag for Isabella to take back to the clinic. I knew very well Isabella could afford to order in whatever she wanted, but it still felt like the right thing to do.

"Why don't you show Greer your room, Hayden?" Isabella asked. "If you turn me more toward the sun, I can just enjoy it a bit longer in the meantime." Her words were casual, but something told me Isabella really wanted me to see Hayden's room for some reason.

"Okay." Hayden stood and turned the wheelchair, then showed me through the house.

The furniture was antique, some dating back two hundred years, I estimated. European figurines and glass cabinets with Dresden china spoke once again of old money. The rugs were Persian and the floors hardwood of the old kind. Chandeliers hung in every room we passed, and someone had to be tending to the house regularly, as I didn't see dust anywhere and no furniture was covered.

"Here. This is my room." Hayden opened a door at the far end of a long hallway.

I stepped inside, not knowing what to expect. My jaw dropped as I regarded it. I slowly spun a full rotation, and the more I looked, the more I wanted to see.

"Oh, my dear God. Hayden…" I had to hold on to her. Wrapping an arm around her shoulder, I took in the walls in the approximately 170-square-foot room. Every single wall space was covered with paintings. Oils, acrylics, watercolors, pencil and charcoal sketches, even crayon drawings were pinned or nailed to the wall.

Shaking my head, I knew I had to start somewhere. The sheer number of pieces overwhelmed me. "Where do I start?" I asked Hayden, slipping my arm down to hold her hand.

"If you mean chronologically, there." Hayden pointed at the far left corner. "Go clockwise."

So I did. It didn't take me long to realize these paintings and sketches were Hayden's diary of sorts. The first painting was that of an open window with billowing curtains. Sun shone in on flowerpots and a small female child made of china. The figurine had begun to crack at the bottom, or perhaps the sun was healing it—I could only guess. I kept looking at each painting, and the next that really caught my eye was of a little girl covering her eyes. Her mouth was open as if attempting to scream, and at her feet was that broken, torn ragdoll I'd seen in another of Hayden's paintings.

After I had looked at half of the paintings, I had to take a break. My mind was filled with images of despair and of exuberant hope, and I was reeling from them. Not thinking about how I might startle Hayden, I turned and hugged her close. "Oh, God." I needed to hold her, mainly because I wanted to make sure she was here, that she had survived all the things that had happened to her.

Hayden slowly wrapped her arms around me. "Are you crying?"

"No. Well, a little, maybe. Your paintings are so strong that they bring all kinds of feelings to the surface. And that's a good thing," I added. "I imagine myself feeling what you went through. You have an extraordinary gift for showing the viewer such things."

"I see." Her voice indicated that she took my word for it, but also that she didn't quite understand what I meant.

"Normally, I ask my artists what they mean or were thinking regarding a certain art piece, but in your case, that's redundant. You've already shown me with each brushstroke."

Hayden pressed her lips to my cheek. I was so full of emotions that I turned my head and captured her lips. Lacing my fingers in her hair, the passion that filled me whenever I was around her took over. Sliding the tip of my tongue whisper-light against her lower lip, I coaxed her to open her mouth for me. Her tongue met mine, willing and eager, and then we were truly kissing. Holding her closer to me, I felt the outline of her slender, yet curvaceous body. I moaned as I explored her mouth; it tasted sweet and slightly of coffee, and I caressed her back with my hands. Her soft breasts pressed against mine, making my nipples harden and burn where they rubbed against the fabric of my sports bra.

Eventually it wasn't enough to breathe just through my nose, and I ended the kiss, gasping for air. Hayden seemed just as out of breath and clung to my upper arms. Her cheeks flushed a becoming pink, and her full lips were damp and swollen.

As it turned out, I couldn't let go of Hayden quite yet. I had to hold her and slowly pulled her closer again, looking for signs of potential discomfort on her part. Instead, Hayden willingly wrapped her arms around my neck and buried her face in my hair.

"You feel so good," I murmured. "I love holding you. Kissing you." This was the first time I'd voiced anything about our physical closeness.

"I like kissing and holding you also, Greer." Now kissing my hair, Hayden inhaled deeply. "And you smell very nice."

I had to chuckle. Suddenly so happy, I tipped my head back and ran my fingertips along her jawline. "I guess I should look at the rest so we don't let Isabella sit alone in the garden for too long."

"Okay."

I kept holding her as I gazed at the rest of her paintings. A recurring theme was the ragdoll, either broken or torn, or looking healthy and glowing. It didn't escape me how much *pink* and other pastels were displayed in the background when the doll looked raggedy. A subtle way to hint at her mother, I guessed. The average spectator would never see the connection, of course, but even so, the bright pastels behind the doll were enough to create interest and conflicting emotions.

The very last paintings, two acrylics, radiated something I interpreted as panic. Swirls, not pretty or decorative, but rather harsh and dizzying, surrounded a small unicorn. The animal was up on its hind legs, swerving its hoofs against the vortices, its eyes wild, with the whites glaring brightly. In an accompanying piece, the unicorn was down on its side against complete darkness. To the sides I could see light, perhaps stars, but ahead, yellow, dried tufts of grass, broken up in places by sharp-edged stones, led to only a blue-black darkness. The unicorn's half-closed eyes looked right at me, and that's when I saw its irises were icy gray.

"The next day I moved into the school gym hall," Hayden said quietly. "I left all these paintings here, as well as some bigger ones in Nana's garage. I took two suitcases with me and began buying paints and more easels. Until then I'd worked over there." She pointed at the part of the room where light came in through two corner windows. "I haven't been back here since—until today."

"I'm glad we came. We'll have to do it again soon. Summer will be here, and we should make sure Isabella can visit more often." I kissed her lightly.

"Yes." Hayden kissed me back. "Thank you."

As we walked back to Isabella, I thought of a multitude of ways I could help these women in the future. Even if it was a simple thing such as having coffee in the sun—when you couldn't manage that on your own, it meant a lot.

❖

"Come up to the studio." That same evening, Hayden stood in the doorway to my office. "Please," she added belatedly, making me smile.

"All right. Have something to show me?"

"Yes."

We walked up the stairs. The setting sun painted the sky a stunning pink and purple. This was usually when Hayden quit painting for the day, and I figured I should put up daylight light fixtures for her if she wanted to work later. I knew many artists who swore by them. I could always suggest it, anyway.

"I have the second painting for Chicago ready," Hayden said, her voice casual as usual.

I stopped walking so abruptly that she walked into my right side. "You do? You're done?"

"Yes." Smiling faintly, Hayden took my hand. "Come." She pulled me through the door to the studio and then let go. I rounded the easel closest to me, having no idea what I would see.

A field of sunflowers created the background for a statuesque woman, backlit by the sunlight and seen from the right. Her hands reached straight up, palms almost together, and her dark hair ran down her back to her waist. I sat down on a stool and kept looking at it with Hayden standing patiently by my side.

The woman's clothes, lacy and frilly, lay in shreds at her feet. Instead she wore sewn-together pieces of sunflowers. They followed the outline of her body, accentuating her breasts and pubic area. In the dark shadows among the roots of the flowers, small furry animals—I couldn't tell quite what they were, but they looked like fantasy creatures to me—scurried and peeked through.

"Oh, Hayden." I often found myself emotional and taken with a work of art, but now, as this was so brilliantly executed and was *Hayden's* painting, I had to blink away tears. "It's absolutely show-worthy. It's more than that. It's amazing."

"Good." Hayden took a deep breath. "Thank you." She placed two brushes on the bench in the corner behind us, and only now did I realize she'd been clutching them. So, she'd been nervous about what my verdict would be?

"No," I said in response to her words. "Thank *you*. I'm not sure you realize what a privilege it is for anyone, me included, to see something like this. Every detail is exquisite, no brushstroke is redundant, and the emotions you evoke in me with this…I'm sure others will feel similarly."

"It's hard for me to judge my own work. Nana says I go into a zone when I work. I'm not sure what she means, but I know I'm focused and don't hear or see what goes on around me."

"That's exactly what she means. That's your own private zone where you create what matters to you."

Hayden tilted her head. "I'm in the same zone when we kiss."

My heart skipped several beats and then rushed on in painfully quick contractions. "Me too," I said quietly. "It's far too easy for me to lose myself in you."

"You don't lose anything, or yourself, in me." Hayden frowned now. "When we kiss, I know exactly where you are, and you are complete."

I smiled wistfully. "Yes, of course. What I meant was, I lose sight of everything else but you."

Looking uncertain now, Hayden reached for a brush. I wanted to kick myself for managing to make my explanation sound negative, so I placed a calming hand on hers.

"I love being in the zone with you." I hoped she'd understand what I meant. Slowly the hand beneath mine let go of the brush but still hovered above it. "I'm attracted to you, to everything about you."

The light reignited in Hayden's eyes. This was such a gift. No pretense, no lies, and no games. I could take at face value what Hayden said and her response to my words and my kisses.

"You're beautiful, Greer," Hayden whispered and let go of the brush completely as she held me close. "I like how you look at my art. You take your time and see it…like in the zone."

"It's impossible not to. I think you'll find others reacting the same way when we show it in Chicago." Something dawned on me. "Have you flown before?"

"Yes."

Oh, thank God. I'd worried about that ever since India ordered our tickets to Chicago. It was a direct flight, but those commuter airplanes were still often crowded. "Good. Great." I tucked a wayward lock of hair behind her ear. "Where did you go?"

"I've flown to my grandmother's summer house on Martha's Vineyard in the company helicopter many times."

Of course. Wanting to thud my head against one of the windowpanes, I had to smile in spite of everything. Taking Hayden to Logan airport, then onto a flight, and, oh God, guiding her through O'Hare airport. One of the most crowded, busiest airports in the world. I just couldn't do that to her. I decided to text India as soon as possible. We needed to arrange for special service so as not to have to sedate Hayden. I could hear India in my mind. "When all else fails, double dose of Benadryl."

We stood there together for a while, until it was impossible to make out any details of the paintings as the sun slowly set. Walking inside, I let go of Hayden, but she kept my hand in hers. At the door of my study, she let go after kissing the back of my hand. I came close to pulling her in for another soul-searing kiss, but I knew taking it slowly was better, if more frustrating. I didn't doubt Hayden would welcome me into her bed, but it was too soon.

Sitting down at my desk, I thought of her newest painting and compared it to the ones I'd seen in her old room earlier. I hadn't seen all of the paintings there, as some of them were put up in several layers in some places. Her earliest work had lacked the technique she now possessed, but the ability to induce emotions had always been there. Now, she painted like a much older person, like someone who'd spent a lifetime observing the world with its inhabitants.

I gripped the computer mouse tightly as it dawned on me what I was about to do. I was going to show the art world and the general public this young woman's extraordinary talent. By doing so, I would help set her free. But once she was flying solo out in the world on the wings of her art and her talent, buoyed by her right to her own life, she might move farther and farther away from me.

Swallowing hard, I vowed to be selfless if that happened. It would no doubt kill me, but so many people had stood in her way, and I sure as hell didn't intend to be one of them.

CHAPTER SEVENTEEN

Another week passed, consisting of Hayden going over to Penelope's to work on her portrait, of us cohabitating, and, of course, the dreaded Thursday when we taught the master class. I actually offered Hayden a way out of the teaching part, but her response was so frantic, I dropped it instantly. She took all promises very seriously, and, for her, it seemed a mortal sin to go back on her word. This made me think such things might have happened a lot to Hayden when she was a little girl.

We spent the evenings, after sunset when it was impossible for her to paint, together. They were getting increasingly warmer and we both enjoyed the roof a lot. Hayden would arrange a tray of cheeses and grapes, and wine—for me—plus mineral water— for her.

Of course we sat on the couch together, and it didn't take us long to find our way into each other's arms. This was where we sat now, indoors this time, as it was raining. I had a TV room on the second floor, and, after the kitchen, this was Hayden's favorite indoor place. She seemed to relish making all kinds of treats, and, if I was home, she used the stove and the oven to create a variety of food. She followed recipes meticulously, and if one ingredient was missing, she simply threw out the whole dish. I tried to convince her it was okay to improvise but soon realized this wasn't going to happen.

My cell phone buzzed and I saw India's name on the display. Answering "Hello," I heard her laugh.

"I'm still hoping to hear you one day answer with 'Greer here,'" she said.

"Funny." I shook my head but had to laugh with her.

"Anyway, I'm calling because I finally have confirmation that you and Hayden will have a special escort through the airports. Eventually I got a hold of this terrific woman who turned out to have an autistic son, and she knew exactly what I was asking for. So, she'll take care of you in person, and she's communicated with O'Hare as well. I'll drive you to Logan here, and you'll have limo service in Chicago." She drew a deep breath after her long and fast speech.

"You're amazing." I didn't often praise her like that, but without India's ability to carry out these things, I wouldn't be nearly as efficient or successful. "Just so you know, an extra summer bonus is heading your way."

"Wh-what? No. I mean cool, absolutely, but you pay me well, Greer."

"You deserve that, and more. No arguing."

"All right. Now, how's Hayden feeling about the trip and flying commercially?" India lowered her voice as if she thought Hayden might overhear.

"I don't see any special signs of stress. She's in the kitchen right now, making dinner."

"Again? Wow, she sure likes to cook."

"Yeah, who knew? As long as it makes her happy, I'm all for it." And this was true. I thought this might be yet another creative outlet for her.

"Okay, I'll let you go since it turns out dinner's ready here too. Mac and cheese à la Erica. I'll pick you up at eight tomorrow. Bright and early."

"Thank you, India. Enjoy your dinner."

"Oh, I will," India said, sounding so dreamy I wondered if she was indeed thinking of the mac and cheese. "Ciao."

I wandered into the kitchen, where I found Hayden in the last stages of setting the table. She'd folded the napkins into perfect bishop's hats and even placed two tall, white candles in pewter holders. Everything looked lovely, and my heart did yet another twirl in my chest.

"Candlelit dinner, I see?"

"Yes. I read it's considered romantic." Hayden looked pleased. "I knew I should wait to light the candles until you got here, since I think the same rules apply to fire as to cooking with the stove and oven."

"Good thinking. Why don't I light them now?" I didn't wait for her to reply but took the large lighter I used for the outdoor charcoal grill and lit the candles. "Very cozy. I don't think we need the overhead light." I switched it off, and the candlelight cast a soft glow around the breakfast nook. "See?"

"Beautiful. Now sit."

"Yes, ma'am." I winked at her and sat down at the table.

"I'm turning off the last burner now and shutting off the oven," Hayden said.

"Good."

Hayden busied herself with our plates, and after a minute, she brought me gravlax on toast with lettuce and a dill-mustard sauce. I ate with enthusiasm and hummed around each bite. "Very good."

"A Swedish delicacy." Hayden's eyes shone in the candlelight. She had never looked more beautiful, and I wanted to slow down time and sit here and look at her forever.

The main course turned out to be a Thai dish with large shrimp, vegetables, and egg noodles. By now I was getting almost too full, but the flavors made it hard to stop eating. "Goodness, we might just have to make you apply to *Master Chef*, given you can cook like this." I didn't look up as I said it, but her tiny gasp proved my attempt at a joke had crashed and burned.

"You wish to send me away?" Hayden's eyes grew huge.

"No, no. I was joking. I meant it as a compliment since you spoil me by cooking so well."

Hayden had gripped her utensils hard for a second but now visibly relaxed, her expression softening. "I like it."

"So do I. And just so we're clear, I don't want to send you away, anywhere." I raised my glass to her. "Cheers."

"Cheers." Clinking our glasses gently, Hayden sipped her mineral water.

"You all packed for tomorrow?" I eyed her for signs of stress or worry.

"Yes. Five outfits, three pairs of shoes, pajamas—"

"I believe you." I held up my hand, gently interrupting the list. "I'm glad we thought of bringing more clothes from your closet at the house. You have some beautiful things."

"Nana insisted I go shopping every fall and spring. She said I had an image as a Calthorpe to uphold, and even if I didn't attend the functions with the rest of the family, when I was out in public she wanted me to 'look the part.' I often asked her what part she meant, but she just said 'my part.' I still don't understand." Shrugging, Hayden leaned back. "The few functions I did attend didn't end well. Mother kept introducing me to people even though Nana told her it wasn't a good idea."

"A lot of people will be at the gallery in Chicago, but I have several ideas how we can minimize how many approach you at a time. I won't leave your side, as the young man showing his paintings next to yours is fully capable of doing his own thing with his agent."

"Agent?" Hayden's eyebrows went up. "Will I need an agent?"

"Only if you think so. An agent takes care of your interests and makes sure people like me pay you the best money possible. They do take a certain percentage for their services, though."

"Then I don't need an agent. I have Dominic and you. That's enough." Hayden's certainty made me smile tenderly.

"Want to have some coffee on the roof or in the TV room?" I asked as I rose to clear the table.

"The TV room. I like watching television with you. If you have time."

"I do."

"I'll go check out the listings." Hayden hurried toward the TV room.

I took care of the dishes while the coffee brewer produced strong Gevalia. Pouring milk in our mugs to mellow the taste a bit, I carried the mugs to Hayden, who had already curled up on the couch. After I placed them on the coffee table, I sat down next to her. "What are we watching?"

"*NCIS*. Do you like it?"

"Yes." I took my mug and sipped my coffee. Hayden followed my example but also lifted my free arm and wrapped it around her shoulders. Resting her head against me, she sighed contentedly and drank from her mug. I smiled into mine as the show started. Hayden felt warm and soft against me, and I let my hand play with her hair. She tipped her head back and smiled up at me. I kissed her lightly. "Who knew you were a snuggle-bunny?"

"I didn't. Nobody does. You're the first person I've ever snuggled with."

"I'm very lucky." I meant it.

"Me too."

We watched *NCIS* and then an old episode of *CSI*, but then I noticed Hayden becoming suspiciously heavy against me. "Are you falling asleep, Hayden?" I murmured against her hair.

"Mmm."

"Why don't we go to bed? We have to get up early tomorrow. India will fetch us at eight."

"Mmm."

"Hayden?" I laced my fingers through her hair and gently scratched her scalp. "Wake up. It's time to go to bed."

"That doesn't make sense," she murmured but sat up, looking at me through her eyelashes. "Tired."

"I can see that. Come on." She did look dazed. I helped her up, and she stumbled toward her room and closed the door. I waited a few moments, knowing she'd open it again, and she did. "Good night, Greer. Sleep well."

"You too, Hayden." I walked over to her and kissed her forehead. To my surprise, Hayden flung both arms around my neck and kissed my lips with a sudden onset of passion. I found myself pressed against the door frame, her hands cupping my cheeks gently as she explored my mouth.

"You make me shiver," Hayden whispered huskily against my lips. "You make my body react in so many different ways. When we kiss I...I ache inside. It's like pain, but not in a bad way. It makes me want to continue this until the ache goes away, but I also don't want it to end."

"That sums it up for me too," I said, holding her close. "You make me ache too, in the best of ways. It's at times like this when all I want is to take you to bed and make love to you all night."

"Why don't you? It's what I want too."

I could hardly breathe. Her words, so honest and easy to believe, made her twice as hard to resist. "Because it's too soon." I tried to explain, but it was hard when my entire system screamed for me to take her word for it. "So many new things are happening to you right now, Hayden. Once we've been to Chicago and you feel more settled in, we'll revisit this."

Tilting her head, Hayden frowned. "And if Chicago isn't the success you expect? Am I still of interest to you then?" Her eyes grew bigger. "Is the Chicago showing an audition for more than my art?"

Shocked at how her analytical mind reached these conclusions, I realized I had only myself to blame. By assuming she understood some things that she didn't, and by not being direct enough about my expectations and intentions when it came to our deeply personal relationship, I had left enough space for her to guess. Her questions were as logical as they were heartbreaking.

I held her close and looked into her eyes. "Listen, darling. I know you'll succeed with your art, but that has nothing to do with the fact I want you here with me. I won't insult your intelligence and claim your amazing talent doesn't factor in when it comes to how I feel about you—after all, it was your paintings that sparked my interest to begin with. Your art is part of you. But *you* keep my interest, you as a person. When we kiss, I forget about everything else, and that won't change, no matter how your career turns out. You're not going to Chicago for me to find out if you're good enough to be my potential lover, my…partner. It's the truth. I promise."

Hayden was still cupping my cheeks, and now she ran her thumbs across them, beneath my eyes. Only then did I notice I was crying.

"I didn't mean to make you cry, Greer," Hayden said, looking stricken. "I had to know what to expect as I want to be your lover. Partner. If I fail at that, I don't know what that would do to me. Someone I knew once said I wasn't girlfriend material. I didn't understand at first what that meant, but when I looked it up, I knew he was right. Considering what young couples do while dating—traveling, attending parties, movies, and the theater, and shopping…I wouldn't cope very well with that. As you're much older than that boy, I hoped you already knew this about me and would still accept me."

I hid my smile against her forehead at her bluntness about my age. "I do. I know all that, and we can work around it. And besides, I hate shopping—especially for clothes."

"Yes. Good."

"And now, it's time to get some sleep." I kissed her lightly. "Don't worry about anything. India's taken care of everything, and I think we'll have a good time in Chicago. We'll take lots of pictures and show Isabella."

"Yes." Brightening, Hayden turned to walk back to her room. As I began to close the door, she stopped me. "No. Leave it open. Please."

"All right." I decided to do the same. No more closed doors or walls between us. The symbolic act might be lost on Hayden— but then again, it might not.

As I got ready for bed, I thought of how Hayden, complex and challenging, had intrigued me from day one. What I hadn't counted on those first days was how quickly and completely she'd captured my heart. The idea of not having her in my life was too painful to even go near. I wasn't superstitious, but I feared if I gave voice to the fear of losing her, I would irreparably jinx everything.

CHAPTER EIGHTEEN

Logan Airport was as busy as always. People waited in line to check in and go through security, and I found it interesting how many people always over-packed or needed to debate the luggage fees.

India had taken care of everything. Erica dropped us off at United's entrance, and Hayden and I stayed by the car while India went to locate the woman in charge of assistance. We were already checked in—another thing India had fixed online—and only had carry-on luggage.

Hayden was pale but composed. Gripping the brushes in her jacket pockets, she studied the busy travelers with both anguish and interest.

A cab pulled up next to us and a woman in a business suit jumped out, furiously tugging a carry-on roller bag from the backseat. She pressed a computer bag down on top of the extendable handle and hurried toward the entrance. As soon as I saw her shove her way through a group of teenagers, I knew our first challenge was here, as a young girl lost her balance and staggered backward, toward Hayden.

I stepped forward and caught the girl with both hands. "Whoops," I said merrily. "Busy lady."

"Yeah, did you see that?" the girl said, glowering. "And they say kids today are rude. Ha!"

"Indeed." I helped her back to her friends and returned to

Hayden. "See, it's going to be crowded in here, but I'm by your side, and soon we'll meet the woman who'll guide us on a special route. We still might bump into people, though. Remember what we talked about this morning?" I wasn't being condescending. Hayden looked like she needed to remind herself of our game plan. Flanked by India and Erica, she wasn't focusing but had started to breathe faster.

"If I get upset, I'll grab hold of you. You'll take care of it." Her voice was staccato and monotone.

"And when we go through security?"

"I'll be on my own going through the metal detector and the body-scan. You'll go through first."

"And I'll watch you the whole time, all right? You'll be fine."

"Okay." She took a deep breath and gave me her polite smile, but it was better than nothing.

"Hayden Rowe?" a woman asked, approaching us with India. "I'm Maryanne Thompson. I'm going to assist you and help you aboard the plane."

"Thank you." I introduced myself and then motioned at Hayden. "This is Hayden. If you can find a route with the least amount of people, that'd be great." I wasn't going to tell this woman anything about Hayden she didn't need to know. She might think Hayden was agoraphobic, and that was fine with me as long as she did her job well.

India and Erica kissed my cheek, and then India did the same with Hayden. I would've thought that was unadvisable, as she was so jittery, but it seemed to help her refocus. "Have fun now, Hayden. That's the most important part. Don't think about anything else but the fun part of it all."

"Okay." Hayden smiled a real smile toward my friends, who were becoming her friends as well. "Thank you for driving us." She shot me a triumphant glance at remembering the niceties, and I winked at her.

After making sure we had our boarding passes, Maryanne

led the way through a part of the airport where hardly anyone stood in line. A wheelchair symbol suggested this section was also for anyone needing special assistance. As we wound our way through the roped-off area, Hayden right behind me, I kept scanning what was ahead. Only two people in wheelchairs were before us in line at the security check, which was a blessing.

As we'd planned, I went through first. I was putting my watch back on when it was Hayden's turn.

"You have to put your jacket in a bin, ma'am," a man said, and approached her with an empty one.

Hayden looked at me, panic beginning to stir in her darkening eyes. I knew immediately what she was worried about. Her brushes. She was clutching them.

"Hayden. Just take your jacket off. It'll go through in a minute, and you'll have it back and your items too." I spoke slowly, making sure she was looking at me. "It'll be okay. Just do it as quickly as you can."

Hayden tore off her jacket, bunching it up and shoving it into the bin. Then she hurried through the metal detector and stopped in the body-scan machine. Glancing down, she placed her feet exactly in the outlined foot symbols on the floor.

"Arms out from your body, please." A young woman handling the machine spoke gently. "That's it. Thank you. You're done."

I was ready waiting with her jacket, and I don't think I've seen anyone put a piece of clothing on so fast before. Hands pushed deep into her pockets, her face relaxed as she found her brushes. After that, Maryanne guided us to an electric cart and we climbed onto it. At this point, I realized I was tense as well and forced myself to relax. Hayden sat pressed tightly against me, holding on to her carry-on bag with one hand and her brushes with the other.

"You're doing really well, darling," I murmured. "We'll be at the gate soon. It's time to board the plane when we get there, I believe."

The gate staff pre-boarded us as soon as we stepped off the cart, and I made sure Hayden got the window seat. Slowly, she began to relax, and I was so proud of her I could sing it from the rooftops. The woman who feared crowds and unknown territory had braved a damn airport, and now all I could do was pray that maneuvering through O'Hare would go just as well.

The two-and-a-half-hour flight was initially uneventful. Hayden was sketching in her ever-present sketch pad, and when the flight attendant served us beverages and offered us magazines, she declined the magazines, but of course asked for mineral water, glaring at the poor woman. We didn't talk much, only a few words every now and then, but it was a comfortable silence. I couldn't have imagined the flight going any better until we started to descend.

Turbulence hit us out of nowhere, and the flight attendants had to take their seats. This was something I hadn't counted on, which of course was ridiculous as turbulence was a common occurrence. Casting a glance at Hayden, I saw she was calm and unaffected. I, on the other hand, wasn't. I didn't have a problem with flying, but I hated turbulence and what it did with the plane, with a passion. As the plane shook and made everything loose around us rattle, I gripped my armrests tightly, digging my fingers into the leather.

"Greer?" Hayden took my hand, actually prying it off the armrest. "What's going on?"

"Just turbulence." I spoke through clenched teeth. "It's all right. We'll be fine."

"I know. Why are you so pale?"

"I'm not too thrilled with it. To be honest, it frightens me."

"The planes are built to handle it."

"It's not an entirely rational fear, I know." I took some deep breaths. "I'll be fine."

"Yes. You will. So will I." Hayden studied me for a moment, then leaned in and kissed my cheek. "Nothing bad will happen.

I'm here." She smiled slowly, as if testing to see if what she'd said was okay.

"Thank goodness for that," I said and squeezed her hand, returning her smile.

The plane leveled out as we descended below the clouds. I kept hold of Hayden's hand until we were on the ground. It felt far too good to let go.

As it turned out, when we landed at O'Hare, two people were waiting for us and whisked us through the airport. We had to go on one of the trains, but clearly Maryanne had called ahead, and the two men made sure we had an entire section to ourselves. When we reached the domestic-arrival area, I spotted a sign saying LANDON-ROWE immediately. Seeing our surnames together like that made me smile as my heart did its now familiar twirl where Hayden was concerned.

"This is our ride." I placed my hand at the small of Hayden's back and walked over to the tall woman holding the sign. "I'm Greer Landon," I said. "This is Hayden Rowe."

"My name's Tyra. Welcome to the Windy City, Ms. Landon, Ms. Rowe. Let me take your bags."

"No." Taking a step back, Hayden held on to her roller bag. She looked at me and then back at Tyra. "Thank you."

"No problem, ma'am. This way." Tyra looked as congenial and polite as before and led us out to where the limousine was waiting. Long, sleek, and black, it provided us with an air-conditioned and calm environment. "Just to double-check, it's the Whitehall Hotel, right?"

"Yes, thank you." I relaxed into the backrest and closed my eyes briefly. I'd come close to buying a condo in Chicago many times, as I came here often, but I liked the Whitehall, and it was conveniently located on the same street as the gallery.

I kicked off my shoes. First part of this trip done. Tonight was the big opening of the remodeled Chicago Landon Gallery. It had been six months since it closed temporarily. I checked my watch. Twelve thirty. I'd have to head over to the gallery around five p.m. to make sure everything was all right. The exhibition started at seven and would continue until midnight. I'd received good news about the status of all the artwork, including Hayden's, whose shipping I'd overseen myself.

Now I regarded Hayden more closely. She wasn't pale and didn't seem stressed. "How about we order a light lunch from room service and then have a nap?"

"Yes. I'm thirsty."

"Why didn't you tell me? Here's a whole fridge with different drinks." I opened the lid to a long, narrow refrigerator. "Don't tell me. Mineral water?"

"Yes." Hayden greedily reached for the small bottle and unscrewed the cap. Drinking in big gulps, she emptied it in a few moments. It reminded me that she hadn't had much to drink on the flight, as the flight attendant had somehow managed to intimidate her. That or simply annoy her, I wasn't sure.

"Better?" I said, and smiled. Her lips glistened from the moisture lingering there, and she looked stunning.

"Yes." She hesitated and then scooted forward and knocked on the partition. She waited for it to lower and then wiggled the empty bottle. "Thank you."

Blinking, Tyra then grinned. "You're very welcome, Ms. Rowe."

"My name's Hayden."

"Then you're welcome, Hayden." Tyra kept her eyes on the road but nodded in a friendly manner at Hayden via the rearview mirror.

The Whitehall desk clerk recognized me on sight, which made the check-in procedure quick and painless. They had my information and credit card on file. Hayden stood glued to my side as our bellhop fetched our keycards. He wheeled the cart into the elevator, and I made sure Hayden was on the other side of it. After riding up to the eleventh floor, we stepped into the large hotel room holding two queen-size beds. I'd offered Hayden her own room, but I couldn't persuade her even if the room had been an adjoining one.

"I don't know this hotel. I've never stayed there. Please, we can share. I'll be very quiet. I won't disturb you." It had bothered me greatly how young and girlish her voice had become as she'd practically begged me to share a room. Of course, I'd reassured her we could get a room with two beds instead. It was only for the weekend, after all. Two nights.

Now, Hayden was unpacking already as I tipped the bellhop. She shook her clothes out and refolded the ones going into the dresser, only to repeat the same thing with the clothes to be put on hangers. Her clothes traveled well, so nothing looked like it needed ironing.

I followed her example, and once I hung my clothes next to her, it dawned on me how right that looked. Her clothes to the right, mine to the left. As I turned to see what she was up to, I saw she was already fiddling with the remote, looking excited at the prospect of exploring the channels.

"What do you want to eat, Hayden?" I asked as I sat down at the desk, opening the information binder.

"Soup. Bread. Mineral water."

"Sounds good to me. They have minestrone, lobster bisque, and vegetable soup."

"Lobster bisque."

"All right." I placed the order and then walked into the bathroom to wash my hands. As I turned to dry them, Hayden was politely waiting her turn, standing just outside the door opening. "Hey, if the door's open, you can come in without asking. Okay?"

"Okay." Hayden stepped inside and washed her hands. "When are we going to the gallery?"

"At five. I suggest you bring a sketch pad or something in case you get bored while I make sure everything's going as planned."

"Okay."

Returning to the main room, Hayden curled up on the bed

to watch TV while we waited for our lunch. I sat down at the desk again, this time pulling out my laptop. Then I fired off a text message on my phone to India and one to Isabella, telling them we'd arrived safely and all was well.

After our lunch, Hayden helped me push the cart out into the corridor and I called the desk, asking for a wake-up call at 3:45. That would give us plenty of time to get ready and walk over to the gallery.

Hayden was watching TV again with the sound almost off. I took a blanket from the closet and curled up on the other bed, suddenly so tired I could barely see. Of course, I'd stressed about the trip as much as Hayden had, in my own way. I was so relieved she'd done so well while facing her demons, I was exhausted.

I didn't know how long I'd slept when something woke me. At first I thought perhaps it was the wake-up call, but then I heard a muted whimper from my right. Turning, I glanced over at Hayden, who was asleep, hugging a pillow in her arms. I thought she must be dreaming, and only when I saw her face contort did I realize it wasn't a good dream. She didn't talk in her sleep, but she kept holding on to the pillow and whimpering. Her right hand gripped for what I imagined were the paintbrushes that had fallen onto the floor. After a few moments, I couldn't bear the anguish emanating from her any longer. I slipped out of my bed and crossed over to hers.

"Hayden? You're dreaming, darling." I cautiously stroked her hair, not knowing if she'd swing at me. She didn't, but I felt dampness at the temples. Her cheeks were also damp and hot to the touch. This wouldn't do. "Hey, wake up. You're safe. You did so well today, and you're safe."

Her eyes shot open, red-rimmed and huge in her flustered face. "I'll be good," she said, forcing the words out as if her vocal chords hurt. "I'll be good. I promise."

Good? What did that mean? Why would she say something like that? What the hell had happened in her past that she'd need to say such a thing? I ached for her and wanted to hit someone at the same time. She couldn't be quite awake yet, I thought, caressing her cheek. Sitting down on the side of the bed, so as not to hover above her, I held her shoulders and squeezed gently. "Are you awake? It's Greer. We're in Chicago, having a nap before we're off to the gallery. Hayden?" I picked up the brushes off the floor and pressed them into her hand.

"Yes. Okay. I'm awake." Her body was slowly relaxing, but she was still shaking.

"Good. That was some nightmare. You all right?" I pushed the damp hair from her face.

"Almost."

"Anything I can do to help?" I meant like a hug or something, but Hayden scooted back and held out her arms after tossing the pillow to the foot of the bed. This could backfire, but how could I deny her? What's more—how could I ever resist her? I lay down next to her and took her in my arms, brushes and all. "There. Much better."

"Yes."

"It's only two thirty. We can sleep some more." I cupped the back of her neck and massaged her scalp with gentle fingertips. "I have you."

"Yes."

"Are you comfortable like this?" I certainly was. I couldn't remember ever being this at ease and enjoying someone else's presence this much.

"Yes." Hayden shifted slightly and moved her right arm. Her hand ended up nestled between my breasts, which threw the concept of well-being out the window. Now my heart started pounding and it was my turn to tremble.

Hayden might have thought I needed some form of comfort, because she started moving her hand up and down where it lay, caressing along my sternum. I wore only a tank top under my shirt, which made the touch feel even more intimate.

"You're shaking." Hayden pushed up on her elbow and looked down at me. "Why?"

"Hmm. You're touching me and it feels…very good." Far too good. I wanted to take her hand and have it cup my breast, but of course I didn't.

"This?" Hayden didn't stop but expanded the caress. She let her hand go down to my stomach, touched me from side to side, and then moved up to my chest again. "Does this feel good too?"

"Yes," I said, my voice little more than a croak. "Oh, God. Hayden, you're…"

And then she kissed me. Soft and gentle at first, but by no means innocently, she parted my lips and I was completely lost in her. Her mouth was warm, sweet, and so intoxicating; I knew in my heart I would never get enough of her. Hayden's hair fell forward around us, just long enough to create even more intimacy.

My hands had been inactive until now, but it was impossible not to reciprocate the touches. As I held her waist, I found her shirt had ridden up and uncovered naked, warm skin. It was satin smooth under my hand, and I ran it up and down as far as the bunched-up fabric would allow me.

Hayden let go of my lips, and I was about to moan my objection to being deserted when her lips began a new journey. She kissed my jawline, down my neck, and on down to the indentation just below. I heard her inhale and murmur something about how good I smelled. Her own scent engulfed me and drew me farther in. I found the top button of her shirt, popped it open, and then found another one, unfastening that one as well. Now I had access to her entire front, but somehow, knowing that I did stopped me from taking it further.

I pulled my hand out from under her shirt and used it to gently tug her closer so she could kiss me again. As we explored each other's mouths, I found I had never loved kissing anyone as I did Hayden. To me, kissing was more intimate than any sexual act. So, engaging in this prolonged caressing of the lips, the tongue, tasting her…it shattered what little protection I had left. After all these years of safeguarding my heart, of loving only my business and caring for my friends, the armor I'd constructed was disintegrating.

No matter what the future held, I confessed something to myself on that luxurious queen-size bed in Chicago, with my lips pressed hotly against hers—I was falling in love with Hayden.

CHAPTER NINETEEN

The gallery quickly filled with art lovers, critics, and the curious public. Their buzzing voices created a cacophony of sound that was quickly giving me a headache. I stayed away from the champagne and stuck to mineral water, just like Hayden. As I'd promised, I didn't leave her side but stood on the mezzanine with her, a pathway on the second floor stretching the entire length of the gallery, overlooking the people below.

They strolled by Andreas Holmer's paintings, stopping every now and then to peruse them, pointing, discussing, and those who saw him in the midst of them seemed to let him know what they thought. Judging from Andreas's expression, the comments were beneficial.

I found myself holding my breath as the first group wandered into the last of the large rooms, which in turn led back to where they'd started in the main hall. I'd arranged Hayden's paintings so they would be the last thing the viewers saw, with plenty of space for the visitors to stand and gaze at them.

I also had the gallery staff corral her paintings by roping them off with a tulle fabric pulled through the posts. A photo of Hayden I'd borrowed from her house hung to the left of her painting of a girl and a white picket fence. Looking at the photo next to the name of the painting reminded me of the interesting discussion we'd had while on the way over to the gallery, once I'd realized neither of her pieces had a name.

"Come up with something," I said as we walked to the gallery. "A girl. A white picket fence. Her wondering what's out there. The ragdoll. Does she fear the unknown?"

"Both. She wants to know what's beyond her walls, but she's told it'd be dangerous." Hayden grew quiet and I let her think. "All right. *Perilous Wonder*."

I blinked. That was quick. "All right. Sounds good to me. And the sunflower painting?"

"Do what you did before."

"What do you mean?" I glanced over at her, trying to figure out what she was asking.

"Tell me the details like you did with the first painting. That's when the name appeared in my head." Hayden took my hand and squeezed it gently.

"Ah. Okay. A woman. Reaching for the sky. Field of sunflowers. Small furry creatures observing her. Sunlight."

Hayden nodded slowly and was silent again. I enjoyed walking down the street with her, still holding hands, not caring one bit if anyone noticed. I'd hold her hand as long as she'd let me.

"*Sun Spirit*."

"I can tell you're going to be brilliant at this." I grinned. "That's a great name for that painting. I'll have the staff make the signs for it as soon as we're there.

Hayden returned my smile, and right then she looked so joyful and free, I wished I could freeze the moment and have her always feel like that.

Now I saw the first visitors leave Andreas's last painting, smiling favorably, and head into the last part. They stopped, their expressions changing from interested to mesmerized as they looked back at Andreas's paintings still in view and back again at *Perilous Wonder*. A woman leaned forward to study Hayden's photo and read out loud the short biography printed beneath it. Her voice carried above the buzz.

"Who's this? Have you ever heard of her, Scott?"

The man also peered closely at Hayden's photo and shook his head. "No. Did it say anything about her in the program?"

It did. I had added a small section with information about Hayden, clearly stating she was making her pre-debut as a painter courtesy of Andreas Holmer.

More visitors showed up, all of them stopping, staring, browsing through the program, and looking around as if to spot the artist.

"Time to go downstairs, darling," I said quietly. "Remember, we're staying behind the roped-off area, and if you feel overwhelmed by too much attention, just take a break and we'll walk back up here. All right?"

"Okay." Hayden stuck her hands into the deep pockets of her flowing white dress. She looked spectacular in the white ankle boots that matched the thigh-length dress perfectly. I'd put her hair up in a loose twist, letting soft locks frame her face. When I'd asked her about using makeup, she'd looked suspiciously at my makeup kit.

"I've never used it."

"But you're a painter—this isn't much different. You won't need any foundation, just a little bit of eye shadow and mascara. If you don't like it, you can wash it right off."

"Okay." Hayden trustingly lifted her face to me where she sat on the stool in the bathroom. I applied some light-brown eye shadow to accentuate her deeply set eyes. Two layers of mascara made her impossibly dense lashes look like she could catch butterflies with them. A pink lip gloss made her full lips glow, and watching her did strange things to my entire system. She suddenly appeared worldly, unless you took the time to read her eyes. When I did, my Hayden, the woman I felt I knew better than I'd known anyone, was still very much there.

"What do you think?" I turned her toward the mirror. It was fun to see her mouth go a little slack at the surprise.

"I look different. Still me, but different."

"Want to keep it?"

"Yes."

"All right. My turn." I put more makeup on myself. I was paler than she was and needed bronzer and blush to not fade out among all the lights that would be illuminating the art pieces at the gallery. When I finished, I turned to Hayden for inspection. "Good enough?"

"Also different. Very beautiful, but when I kiss you again later, we should wash up first."

I laughed breathlessly as we left the bathroom to get dressed. Later. Oh, bliss.

Now I walked down the staircase cleverly leading the way to the roped-in area where Hayden's paintings were displayed.

"Ms. Landon! Is this the young artist? Is this Hayden Rowe?" Several people pounced on us, and I felt more than saw Hayden come to a full stop.

"Yes, it is. Careful now, one at a time. Don't scare her." I blinked as I said it, as I hoped they'd think I meant Hayden was simply a shy girl, new to the scene.

"Ms. Rowe, where have you been hiding?" asked a woman in a red suit. Her name eluded me, but I recognized her as a renowned Chicago art critic.

"In a gym hall in Boston," Hayden replied, her voice steady, but her back pressed to the wall next to *Sun Spirit*.

"Really?" Looking taken aback, the woman smiled uncertainly. "And is that where you created these masterpieces?"

I nearly swallowed my tongue. To hear Red Suit—who rarely even bothered with new artists, let alone giving them any praise whatsoever—call Hayden's art masterpieces floored me.

"Only *Perilous Wonder*," Hayden said. "I painted *Sun Spirit* in my new studio."

"Now, now, Elsa. Don't monopolize the poor girl," a short, stocky man said. "I'm Dennis Lombard. Here's my card. I don't know who your current agent is, but I'm sure they can't be doing as good a job for you as I can." He winked at Hayden in a paternal way.

Hayden accepted the card and read it thoroughly. Looking up, she shook her head and handed it back. "I don't need it. I don't have an agent and I don't want one." She paused. "But it was polite of you to offer."

Elsa Red Suit snorted. "She showed you, Dennis." She turned to me. "When's Ms. Rowe having her exclusive exhibition? Will that be here or in Boston?"

"We haven't come up with a date yet, or which venue. If I'm to make a guess, I'd say this fall."

"These are both oils," a young man said. "Is that your favorite medium, Ms. Rowe?"

"No."

He waited for Hayden to continue, and when she didn't elaborate, he tried again. "Which other mediums do you work with?"

"Acrylics, watercolor, charcoal, pencil, crayons, and pastels."

"Wow, that's impressive. I'm Jason Rhys." He extended his hand to Hayden, who now took a step sideways to put more distance between them.

"I'm Hayden Rowe," she said and gave her polite crocodile grin.

Slowly he lowered his hand, frowning. "How come this is the first we've heard of you?" His voice had changed, now sounding sharper, and I wasn't so sure he was such an admirer after all.

"I've been busy painting." Hayden glanced at me, clearly needing reassurance.

"Hayden is a very hard-working artist, and I was lucky to stumble across her art only weeks ago. I don't think she realized how good she is—it's as simple as that." Out of the corner of my eyes I saw her squeeze her brushes in the deep pockets of her dress.

More people entered the room, making it impossible for Jason, Elsa Red Suit, and Dennis Lombard to remain by the roped-off area. The following people were kind and appreciative, pouring accolades over Hayden, who eventually started to look exhausted. I decided she'd had enough for now, and frankly so had I. She would have one more opportunity tomorrow to meet her adoring new fans.

"Thank you, everybody, but we have to leave," I said, trying my best to sound sorry. "I'm sure my staff and Andreas Holmer are ready to answer any questions you may have. Please feel free to have some more champagne." I took Hayden by the hand and ushered her up the stairs. We didn't linger on the mezzanine but walked into the small lounge area leading into my office.

"You did great, Hayden," I said, and hugged her. "I'm so proud of you, since I know this was hard on you."

"I liked part of it. I didn't like Jason Rhys."

"I could tell."

"How?" Hayden sat down on the couch and reached for another bottle of water.

"Well, first of all, I didn't care for his attitude either, even if I couldn't put my finger on what bothered me about him exactly."

"I can rarely put my finger on anything that bothers me. Nor do I want to. I usually stay away from things, or people, that bother me. When it's possible. When it's not my mother."

"You know," I said, and sat down next to her, "I think putting some distance between you and your mother might be a good thing in the long run. Once she comes to terms with the fact that you're not living at the school anymore, that you've started your career, she might come around and see that you're a grown woman. An adult in charge of her own life."

Hayden tilted her head and considered my words. "I don't think so. My mother has never accepted any skills in any way. She thinks I'm naïve and incapable of making my own decisions." She looked sorrowfully at me. "I used to try to convince her, despite Nana's objections, but Mother…never listens. Not to anyone, and never, ever to me."

I wanted to reach all the way back to Boston and throttle

the woman who'd hurt Hayden so badly over the years. Instead I channeled my emotions into my love for her. Hugging her close, I felt Hayden's heart hammer against my chest. I pressed my lips against hers and she opened her mouth immediately, kissing me back.

Eventually letting go of her, I cupped her cheeks. "I will always do my best to listen to you, Hayden. I know you're fully capable of making your own decisions and living your life the way you see fit."

"I see you in my life." Hayden turned her head and kissed the palm of my right hand. "I see how you fit into my life."

"Oh, God, Hayden. You drive me up the wall..." I nuzzled her neck, inhaling the scent of her. Clean, fresh, and faintly citrusy.

"When we are back at the hotel, I can do that if you want." Hayden's eyes glittered now, and I could have sworn she looked... naughty.

"Do what, darling?" I wiped some smeared lip gloss from her chin.

"Have you against the wall." She blushed faintly.

I was at a loss for words and completely dumbfounded. This woman would no doubt be the death of me, but who was I to complain? I was ready to be around her in whatever capacity she would want. "All right. Let's walk back to the Whitehall. Something tells me we better use the back exit. You're already such a rock star, they won't let us leave if we try the front door."

Hayden nodded emphatically. "Room service again?" she asked, sounding hopeful.

"Absolutely. I think we've seen enough people for today."

She smiled genuinely and brightly as she pulled me up from the couch. "Hurry, then."

"Okay, okay. Where's the fire?" I laughed and reached for our coats from the rack.

"In my chest, down through my stomach, and between my—"

I kissed her before she continued because, damn it, she was making me blush, and she reignited fires in me as well, by being so up front. And still, how else did I expect Hayden to be, if not blunt? I scolded myself. I shouldn't interrupt her when we were alone. In public, perhaps, if it would cause her sincere embarrassment, but like this, just between us, she should be able to say whatever she wanted.

"Yes?" I urged her to continue.

"Between my legs," Hayden said readily.

"No wonder you're in a hurry. Let's go."

As we walked through the corridor leading to the back stairs, I sent a few text messages, to my gallery staff and to India and Isabella. Once I finished, I could relax and focus on the only one who mattered.

Hayden.

CHAPTER TWENTY

I delicately wiped my mouth on the napkin and dropped it next to the plate. The entire meal, I had studied Hayden unabashedly—her hair, her face, and upper body—over and over as we ate. She didn't seem to mind, as she too looked at me. Now, my eyes had settled on hers, watching the gray irises go darker by the minute.

"That's it for me." I drank the last of my Bordeaux as I let my gaze sink deeper into hers. Unable to muster much appetite, at least not for food, I placed the lid back on my plate.

"Me too." Hayden stood and began putting the plates back on the cart. I rose to help, and then we did a repeat maneuver from earlier in the day by pushing it out into the corridor. "I'm going to wash off the makeup." Hayden looked encouragingly at me.

I chuckled. "Good idea. Mind if I join you?" I knew Hayden's routines before bedtime were set as if by royal decree. Having observed her a few times, I'd noticed she always did things in the same order and the same manner. Perhaps it gave her a sense of safety or control.

"No. I don't mind."

So, there we stood, shoulder to shoulder, makeup wipes in hand as we washed away our official selves. I nearly poked one of my eyes out as I kept watching her in the mirror rather than what I was doing. After finishing, I went back out into our room and turned off all the lamps but the ones on the nightstands. Admitting to myself I was nervous, I also realized we hadn't talked about our experience or lack thereof. I, for one, hadn't been with anyone in longer than I cared to confess. Hayden wouldn't care either way, and she wouldn't care about me feeling self-conscious about my semi-self-imposed celibacy. Still, this wasn't the main issue for me. What if Hayden was completely inexperienced? How did I ask this? Would such a question offend her?

I reeled myself in. I knew the answers to the last two questions. I should simply ask her. Hayden wouldn't be offended. To her, they were merely questions. She wouldn't invent any perceived judgment on my part.

Hayden came out of the bathroom smelling freshly of toothpaste. Damn it. Forgot. I hurried past her, eager to brush my teeth and—who was I kidding—grateful for a reprieve. As I returned to the room, she was sitting on her bed, looking at me. I sat down next to her and took her hand.

"Hayden, I have a question. Perhaps more than one."

"Yes?"

"Have you had sex before?"

"Yes."

Blinking, as this was somehow not the answer I'd expected, I wasn't sure if I was jealous or relieved. The former, of course, was utterly ridiculous, I told myself.

"I wanted to ask," I explained, albeit not very well. "Because if you hadn't, I might have, you know, not hurt you exactly, but inadvertently done something to—"

Hayden's smiling lips descended on mine and shut me up. Clearly, I'd made my point, and she wasn't going to wait for me to find any semblance of eloquence.

"Mmm." Hayden murmured into my mouth. The humming sound drove sparks of desire into my abdomen where they exploded and gave birth to yet more sparks, infusing my entire system. So this must be the fire she spoke of.

Hayden began unfastening my blouse, pulling it out of my

skirt. I helped by shrugging it off. At the same time, I unzipped her dress, wanting to see more of her, *touch* more of her. I couldn't wait for her dress to come off, so I kissed her. This was where the true intimacy lay. Soft, long, and, oh my God, such deep kisses. She responded like she'd been starving for me as much as I had for her.

Cool air engulfed my upper body and I knew my shirt was off. Wearing only my lace bra, I shivered, but not because I was cold. It was the heat she induced by her mere touch, and it made me shiver. Her fingertips seemed to paint my skin wherever they explored it. Slow circles across my collarbones, light strokes against the outline of my bra.

Impatient, I wanted her touch more than anything. Pushing down the shoulder straps of my bra, I unhooked it in the front and let it fall. Hayden's gasp was encouraging.

"Beautiful." She cupped my left breast reverently and then pressed her lips just above it. As this made it possible for me to fully unzip her dress, I pushed it down her arms. Unlike mine, her bra was simple cotton, but so pretty. It had to go. I reached behind her and unclasped it. As it fell into her lap, I sat on the bed next to her, kissing and tracing her jawline and neck with my lips, inhaling that special, clean-and-fruity scent of hers, forever tinged with paint, it seemed—or most likely that was only in my mind.

Her breasts, firm and high and just the right size for my palms, showed how aroused she was. Dark and pebbled, her nipples painted their own secret patterns in my palms. Hayden inhaled sharply and tipped her head back as I explored every part of her upper body with hands and lips. When she finally whimpered and stood, I stared at her, confused. It didn't take me long to realize all she wanted was to get naked. As she stood there, pale-skinned and so gorgeous I forgot to breathe, she pulled me to my feet. My blouse fell to the floor. I was shuddering so badly, I had to have her unzip my skirt and pull it down my hips. I started to roll down one of my stockings, but she pushed my hands out of the way. My heart thundered as she sank to her knees before me and peeled my stockings off my legs. Kissing along my legs, she made me groan, and for a moment I thought my legs would give out from under me. Her warm, steady hands peeled down my lace panties and pushed them slowly down my thighs. She looked up at me as she made the removal a caress.

I stepped out of my underwear, holding on to her shoulders, and she folded them neatly, placing them behind her on the other bed. Her breath gushed over my pubic hairs as she bent forward, kissing the crease above my left thigh. She kissed all the way from one hipbone to the other. Nuzzling me farther down, she nipped at the inside of my thighs, making me whimper. Her breath, so hot it ought to blister my skin, made me slide my fingers into her hair. I'd dreamed of this, so many times. In my dreams, both awake and at night, I'd been the instigator, but this…this was so mind-blowing, I knew I couldn't remain on my feet much longer.

I pulled her up, and now it was my turn to kiss her skin as I knelt before her. I helped her get out of her boots and step out of her dress. Folding it, I managed a fairly good throw and draped it over a chair. When I turned back, she'd begun to remove her panties.

"Allow me," I said huskily and tugged the cotton briefs down her long legs. Her skin was young, silky, and flawless. I placed open-mouth kisses as I got rid of her underwear, placing it next to my own. Now equally naked, I was torn between looking at every inch of her or pulling her into my arms. As it turned out, Hayden made the choice for me by taking my hand and tugging me toward her bed. She guided me to lie down, and I felt safe in letting her lead, which was so unlike me.

I kept looking at her, and the beauty of her angular face, her kiss-swollen lips, and her tousled hair was close to painful. If I could've painted like her, this would be my Holy Grail moment. She looked at me so intently, searching my face for something—what, I had no clue, but I hoped she saw my love for her in my eyes. I wanted to tell her, I really did, but the words, so huge, so overwhelming, eluded me. I tried to infuse all my feelings in how I touched her, how my hands mapped her skin and committed it to memory.

As she straddled my hips, her neat, dark curls, matted against her with the wetness, made me want to roll us over instantly. I wanted to explore just how far this wetness had spread and see if I could make her lose control like I was about to any moment now. Hayden continued to stroke along my body with her fingertips, and it felt as if she were painting on me. If she ever asked me to pose nude, I wondered if this was how I'd feel. Her hands were so soft, so hot, and I couldn't lie still anymore. When she reached my breasts, I arched against her, eager for her to caress me with greater intimacy. Smiling now, she cupped my breasts; she bent over me and took the right one into her mouth. Her hips began to roll against me, grinding the front of her drenched folds against me. Crying out, I slid both hands into her hair, holding her in place.

"Yes, yes," I said, moaning. "Oh, God, Hayden."

"Mmm." She hummed around my nipple, twirling her tongue around it, devouring me—there was simply no other word for it. She let go and stretched out fully on top of me, capturing my lips with hers. Her tongue demanded entrance and I met it with mine. At the same time, I pressed my heels into the mattress to gain momentum, rolling us. Now the one on top, I set out to explore her.

I didn't waste time but licked the same trail she'd used, yet in reverse, ending up with my mouth closing around one of her nipples. Hayden gasped and wrapped her legs around me. This maneuver pressed our pubic bones together again. My own wetness mingled with hers and the sensation intoxicated me.

"I need you." In a sense, I was asking permission, not quite sure why I felt I should. Hayden made room for me, eagerly parting her legs. She pulled her knees up and didn't take her eyes off mine as I cupped her labia, merely holding her for a few moments.

"I need you too. I need you more," Hayden said, sounding husky.

"Oh, God." I slipped my fingers in between her folds. The heat, the abundant wetness, almost made me come. Her arousal, given so freely, sent shivers throughout my body. I licked her nipples, going back and forth, as I spread the moisture between her legs everywhere. When I brushed against her clitoris, she jerked and moaned unabashedly. Her lips parted, her eyes wide open, she gazed at something far away. I'd never seen her this flustered, and the way her legs moved around me, impatient, erratic movements, urged me on.

"Like this? You have to tell me." Out of breath, I rolled my fingertips around her clit.

"Yes. Like that, but more." Undulating her hips, it was clear Hayden was trying to increase the pressure.

I circled her clit and gently flicked it with my thumb every now and then. I could feel my own moisture coating my thighs. I was so turned on that I was close to coming. Locking her arms around my neck, Hayden pulled me down and kissed me. Her tongue explored my mouth as she slid one hand down and pressed on top of mine. As I circled her entrance, her wetness sucked my fingertip in. I let my index finger enter her slowly, very slowly. I damn near fainted. I was inside the woman I loved. She welcomed me, trusted me to love her well, and I sobbed as I slid my finger all the way in. Hayden was so tight and her muscles trembled, already on the brink of coming.

"Oh, oh!" Arching, Hayden began to shake. I pressed my thumb against the now-rock-hard clitoris, gently massaging it. "Greer…Greer…yes, just like that. I like it…like that…"

I smiled into her neck, straddling her thigh with my hips, riding it. "Just let it come, darling. When you're ready—" My voice was barely audible even to myself.

"I'm ready now, Greer." Hayden wailed the words and lifted us both off the bed. "Now!" Convulsing, she pulled my finger farther in, as if milking it. I gladly obliged her, giving her what she needed. I kissed her neck, her cheeks, and when her breathing began to slow down a little, I kissed her lips. She was stunning where she lay beneath me, flushed and her skin aglow with beads of perspiration.

Finally, she stopped shuddering. "I've never felt such an intense orgasm before," she whispered.

"Then I'm glad you did now." I was. And infused with a good portion of cocky pride mixed with tremendous joy, I had to confess. I really wanted to be the only one who brought Hayden this kind of pleasure.

"You haven't climaxed yet," Hayden said, and scooted out from under me. "It's your turn."

"You're so beautiful." I pulled her on top of me and wrapped my legs around her. Rubbing my center against hers, I moaned. "And you feel so good."

"As do you." Hayden slid her hand down between us, much like I'd done with her. "Like this?" She pressed her hand against me.

"Oh, God, yes. Any way you touch me is fine. I'm—I'm so turned on by you, by watching you come, it's not going to take much."

She slipped two fingers inside and began moving, like an ocean wave back and forth, in and out. Hayden moaned as she let her palm rub against my clit. "Greer. So hot." She looked down at me, her lips quivering. "And so beautiful. Do I give you pleasure?" A tiny frown appeared between her eyebrows.

"You give me more than that." I wasn't going to put words in her mouth, but her touch was as loving as it was hot. I pressed my head back into the pillow, crying out. Having ached for her so intensely and now having her finally here with me, making me hers, I was teetering on the brink of the unknown. It was as if this lovemaking sealed something for me, cemented how I felt with each stroke against my inflamed folds.

Whimpering, I felt the orgasm start in my clitoris and then begin to spread. A thousand needles whispered over my thighs and abdomen, making me shake all over. I knew I was calling out her name over and over, but I didn't care if anyone heard me. A second orgasm immediately followed the first and this one wasn't as intense, but it was fuller somehow. I pulled her farther into my arms so I could kiss her, hold her.

"Hayden, you—you're amazing. You're wonderful." I wanted to tell her I loved her, but something held me back. "You're everything." Pressing my face into her neck, I curled up around her.

"You're all those things," Hayden whispered, her voice sounding tear-filled. "You're everything as well."

So happy in this perfect moment, I tugged at the blanket at our feet and pulled it over us. Safe and warm in the cocoon I'd created, I kissed her slowly, dreamily.

"Are we lovers now?" Hayden asked.

"Yes, I believe we are," I replied, and pressed my lips to her shoulder. "Happy?"

"Yes."

"Good. Me too." I smiled against her skin. She smelled of soap and sex, and it was the most enticing blend I'd ever encountered.

We lay there, and I was lost in my thoughts when she started talking.

"When I moved to live with Nana, I had only received hugs from my brother every now and then. I liked his hugs and had heard about how important human touch is for our mental development. I explained this to Nana, who was of the same opinion. We made hugs a daily effort, and after several weeks, I got used to it. Longed for it."

"That's only human. Totally normal," I said.

"Yes." Hayden snuggled closer. "But this is more. It's more than just a need or a want. I can't explain it, but it's *more*."

She was right. Even if she couldn't put it into words and didn't speak of love, she was right. I, on the other hand, knew that, for me, it was love and had been almost from day one. If anyone had told me I'd experience something akin to "love at first sight," I wouldn't just have scoffed; I would've mocked them for even suggesting such a thing existed in real life. And here I was, so in love, so enamored, with Hayden.

Hayden, who now was half asleep against me. I reached out and took a few of her paintbrushes, placing them under her pillow for easy access. I turned off the bed lamp closest to us and let the other one remain lit.

After I made sure the soft blanket covered us both, I wrapped my arms around her and closed my eyes. Hayden stirred, and her left leg slipped in between mine. That was all it took. I slid down, cupping her breasts, and gently pushed them together. Licking at her nipples, I heard her breath hitch and then she moaned, "Greer."

I rubbed myself against her knee, coating Hayden's skin with new wetness. She reciprocated by cupping my butt cheek with one hand, and the way she massaged it and pulled at it intensified the sensation between my legs.

"I can't get enough of you. It's as simple as that," I whispered.

"I want you again." Hayden growled, and the unexpected, sexy sound made a small, pre-orgasmic twitch deep inside me erupt. She pushed me off her leg and scooted down, taking the blanket with her. She buried her mouth and nose between my legs, and I spread them wide. I hadn't expected this either, but this was Hayden, my girl, and I could never deny her—why would I want to? As she entered me with several fingers and sucked my clit in between her full lips, I knew I wouldn't last. I had no self-control, and for once, I thought self-control was highly overrated.

When I came, I called out her name, vowing to reciprocate in kind. I just knew that tasting Hayden would be as sweet as the woman herself.

Chapter Twenty-one

Two days later, on Sunday afternoon, Hayden and I stepped out of India's car in front of our house. The revelation that I saw the house as ours made me swallow and then smile.

Hayden looked tired, her eyes red and with dark circles underneath them. She glanced over toward Penelope's house, and I figured if there was any way for Hayden to regain her bearings after yet another crowd-infested airport experience—even if she had handled it well—a session, or at least a chat, with Penelope would do it.

"Why don't you see what Penelope's been up to this weekend, Hayden?" I asked as I pulled out our bags.

"Okay." She started walking, and I smiled when she stopped suddenly, pivoted, and returned to, as I thought, kiss my cheek. Instead she kissed me passionately on the lips and then resumed her jog toward the Moore residence.

"And I guess you two are getting along *really* well?" India hoisted my messenger bag and handed me my keys. "Boss, that was some kiss."

"Hmm. Well. She never does anything halfway." I opened the door and switched off the alarm. In fact, having made love with Hayden several times since Friday evening, I was deliciously sore but kept that fact to myself.

"Erica says to invite you guys to dinner on Tuesday, if that's doable." India, according to our habit, carried out her assistant duties at my home as well and grabbed my house phone to listen for messages, pen in hand.

"That sounds great. I think Hayden will like it. Just stock up on mineral water." Kicking off my shoes, I smiled with relief, but when I turned to her I saw a deep frown form on India's face. She hung up the phone, staring at me.

"Fuck. We've got to get over to wherever Hayden was going. Penelope, right? The author?"

"What? Why?" I was already shoving my feet back into my discarded shoes.

"That was Penelope. Edward, that's her husband, I believe?"

"Yes?" My heart plummeted.

"He passed away yesterday."

"Wh-what?"

"She said she didn't want to ruin the showing in Chicago for you but wanted you to know as soon as you came home."

I ran. After I stormed out the door, I hurried down the sidewalk trying to catch up to Hayden. I wanted to be there when she found out. But Hayden had been running over to Penelope's and had reached her house within minutes. As I rushed up the path to Penelope's front door, I saw it was half open. With India right behind me, I stopped inside the hallway, where Penelope was holding on tight to Hayden's hands.

"Ah, Greer came along too. And you girls brought a friend." Penelope shook her head at me, and I realized she hadn't broken the news to Hayden yet.

"Hi, Penelope." I greeted her softly and introduced India.

Penelope shook India's hand and then turned back to Hayden. "Now, why don't we go and sit in the conservatory, all four of us?"

"Something's wrong, Greer," Hayden said to me, her eyes darkening. "Something has changed in Penelope's face since I painted her last and—"

I came up on her other side. "Let's go with Penelope."

"Why are you here? You're out of breath. Did you run?" Her

eyes narrowing with suspicion, Hayden glanced back and forth between Penelope and me.

Penelope didn't sit down but merely turned to Hayden when we stood in the center of the beautiful conservatory Hayden enjoyed so much. "Hayden? Edward died yesterday morning, probably around six. He suffered a major heart attack and was dead before the paramedics arrived." She spoke with sorrow, but also with dignity and love. "And he would have died alone, had it not been for the sketch you made of me." She blinked away tears, cupping Hayden's cheeks. "He was holding it against his chest, which comforts me. The last two days before he passed away, he only recognized me in that portrait—not me in person. I think he felt I was with him."

"Edward is dead." Hayden looked at me over Penelope's shoulder, telling me as if she didn't think I'd heard. "He's gone."

"I know, darling." I wanted to hug her to me, hold her close, but I could tell Penelope needed the contact, and perhaps Hayden did too.

Hayden cupped Penelope's shoulders and kissed her cheek. "I'm so sorry. Are you very lonely?"

"I don't think I've come to that yet, child. It's very quiet, though. I'm used to Edward yelling for me when I'm not there, or snoring when I sat next to him, writing."

"You can come home with us. Greer has several guest rooms." Hayden sent me a look that said "right?" in a very clear way.

I nodded. "Yes, you shouldn't be alone."

"Oh, I'm all right. All his caregivers still come according to their schedule. They're so loyal." Penelope wrapped her arm around Hayden's shoulder. "What I would *love* is some distraction. Please tell me about Chicago, the showing, all of it."

We sat down on the cushioned wrought-iron chairs. India offered to locate the kitchen and make some coffee, but Penelope insisted on the current caregiver doing it.

"Well, Hayden? Go on." Penelope sat close to Hayden

and held her hand. I had the feeling we'd shown up just when Penelope needed us the most.

"The visitors liked my paintings." Hayden nodded with emphasis. "Even the critics that Greer says are very picky. She calls them hard-nosed."

"I'm sure they can be."

"People asked me about my technique, where I come from, where I'd been hiding, who I'd studied with, and all kinds of questions. Some were hard to answer."

"Which ones?" Penelope asked, but was interrupted by a young man carrying a tray of coffee and biscuits. She motioned for him to place the tray on the table. "Do take a break and put your feet up, Larry," she told the man. "You've been at it all day."

"Thanks, Penelope." Larry nodded politely at us and left.

"Which ones?" Penelope asked Hayden again.

"Some asked where my inspiration came from. It was hard to answer when it came to *Perilous Wonder*, but easy for *Sun Spirit*. That one shows some of how Greer makes me feel. Not all of it, but some."

I had been pouring us all some coffee, but now I snapped my eyes up to look at Hayden. I'd thought it was about her coming out of her shell, and even if I had a lot to do with it, I didn't know I was part of her inspiration. This realization created a glowing bundle in the center of my chest, and I knew I was smiling like a fool. "She sold both of them," I said, so proud of Hayden that my grin grew even bigger.

"Oh, Hayden, that's wonderful. I'm so glad I got to see them before Greer shipped them off to Chicago." Penelope beamed, something I would have thought impossible only moments ago. Clearly the distraction of Hayden's success was working.

"What else took place?" Penelope asked and sipped her coffee.

"I had sex with Greer. Several times." Hayden looked pleased. "That was the best part of the weekend."

A fine mist of coffee sprayed from Penelope and India. I

wanted to tip my chair over and hide behind a damn palm tree or something. Hayden in turn looked obliviously, if a bit curiously, at the other two.

"How—how nice." Penelope attempted another sip before she put her cup down. "So, the two of you are, eh…an item?"

"No." Hayden regarded the coffee with hesitation. "We're lovers." She spoke with clear satisfaction.

"Yes. Of course," Penelope said weakly.

"Of course," India echoed, glancing at me, her eyes sparkling.

"We've taken yet another step in our relationship," I said, doing my best to sound casual. I was fully aware that life with Hayden would mean social awkwardness on a daily basis—or close to it. And I wanted a life with Hayden more than I'd ever wanted anything else. What was a little embarrassment compared with that? Besides, when Hayden disclosed our new status with such a happy face, how could I bother with the social *do*s and *don't*s?

"I'm very excited for you." Penelope squeezed my arm. "Are you planning what comes after this yet?"

I flinched. What was she talking about? Our relationship?

Penelope smiled broadly at my apparent confusion. "In regard to Hayden's work? Is she going to have a showing of her own?"

"Oh, *that*," I said, relieved, then shooting India, who was snorting, a dark glance. "What do you say, Hayden? When you feel the time is right, do you want to show some more of your art?"

"Yes. Here in Boston. No flying," Hayden said as she munched on a biscuit. "Pardon me."

"No flying. I think we can find many ways around that if we plan well. That's why we keep India around." I patted India vigorously on the back as payback for the snickering.

"I'm determined to become your first Bostonian art collector and customer," Penelope said. I could tell she was starting to fade now, her eyes drooping a bit at the outer corners.

"Thank you, Penelope. Now, we should unpack and let you get some rest." I stood and took her hand. "Please, are you sure you don't want to spend a few nights at my house? You'll be close to your own place but not alone." I thought of how to bring up the funeral arrangements without sounding too forward. "Penelope, don't hesitate to have the three of us help you with anything you need done regarding Edward's funeral. We're happy to help." I knew I could speak with such certainty for all of us.

"Thank you. I'll keep that in mind. My lawyers will handle the practical matters, and Edward and I have living wills. His is pretty specific about all the details, which helps. Thanks, both of you, for asking. I'm fine here." She paused and then glanced at Hayden. "But if you'd come over tomorrow and work on your painting, that'd be wonderful. If you have time, of course."

"Okay. I have time. Even if I didn't, I would reschedule." Hayden leaned sideways and hugged Penelope. "Call us if you feel lonely." She tilted her head. "Please."

"I will, dear. I promise."

"Good."

As we said good-bye and left Penelope's house, India wiped at suddenly damp cheeks. "Damn it. I hadn't even met the guy and I feel sad. What a terrific lady she is. Now I can brag to Erica that I met Penelope Moore." She smiled, misty-eyed.

"We might even ask Penelope to join us, or I should say you, for dinner on Tuesday," I said. "What do you think? Good idea?"

"Good idea," Hayden said. "She shouldn't be alone too much. Caregivers are practical, but they're not family or friends."

"True." I knew she was also thinking about her grandmother. "Are you driving over to see Nana while I'm at the gallery tomorrow?"

"Yes." Looking more at ease, Hayden smiled. "She wants all the details too."

Oh, God. I reminded myself it wasn't my place to edit Hayden. Her grandmother had certainly heard Hayden describe things that fell under the "too much information" tag many times. I just had to play it cool the next time I saw Isabella.

❖

I found myself fiddling longer than usual in the bathroom when it was time for bed. We'd finished the evening by watching yet another crime show. Hayden preferred the less-gory shows, which was a relief, as I didn't enjoy watching someone poke around in a decaying corpse too much. Now I brushed my hair for the third time, uncertain how the evening would play out. Perhaps Hayden wanted to keep her newfound freedom and sleep in her own room? Or was I overthinking it and should just crawl into bed with her, in either of our rooms? Perhaps invite her to mine?

Hayden rapped her fingers against the doorframe to the bathroom. "Greer?"

"Yes?" I dropped my hairbrush in the sink, and knowing I blushed at suddenly being so clumsy, I carefully placed it in its drawer.

"Now that we're home, which bed are we going to use?"

So I wasn't the only one wondering—that was a relief. Laughing, I wrapped my arms around her. "It really doesn't matter. I think you should keep your room as your own space, no matter what, but I'd love if you slept here with me in the master suite." I motioned toward my queen-size bed. "What do you think?"

"I like it." Grabbing my hand, Hayden tugged me toward the bed. "Is your bed as soft as mine? Which side do you sleep on? I favor my right side."

"Then left's fine by me." I grinned, suddenly so happy I thought I might self-combust. I wanted to tell her I loved her but held off. I'd never heard Hayden use the word, not even about Isabella or her brother. People said the word carelessly and often—loving food, films, items—and because Hayden never used it…the value of the word grew. I admitted to myself I also feared she might never be able to truly express it to me. Never in a million years would I want her to say it because she thought it was the polite or right thing to do. I tried to tell myself it was just a word and it shouldn't bother me. Gazing into Hayden's happy eyes when we crawled into bed was enough. She was here, with me, and showed me affection and attention with everything she did and said. That was all I really needed.

As Hayden began peeling off my sleepwear, I quickly forgot any misgivings, and all I could focus on was her. She ignited every single part of my body, made me lose my breath with each new caress. Hayden was my lover, my sorceress, and seemed to know just how to touch me. She found the topic of feelings mysterious, but I experienced them clearly through her hands against my skin—or saw them on her canvases.

I wrapped my arms and legs around her as she made me come over and over. Never in my life had I let my guard down like I had with her. She effortlessly broke through my defenses, and once they were down, I let them stay there. Gasping now, trying to replenish the oxygen I'd lost when my body was on fire, I clung to her.

Only when I'd regained my bearings did she allow me to reciprocate. I found it equally amazing at how responsive she was, and then I stopped analyzing and let myself drown in her. After kissing her full lips swollen, I let my mouth travel down her body. Damp, silky, her skin blushed under my caresses. I wanted to explore all of her, needed to map her entire body. Rolling her over, my hands greedy for her, I still kept my touch gentle and tried to read her response. Trembling, Hayden pushed her bottom against me, and I entered her gently. So tight, so hot, she pulled me farther into her heat.

Our sweat-soaked bodies slid against each other, the barely there friction exquisite. Her climax started something in me, a low, humming sensation, and when she pressed her bottom against me, I rode her shamelessly, our moans blending and merging.

"You smell good," Hayden whispered as we finally settled down under the covers.

"I do?" I pressed my lips to her damp forehead.

"Yes. You smell…like Greer. It's a unique scent."

Unique. The word stuck with me while Hayden nuzzled my neck and found a comfortable position. I thought it fit her much better than me.

❖

The next morning, I was out the door half an hour earlier than usual. Hayden was already on the roof, painting, and around ten she would drive to Isabella's. I knew she was eager to see her grandmother, and before I left, I dashed up one more time to kiss her good-bye.

"Drive safely," I said, cupping her bottom as she held the oil brushes away from my suit. "And give Isabella my best."

"I will. And I will." Grinning, Hayden kissed me back. "Don't hit anything on your way to the gallery either."

"I won't."

Hurrying down the stairs, I chuckled at Hayden's attempt at social niceties. She'd done so well in Chicago and still stayed true to herself. I was sure some people had picked up on her directness and literal way of answering questions. So what? Some people found me rude and too direct as well, and I couldn't care less.

India waved a thick stack of notes for me as soon as I arrived. "People love her!"

"Are these all about Hayden?" I took the stack of at least fifty notes.

"Nah, some of them are about Andreas, but I'd say two-thirds are about your girl." She winked at me.

I merely raised an eyebrow and shook my head. "I don't own her, India."

"I know that." She pouted, doing her best cute-puppy face, which looked more like cute-barracuda. "But she's your girl nonetheless. And dang, is she hooked on you. I saw it before you guys flew to Chicago, but when you came through the airport, Hayden all tense about the crowd, she *still* looked at you like you were the one who made the sun go up and the stars glimmer."

"How poetic of you," I muttered. In secret, I found the description charming, if a bit exaggerated. I sat down at my desk and read through the notes one by one. Most of them were from different art dealers, critics, and a few regular journalists interested in doing what they called a human-interest story. I wouldn't recommend the latter to Hayden, as I could already picture their angle. If they'd done their research, they knew more of Hayden from the old tabloids. No doubt they'd portray her as some poor girl who could paint but struggled against horrible odds. She'd hate it, and I'd throttle them if they dared go near her.

As I was on my way to lunch, my cell phone rang. I checked the display and frowned when I saw Oliver Rowe's name.

"Greer Landon," I answered, an ice-cold lump forming in my belly.

"Hi, it's Oliver. Hayden's brother."

"Of course. What can I do for you?"

He sounded rigid as he continued. "I hope I'm wrong about this, but I think Mother's planning something. Knowing her, whatever she's up to can't be good for Hayden."

"Now what?" I couldn't believe the gall of this woman. "What have you heard?"

"Actually, it was my father, who seems to finally get that my mother's obsessed with Hayden. Or I should say, obsessed when it comes to controlling Hayden. He said she was frantic this morning and determined to, as he put it, 'Put a stop to this unseemly affair Hayden is in.' She was out the door before he could stop her."

"God. Has she finally lost it?" I shouldn't have been shocked, but part of me still was.

"I know it sounds insane—and in a way, that's what it is. It's been escalating these last years, ever since Hayden moved out when she was fourteen."

"And now, what's her agenda now?" I hurried to my car. "And where do I need to go? Is Hayden still with Isabella?"

"Yes, I believe so. I've tried calling, but her cell phone goes directly to voice mail."

"I'm on my way there."

"Me too," Oliver said somberly. "I have a bad feeling about this."

So did I.

CHAPTER TWENTY-TWO

I ndia. With me." I waved at her.
   She'd probably heard some of the conversation because she
brought her tablet and was ready to go.

"See you at the clinic," I said to Oliver. "And drive safely."
I hung up and unlocked my SUV. Entering the car, I gripped the
wheel hard, my anger crashing inside me like waves against tall
cliffs.

"Yes, drive safely," India said softly. "Take a few deep
breaths and don't get us killed in traffic. Then you can fill me in
so I can help."

As we hurried to the clinic, I gave India enough information
for her to be up to speed. My heart thundered as I imagined Leyla
tearing into Hayden, and perhaps even Isabella. Hayden would
be a hundred times as upset about the latter, and I swore I'd
persuade them both to take out a restraining order.

"I double-checked that the storage-facility contracts are all
in Hayden's name, so she can't challenge that. I have a feeling
she'd try to get her hands on Hayden's paintings if she could."

We got stuck in lunch-hour traffic, but I consoled myself that
it was bound to affect Leyla too. And it gave me time to pull one
extra rabbit out of the hat. I was very grateful to have a suspicious
mind and a virtual private detective for an assistant.

When we reached the clinic I spotted Oliver's car parked

close to the entrance. I lucked out and found a spot right next to him. We hurried inside. My stomach was in knots no matter how I tried to follow India's advice about deep breaths.

When we entered the corridor leading to Isabella's suite, I heard the sound of raised voices.

"Fuck," I muttered and ran the last of the way. Entering Isabella's living room, I stopped so fast, I almost fell over the fold I created in the Persian rug.

The tableau before me was like something from a Greek drama. To the right stood Leyla, dressed in lilac shoes, skirt suit, and purse. Next to her a tall, skinny man in his late sixties stood holding a set of legal papers.

To the left, Isabella sat, straighter than I'd seen her sit so far, in her leather armchair, flanked by Hayden and Oliver. Behind me a new set of footsteps announced the presence of yet another person, a handsome middle-aged man who seemed to belong to the left.

"Greer!" Hayden held out her hand. I circled Isabella's chair and pressed a quick kiss to the old woman's cheek before I took my place by Hayden's side. India seemed to find a kindred spirit in the handsome man and stood next to him, murmuring something in his ear. He smiled and nodded, only to redirect his laser-like blue eyes on Leyla's representative.

"So, the leeches have gathered around my daughter," Leyla said. "Greer, how you disappoint me. I didn't think you'd show your colors this fast. My daughter, despite her problems, is an heiress, and from a lack of insight into her state of mind, my frail mother-in-law has seen fit to allow her to access her trust fund. Isn't it interesting that you would show such interest in her 'art' just as she gained access to all that money?"

"You're misinformed, Mother." Hayden spoke coldly. "I gained access to my trust fund when I was twenty-one. Five years ago. If Greer wanted to have access to the money, she wasted five years."

Leyla shook her head, managing a pitying glance at her

daughter. "You're too blissfully ignorant of how devious people can be, sweetheart."

"No. You've taught me very well, Mother." Hayden placed a hand on Isabella's shoulder. "You haven't been to see Nana in months, yet you still barge in here, ruining our time together when I was telling her about Chicago—"

"Chicago! There's another example of Greer Landon's method of intimidating and tormenting my child." Leyla now turned to the man next to her. "Make a note of the fact that my daughter is deathly frightened of crowds and unfamiliar people. Still, she's putty in this woman's hands, and Greer Landon drags her halfway across the U.S., traumatizing her for her own gain. Futile gain, at that."

I was standing close to Hayden, my hand at the small of her back. I hadn't planned to speak for her, but since this damn woman was attacking me personally, I couldn't be quiet. "Traumatizing her? Now, let me see, like you did when you locked her up in the gym hall of your school? If you ever found it curious how that key just seemed to disappear, I can tell you I suggested Hayden keep it so you couldn't do it again."

"What? I never—"

"On more than one occasion, Mother. Many times when I was a little girl."

"Don't bring your childhood up," Leyla said. "You were too young to understand."

"I disagree," Isabella said, her voice unsteady but completely audible. "You mistreated this child from the beginning. At first, I gave you the benefit of the doubt, since having a child with special needs, who's a bit different, can be daunting for any parent. But as you and my son didn't grow and learn, and he danced to your tune at every turn, I had to step in."

"You horrible old...bat!" Leyla curled her hands into fists. "The matter at hand today is the petition I intend to file to have Hayden declared incompetent. I should've done it long ago, to save her from people like Greer Landon."

"The same Greer Landon you went out of your way to invite to your school?" the man next to Isabella said, reading from India's tablet. "Oh, my apologies, Ms. Rowe. You may remember me from the custody hearings when Hayden was fourteen? I'm Dominic D'Sartre, head of Sartre, Fartherington & Bloom. Our firm has handled the Calthorpe family's business since 1812. Long history there." He smiled broadly, reminding me of a polite shark. "When Ms. Calthorpe Rowe placed a call to me via her granddaughter, who I'm also delighted to represent, I only had to pull out the documents Mrs. Calthorpe Rowe, her late husband, and I put together when Hayden and her brother were little. As I'm a firm believer in transparency, here's a copy for your attorney. Nice to meet you again, Dennison."

"D'Sartre," the man called Dennison muttered, and nodded briefly.

"This is my administrative assistant, India Duane," I said. "I'm sure India can email you any electronic copies you may require from my company."

"It doesn't matter how many people think they can fool my daughter into thinking they're in her life because they care." Leyla was actually stomping her foot again. This didn't look very good. "I know they're trying to fool her. They tell her she's a gifted painter, and voilà, she's spitting out paintings like toothpicks. Greer Landon drags her across the country to show her off like a one-trick pony, an idiot-savant—"

"Enough!" The deep male voice from the door made us all jump. I stared at Hayden's father, who stood there, shaking, but more from fury than from fear of his wife, I surmised. He looked from Hayden to his mother, his face softening. "I apologize for the commotion, Mother," he said. "How are you doing?"

"I've been in a better mood, but otherwise, I'm doing quite well." Isabella nodded slowly.

Michael Rowe turned to his wife. "Leyla. It's gone far enough. It's time."

"What do you mean?" Leyla's face was pale, but pink roses

burned on the apples of her cheeks. "You know better than anyone what we went through—what *I* went through—"

"I do. And I know what Hayden had to go through. And Oliver. You were so busy trying to fix Hayden, you forgot your firstborn child. I tried to make up for it, but he needed his mother too. It's a miracle he comes to see us at all."

Leyla gasped for air now, drawing breath after breath, her body shaking. It dawned on me now that this woman, who I truly thought I hated, might be unwell. Mentally unwell. Had her ambitions, combined with the past of this whole dysfunctional family, finally pushed her over the edge?

"Mother." Hayden stepped closer to Leyla but kept her distance. She had one hand in her jacket pocket, no doubt squeezing a few good paintbrushes. "There isn't anything wrong with me. You know how I know?"

Leyla, now sitting down on one of the visitor's chairs, merely shook her head.

"Because I like my life. I like to paint. I don't like flying or airports, but when Greer was with me, it was okay. I'm sad about Edward dying, but my new friend Penelope needs my support. And Greer's. And Greer needs me. Not my money. She's already rich. She needs me."

I was grateful Hayden didn't bring up *all* the ways I needed her. I didn't think I could be more proud of the woman I wanted to spend my life with, but now I was. Here I'd driven over, nearly killing India and myself, to get to Hayden and save the day. As it turned out, Hayden was doing a fine job of saving herself. I also knew it was because the people around Hayden empowered her.

Michael Rowe walked up to his daughter. "I'm sorry, Hayden. I shouldn't have let it get this far. I hope you can forgive me one day." He half raised his hand but then let it fall immediately when Hayden took one step back. "Your mother and I are leaving now. There'll be no petitions or lawsuits. You have my word."

"Michael!" Leyla gasped and stood. "You know very well what our duty is—"

"Our duty is to let our grown children get on with their lives. If you're lucky, Hayden may still come to your school to give master classes. If she doesn't, well, I for one will understand."

Leyla was still arguing when he put his arm around her shoulders and led her out into the corridor. Mr. Dennison nodded awkwardly at the rest of us and hurried after the Rowes.

"That was unexpected," Oliver said. "The old man put his foot down in the eleventh hour."

I wrapped my arms around Hayden from behind and hugged her. "Are you all right?"

"Yes. I think. Yes." She was shuddering. "She's not well. I hadn't really understood that before. Today, it was clearly visible around her eyes. She looked...wild."

I agreed. Leyla had looked feral as she spat her opinions and fought to reel Hayden back into the fold. Perhaps she had really thought she was protecting her? Nah. I didn't buy that. Leyla was a social climber and ambitious enough to shame our most ruthless politicians. She might have started out trying to help her daughter at one point, but when she thought Hayden had become a social liability, someone her peers talked about as "that poor Rowe child," she had conveniently hid behind "I just want what's best for you, Hayden."

Isabella rang for coffee. I sure as hell needed a whole thermos for myself after witnessing Hayden take on her mother.

"Now, despite my son's miraculous turnaround, I still want you to keep your ear to the ground, Dominic," Isabella said. "I don't trust her."

"Don't worry. I'm on it, and Hayden has nothing to worry about." Dominic D'Sartre smiled at Hayden. "In fact, from the Chicago newspaper clippings my assistant showed me, you have a lot to look forward to career-wise, Hayden. The showing created quite a buzz about you in the art world."

"A buzz?" Hayden's eyebrows rose. "My paintings cannot induce a different frequency in sound." She looked over at me. "Greer?"

"To create a buzz means that people are talking about your paintings a lot."

"Ah. Another saying." Hayden did exaggerated quotation marks with her bent fingers. Her face made it clear what she thought of cryptic sayings. Not much.

"I don't know about you guys, but I feel totally drained," Oliver said. "And I hardly opened my mouth. I guess that was a long time coming."

"How did it feel to have your father bring out in the open how Leyla let you down when you were a young boy?" India patted his arm.

Oliver blinked hard a few times. "I never knew he noticed. He did make a point of coming to my Little League games and spending time with me, but I never knew he realized how…lost I was when Mother wasn't there. I'm four years older than Hayden, and I saw such a difference in her before I started school, and after. That's when she truly changed."

"Was it my fault?" Hayden whispered, shattering my heart. "I tried to be good, to be as she wanted. I never understood—and still don't—what I did wrong."

"Darling sis," Oliver said, and flung his arms around her. "Don't you think that for a minute. You were a little, tiny girl. I was a young boy. She was the adult. Our father too. Nothing was our fault. Thank God Nana got you out of there. By then I was off to college and you needed rescuing." He pressed his forehead to hers. "And you know what? You don't need that anymore. You're fine just the way you are."

Hayden smiled and hugged him back. This situation was now reaching emotional overload. I stood and took my coffee cup with me to the window. Since I'd met Hayden and been swept off my feet and really hadn't landed yet, if I ever would, my heart had been tossed between so many emotions. I wiped errant tears at the corners of my eyes. For me, Hayden's happiness mattered most. I was honest enough to add myself to that equation, as I couldn't imagine being without her. What if my presence kept

Leyla from calming down? What if I turned out to be the factor that made her continue to launch new attacks at Hayden?

Lanky arms wrapped around me from behind, and the room was suddenly quiet. Hayden's scent of soap and fruit filled my senses and I sighed, knowing full well I was too weak to give her up. Or perhaps strong enough not to let a cow like Leyla Rowe dictate Hayden's and my happiness?

"Are you all right?" Hayden kissed my neck.

"Yes. Thank you. I will be."

"Nana's off to the dining room to have her lunch there. Oliver went with her. Dominic and India are going back to their offices. India took your car."

"She did? Ah, I see. So, just us, huh?"

"Yes."

I pivoted within her arms, placing the coffee cup on the side table. "Why don't we go home? You can paint some. We can check on Penelope."

"And watch some daytime TV." Hayden smiled brightly.

"Of course." I could think of nothing better. "Let's go."

Hand in hand we walked out into the parking lot, where she automatically chose the driver's seat as usual. I certainly didn't mind, as I had concluded Hayden was the better driver.

CHAPTER TWENTY-THREE

I stood in the doorway to the staircase leading up to the old gym
hall where Hayden used to live. It was hard to imagine that was
just weeks ago. I saw the key was still in the lock—on the inside
of the door—and this made me think of when she called me after
being locked up. I shuddered and walked up the staircase, not
quite sure why I needed to see this place again.

It was darker than I remembered. Even if the sun shone
outside, the much-dirtier windows kept the light from getting
through. Imagining Hayden trying to paint here, in less than
stellar conditions, to put it mildly, broke my heart. Especially as
she now had the studio on our rooftop, a place I knew she adored.

I sat down on one of the foldable chairs by the wall and gazed
around the dreary gym hall. So large, desolate, and yet Hayden
had created such miraculous art here. Perhaps it worked for her,
as she always looked inward while painting. Even when she
painted portraits, like the one of Penelope, she was somewhere in
her head, or her heart, or wherever her brilliance lived.

Would I ever truly be invited there? I so longed to share
everything with Hayden, and by that, I meant professing to love,
something I had never done. I've lived my life with such armor
on. Practicing hit-and-run dating, I've never allowed anyone to
remain close. If India and later Erica hadn't been so persistent in
being my friends, I would probably still hold them at arm's length.
With India especially that hadn't worked. She merely decided she

liked me, as a friend, and that I needed someone in my corner. Of course she was right. When she and Erica kept setting me up with different women, and none of them ever worked, mainly because I didn't give them a chance, I focused on business. On success.

And then Hayden came into my life. Now I was the one hopelessly enamored by this young woman who might never be able to fully reciprocate my love for her. I knew Hayden felt every emotion just like any other person would, but she was nonplussed when it came to expressing them and distinguishing what they were.

I knew she loved her grandmother and Oliver, her brother. That was obvious. She said herself she liked Isabella and our friends. It was clear she was attracted to me, romantically and sexually. She trusted me totally, which made me want to hold her and never let anyone hurt her ever again. Of course, Hayden wouldn't respond well to such protectiveness, but be completely dumbfounded and question such weird behavior, no doubt.

Sitting in the gym hall, alone, I admitted to myself I yearned for her to express her love for me. Would I be able to live with her, spend the rest of my life with her as I ached to do, if she could never truly say she loved me? I wanted her to say it because she truly recognized this emotion in herself. That might never happen. Most likely, I would never hear those words from her.

Did that mean I shouldn't tell her I loved her? I knew Hayden would take it in stride, possibly even say "thank you," as she might perceive it as one of those occasions when she should remember to be polite. That would be horrible. And rather ridiculous.

I hid my face in my hands and felt incredibly silly as tears burned behind my eyelids. I forced them back as best I could. If Hayden saw me red-eyed later, she would worry. For misinterpreting and finding it hard to read others many times, she was far too observant when it came to me. I often found her studying me, her head tilted or resting in her hand, and her eyes never left me as I cooked or worked on my laptop. She would take one look at me and ask me, sometimes in front of whoever happened to be there, why my eyes were red and had I been crying.

I was so lost in my thoughts I didn't hear anyone approach, but suddenly she just stood there. Three brushes in each hand, Hayden looked uneasy as she gazed around the room, then returned her focus to me.

"Why are you up here, Greer?" She shifted from one foot to the other.

"I'm not quite sure. You were busy teaching and I needed to stretch my legs. I saw the door was open and…I just came up."

"I don't like it here."

"I don't blame you. Let's go downstairs again." I got up, but she held up one hand and stopped me.

"Wait." Just like I knew she would, she studied me closely. "Your eyes." She frowned and moved the brushes in her right hand over to the ones in her left. Running her fingertips along my eyebrows and down my cheek, it was as if she tried to absorb my feelings by touching me.

I couldn't keep her guessing. It simply wasn't fair. If Hayden and I were going to make it as a couple, I needed to be as transparent as it was humanly possible. "I sat here and thought of both our pasts," I said, and captured her hand. I kissed her palm, charmed by her familiar scent of soap and paint. "It made me sad for a while. You were miserable up here in the gym hall, yet it was where I first got to talk to you properly. If I hadn't barged in here after seeing your painting that Luke and the others had 'borrowed' from you, who knows…?"

Hayden listened intently. "I was unhappy here. Yes. I missed my grandmother. I didn't see Oliver very much. I was alone."

"And now neither of us is alone anymore." I wanted to see that desolate expression on her face disappear so badly, I pinched myself for coming up here and causing her distress in the first place.

"I like where I live now. I like your house."

"*Our* house, Hayden," I reminded her. "Don't you feel it's your home too now?"

Hayden stood silent for a few moments, clearly giving my question due consideration. "I do. I like everything about *our* house. Especially the studio, the kitchen, our bedroom, and the TV room."

"That sums up half of the house, so I take that as an overall approval." I winked to show her I was only teasing. "I'm glad. If you ever want to change anything about it, please tell me. You have a good eye for colors."

"Okay." Hayden took my hand and tugged gently. "Can we go downstairs now? I want to kiss you, but I don't want to do it here. This room doesn't deserve that."

Charmed again at her way of reasoning, I squeezed her hand and we left the gym hall. I knew we would most likely never return there again. As soon as we stepped out into the corridor, Hayden put her arms around me and kissed me. I had already noticed the corridor was empty of students, not that I would've truly cared, but their absence made it even better. I held her close, and the kiss burned all the way to my thighs.

"Mmm." Hayden pulled back a little and smiled. "I like our kisses too."

"That makes two of us." I nuzzled her cheek. "Guess we need to go back to the classroom?"

"Yes, in four minutes."

I merely stood there for a while, inhaling her scent, knowing no matter what, I would make this relationship work because the alternative was unthinkable. A future without Hayden by my side would cause me such pain, I would never entirely recover. I knew this. Had anyone told me I'd feel like this only a few months ago, I would have scoffed at such drama. Now I knew better.

"A mural," Hayden said and smiled broadly.

"What? Where?" Yanked out of my reverie, I tried to catch up.

"On our wall just inside the door, to the left. You have a few paintings there, but that wall lends itself to a mural." Hayden looked so happy about her idea that I chuckled and hugged her hard.

"That's a great idea. Why don't you sketch a few ideas and we'll brainstorm together?"

"Brainstorm? Yes. Lots of ideas." She tapped her temple. "Lots of storms."

As we walked back to our students, I thought of her sudden inspiration. A mural on our wall at the house—something permanent. This possibility made me feel encouraged and infinitely better.

❖

Hayden had been acting uncharacteristically mysterious the last couple of days, and for some reason, I hadn't been allowed into the studio. I'd worked from home the first three days after the showdown at the clinic. Or the Leyla Rowe Meltdown, as India referred to it. Hayden became a woman of even fewer words when I brought the incident up; she clearly didn't want to talk about it. I was worried but had to respect that.

We spent Tuesday evening with Penelope, India, and Erica, the five of us having dinner, which turned out to be an interesting evening. India, like me, was a decent cook, but Erica was phenomenal in the kitchen. Hayden had shadowed her every move, asking questions about the exotic spices, and looked mildly horrified when Erica talked about winging it.

"You have to follow a recipe," Hayden stated, her eyes darting back and forth between Erica's hands and the pots on the stove.

"Nah. I have a basic recipe, but I like to switch things up. Like when you paint, you know? Once you have your technique down, you use it to create new pieces of art."

Hayden's lips formed an *O* as she looked at Erica as if she'd said something Nobel Prize–worthy. "I want to try."

"Sure, go ahead. Pour into your palm so you can estimate how much you'll use, okay?"

"Estimate?" Now uncertain again, Hayden poured some oregano in the palm of her hand. "This makes tomato sauce taste good." Her forehead creased as she debated what to do with it. I followed her every move, so happy she was enjoying herself. Against all odds, the tall, strong Erica didn't intimidate Hayden like she did most other people. "Since there are tomatoes in this pot of vegetables, it might have the same effect in there?" Tilting her head, Hayden looked at Erica for confirmation.

"I agree. Go right ahead."

Hayden carefully sprinkled the oregano into the ratatouille, a broad, genuine smile on her face. She glanced over at Penelope and me. "I'm learning new things."

"Works for me." I raised my glass to her, and she hurried around the kitchen island and grabbed her own glass. Clinking it to mine, Penelope's, and India's, she wrapped her free arm around me. "What are we toasting?"

I thought fast. "To improvisation!"

They echoed my words and we all laughed. I hadn't been that relaxed in years. Me, enjoying a double date with friends? Who would've guessed?

❖

Oliver came by on the Wednesday, bringing news. As it turned out, he had to give it to me, as Hayden wasn't interested. She waved dismissively at both of us from inside her studio, and we knew better than to push her.

"Mother refuses to talk to me. I don't think she's forgiven Father for interfering with her crazy idea either." Oliver sat down across from me in one of my wicker chairs on the roof.

"She's not...well," I said diplomatically.

"That's putting it mildly," Oliver said, his voice sad. "She's never been this irrational. On Monday evening she was close to paranoid, according to Father. He's openly concerned, which is a first."

"Has Hayden always been her focus? Her target?"

"Not the whole time. They didn't even see each other for long periods when Hayden was younger. As she became an adult, Mother was concerned about her rocking the boat. The boat being Mother's social circle of influential friends. She's worked hard, cultivating these relationships with Boston's high society. Being married into the Calthorpe family was just the start for her."

"To such a degree she made life a living hell for Hayden and forced her to keep her talent and creativity a secret." I could see how this fit together.

"And then you entered the scene. On one hand, you're the person she needs for her school to be recognized as one of the best on the East Coast. On the other, you challenge her, contradict her, and what's more, you bring Hayden into the spotlight." Oliver wiped at his eyes, and I could tell his heart was broken over his mother's actions and his sister's situation. It couldn't be easy for Oliver to be the child completely lost in the shuffle through the years.

"I bet you went to an Ivy League college and did everything you could to please your parents." I wasn't sure why I said this, but I suppose I wanted him to know.

"Well, yeah. I figured if I got brilliant grades, well, that'd make them see me…and it'd give Hayden a break." He shrugged. "The thing was, if you look at Hayden's high-school diploma, her grades were way better than mine in most subjects. She never went to college other than a few distance-learning courses, but she did really well in those." Oliver smiled and glanced over his shoulder at his sister. She was still ignoring us, focused on a large canvas. "I'm truly happy she's met you. I've never seen her so out of her shell and happy." He turned back to me. "Do you love her?"

I wanted to say those words to Hayden before I let anyone else know, but this was her brother and he was worried. Oliver had been to hell and back the last few weeks. "I'm going to tell her that, yes," I said, sort of letting him know without using the actual word. "I'm not sure if she'll ever say it to me, but she will hear it."

"She's never spoken of love as far as I know. Not even when it comes to Nana, who until now has been the most important person in her life." Oliver winked at me. "She can easily express when she likes or dislikes something, but the word 'love'…I think in her mind, it's such an abstract word, it's sort of illogical. If that makes sense."

"It does." I nodded slowly. It did. If Hayden never told me she loved me, I would learn to live with that. She showed me in so many ways that she cared about me, and her affection was very passionate and physical.

Oliver left without having had the opportunity to speak to Hayden.

The master class on Thursday went surprisingly well. Leyla wasn't present at the school, so her office manager acted as headmaster. It was as if the entire student body relaxed and did a better job. I doubted anyone would ever dare tell Leyla how detrimental her presence was.

Luke, Ulli, and Mio had set up the classroom according to our instructions. Four objects sat center stage on the dais, and the easels were spread out in a semicircle around them.

"All right," I said, and motioned toward the objects next to me. "We're going to take a vote here. Which one of the objects on the dais do you want to paint? You can use any medium, any technique, but you all need to agree on which one."

Luke's eyes lit up, and he quickly leaned over to Ulli and whispered something. She in turn whispered to Mio, who smiled and nodded vigorously. My suspicions grew as the entire class broke out in smiles and seemed to agree on their choice unanimously. That never happened, normally, during the times I'd done this exercise.

"All right, you clowns," I said, and placed my hands on my

hips. I shot Hayden a look. She appeared calm and held loosely onto a few brushes. "Which item did you choose?"

"We chose you, Ms. Landon," Luke said.

"What?" I wanted to thud my head against the whiteboard behind me. "That's too funny, but—"

"You did say any object on the dais." Ulli grinned and motioned at me, where I stood next to an old kerosene lamp. "You're the most challenging object up there. I think you should be proud of your students for not taking the easy route."

Oh, for the love of... Shaking my head, I knew I was beaten. If I chickened out on this one, I'd lose face, and they knew it. And I didn't want Hayden to think I was a coward. She was entering new territory every single day. I should be able to take this in stride.

"All right. Just so you know, I'll be twice as hard on you as if you'd chosen one of the inanimate objects. I see this face in the mirror every day. You won't be able to wing it. You have four hours, and I get a ten-minute break every hour. And I expect you to fetch me coffee. With milk. No sugar."

"Got it, ma'am." Luke saluted and began squeezing oils onto his palette.

Mio jumped up on the stage and removed the objects next to me and brought me a tall stool. I assumed a comfortable, relaxed pose. They all started working, some painting directly, some creating a few pencil sketches first. Hayden made her rounds among the students, and some of them asked her questions. I didn't realize until then what an amazing opportunity this was for her to teach the master class independently. She moved with such poise and self-confidence, and I figured it had to be because she knew she had something to offer. This was her area of expertise, and clearly these students looked up to her. She was no longer the strange person known as Rude Girl they'd created myths about before.

Reduced to an "object," I merely sat there, letting my mind wander. As usual, it was filled with images of Hayden. I thought of how we'd spent every night in the same bed this last week. When it came to making love, Hayden was as insatiable as she was uninhibited. In her eyes, nothing was wrong or too much. She could go from tender to strong and passionate within minutes, and still she always took me with her. Ever attentive, she focused on my pleasure with complete dedication, making me virtually howl beneath her hands and lips.

I had very rarely sat for portraits or any other artwork, but as I was comfortable and not asked to hold a painful pose, the four hours passed very quickly. Hayden had kept an eye on the time and gave the students a heads-up when only fifteen minutes was left. I was grateful to get up and stretch my legs. During my ten-minute breaks, I'd deliberately refrained from even glancing at any of the students' artwork, but now I was looking forward to it with terror-filled delight.

Luke had painted me with his usual strong, bold style. True to form, he'd managed to incorporate secret patterns showing something entirely different, depending on what part of the painting you focused on. Clearly, he saw something powerful in me, as he made me look quite superior and close to arrogant. It dawned on me that this depiction might be less than flattering for me on a personal level. I supposed unless someone portrayed me as a virtual witch, I had to suck it up. Hayden had already said what I thought, so I mainly concurred with an appreciative nod and moved on.

Ulli surprised me with a soft, stunningly beautiful watercolor rendition of me. My blond hair was like a halo, and she'd switched my chinos and black shirt to a long, sweeping organza dress.

"This is a nice change," I said, smiling at Ulli, who was chewing at the end of a brush, clearly not the first time, as it was totally demolished. "You've used a good technique and actually made me look pretty. No small feat in itself. You should develop your expertise in this medium more as it seems to bring out yet another side of your art."

"Thank you," Ulli said, preening.

If Luke and Ulli surprised me, Mio blew me away. Using only charcoal pencils, she'd created a detailed portrait of me that was close to a photographic likeness. She'd also captured the dreamy look in my eyes. I was glad nobody knew exactly what had brought out that particular expression.

Hayden and I went through all the paintings, and to my delight, we didn't find a single bad one. One actually made me laugh out loud. One of the girls, whose name I could never remember, had painted me as a marionette, someone cutting off the strings with a huge pair of scissors. You couldn't see who was attempting to pull the strings, but a distinct pink cloud hovered above the Greer-marionette. Hayden looked at the painting and then back at me, where I was wiping tears of laughter from my eyes.

"You have a strong point of view and an odd sense of humor. I'd say you've succeeded in impressing Greer as well as making her laugh." She patted me on the back. "Can you breathe properly? You're turning very red."

"No wonder." I choked, literally, on my mirth. Coughing, I managed to compose myself. "Brilliant, eh, what's your name again?"

"Britney."

"Well, Britney, you may have a future in several fields where humor and painting skills are required. Keep it up, and don't let anyone repress this side of your art."

"Yes, ma'am. No, ma'am." It was Britney's turn to go red. "I mean, I'll try not to."

"Good," Hayden said.

Once we'd critiqued the last of the paintings and the students had left the classroom, I turned to Hayden, studying her playfully. "And, my darling, if you'd been painting today, what would you have done?"

"I can't say." Hayden gripped the brushes harder.

Concerned, I closed my briefcase and walked up to her. "What's wrong?"

"Nothing's wrong. Not yet. I mean, it might be. Or not." She was rolling the brushes between her fingers, and I knew I needed to back off a bit.

"All right. Don't worry. You know we always figure things out." We started walking through the corridors toward the parking lot. "You didn't feel like talking with Oliver yesterday?"

"Yes."

"Hmm. Then why didn't you?"

"I was working."

"Ah." I tried to decipher the short sentences. "The painting you're working on—it's important?"

"Yes."

"More so than before?"

"More so than *ever* before." Hayden drew a deep breath. "If Oliver comes today, I can talk to him."

This I understood. "So it's done."

"Yes."

"Will you show me when we get home?"

After a very short hesitation on her part, she said, "Yes."

"All right then. Let's go home. Are you driving?"

She gave me a what-redundant-question-is-that kind of look. "Yes."

"Thought so." I tossed her the keys and she slid into the driver's seat of the Mercedes. She made sure the chair and the mirrors were set correctly, even though she'd driven the car to the school.

❖

At the house, Hayden waited patiently while I put my briefcase away and fetched us two bottles of mineral water. I was getting hooked on it too. I took Hayden's hand in mine as we walked up the stairs to the roof. It was a cloudy day, but the light was still bright enough for me to peruse a painting in her studio.

The canvas was covered, and Hayden slowly removed the

fabric and stepped back. She held the water bottle in one hand and three brushes in the other. Before I even glanced at the painting, I crossed the floor to her and cupped her cheeks. Kissing her gently, but with emphasis, I hummed into the caress. Then I let go and looked into her eyes, wanting her to see how honest I was.

"I love you, Hayden. With all my heart and soul, I love you. I've never said that to another woman before. There was actually a time when I thought I'd never love anyone—ever. You're a miracle to me, Hayden. Not only because I love you, but because you care about me too. You mean everything to me."

Hayden looked into my eyes for a good ten seconds, not saying a word. The silence should've been awkward, but it wasn't. I wondered if she was trying to put words to her feelings. I knew she felt everything like everybody else, but it was hard for her to identify her emotions.

"Greer. Look." She took me gently by the shoulders and turned me around, facing the painting.

I found myself looking at a portrait of me. As I let my eyes dart all over the painting, they welled up with irrepressible tears. Pressing my fingertips to my lips, I tried to take in all the details.

The canvas was large, fifty by thirty-five inches. Hayden had placed me in the center of a meadow, mountains to the left and a big city to the right. In the far background was a forest. She had extended some locks of my blond hair, making them reach the clouds and disappear into the sunlight. Flowers and grass wound themselves up along my legs, morphing into my long shirt. My shadow touched the mountains, and when I leaned closer, I saw one mountaintop was shaved flat. On it was a set of wicker patio furniture and a very familiar studio. The city was, of course, Boston. I recognized the skyline from the Financial District. Here, two people who bore a striking resemblance to India and Erica were enjoying a picnic on the roof of one of the high-rises. On yet another one, I recognized Luke and some of the other students.

Between me and the forest, slightly to the side, I saw Penelope at her desk, writing. Next to her stood a transparent portrait of Edward, looking stronger and younger, and cupping the back of Penelope's head. To my other side, I saw Isabella. Standing up proudly, she held on to Oliver.

My gaze returned to how Hayden had painted me. She hadn't made me prettier, or more beautiful, or painted me into something I was not. She'd used oil, with tiny brushes, and painted me like she saw me. My eyes glowed with love for her. My hands reached for her, palms forward. A faint smile played on my lips, and across my body she'd even painted in my signature messenger bag.

I pivoted and hugged Hayden so hard, she gave a muted whimper. "Oh, God, darling. You're amazing. This painting is… is…" I couldn't find the word. "I love it. I love *you*."

"It's yours. We won't ever sell it." She pulled back some to look at me. "You see?"

And I did. As I held her close, I managed to murmur, "I do." And I did. Perhaps Hayden would never say "I love you," but this was more than that. Way beyond anything I ever could've wished for or expected, Hayden had showed me I was the center of her world.

I vowed to make sure she knew she was the axis mine revolved around.

EPILOGUE

The sun shone through the vines in the ceiling of Penelope Moore's conservatory. In early September, it was nearly too warm to be out here, but Penelope had opened two of the large sliding doors, and a cool breeze made it perfect.

"I was close to speechless," Penelope Moore said, and squeezed my hand. "Can you believe how long the line was to your gallery?"

I couldn't. The opening of Hayden's showing at my Boston gallery had superseded any expectation. The few promotion opportunities I'd managed to convince Hayden to participate in had paid off tenfold. The interesting part was how many of the younger demographic were interested in Hayden's art. I even thought I saw kids as young as preteens in line to get in.

"Penelope's portrait was one of the highlights," Isabella said. She maneuvered her wheelchair with her good hand. "I'd seen most of her earlier work already, of course, but the way you displayed them, Greer, made them feel brand-new."

"We debated whether to hang her paintings chronologically, as she wanted to do initially, but when we talked about it, it seemed better to go by the mood rather than the date." I held my arm around Hayden's shoulders, where we sat on a wooden bench together.

"I had to make Greer put up a not-for-sale sign next to Penelope's portrait." Hayden looked serious. "Some people were very persistent. I told them over and over, but they seemed to think if they offered more money, I'd change my mind. I told them I was richer than them and didn't need it."

I guffawed at the memory. One art collector in particular had stared at Hayden as if she'd sprouted wings and smacked him over the head with the tips.

"I noticed you didn't show Greer's portrait," Isabella said. "Why's that? It's one of your most amazing pieces, my girl."

Hayden looked at me and smiled. We'd both been in total agreement not to display that particular painting, which hung over the fireplace in our home. Turning back to Isabella, Hayden said, "It's too private, Nana. It's how I revealed my true feelings for Greer the first time. Showing family and friends at our house is fine. Displaying to total strangers what's in my heart, how Greer is everything to me, is not fine."

"I see." Isabella's eyes softened. "I won't argue with that—far from it. I think it proves how far you've come, not only with your painting, but also in the way you express your emotions. I'm so very proud of you, Hayden."

"Sorry to interrupt, but coffee and tea are ready in the dining room." Tina, the caregiver Penelope still employed, showed up in the doorway. "Also, India and Erica are here, as well as Oliver and his date."

"Excellent. You are joining us, aren't you, Tina?" Penelope asked as she stood. She took the handles of Isabella's wheelchair and pushed her back into the house.

"Sure. Thank you." Tina took over the wheelchair and helped Isabella maneuver it close to the table. Isabella had lived in Penelope's house for almost two months now. The two of them had found each other through Hayden and me. It didn't take long for Penelope to suggest that Isabella move in with her. She argued the fact that she already had all the equipment needed for the practical side of Isabella's care.

Isabella had agonized over the decision, but when Hayden stated how lonely Penelope must be, she relented. Penelope had spent a week having painters and decorators turn Edward's very male bedroom into a lovely room fit for a flower-loving woman. Hayden brought a painting she'd done of her grandparents when she was fifteen, which brought tears to both older ladies' eyes.

Isabella thrived. Hayden and I visited several times a week—Hayden actually popped over almost every day—just to talk and have coffee together. Even Isabella's physician was amazed at her improvement. The day she moved her left hand for the first time since her stroke, Hayden actually hugged Tina, whom she'd taken a long time to warm up to.

I wondered if Hayden and Oliver missed not having their parents take part in this celebration of Hayden's success and Isabella's improved situation. I knew Oliver had made progress with his father over the last months. Hayden showed no interest in reconciling—not yet. Leyla kept her distance, and I thought that proved the woman wasn't completely unintelligent. I simply couldn't see how Hayden, so honest and without deceit, could ever have a true exchange with her mother, the born narcissist. Leyla would never own up to how much she traumatized her daughter, and Hayden would never accept anything but the naked truth.

Now as we sat around the table, chatting over homemade scones, I tried to think back to the day before I went to the Rowe Art School. I'd been successful and busy, had good friends. I hadn't really missed not having someone in my life—or I'd convinced myself having a partner was more trouble than it was worth.

One day later all that had changed. I'd nearly turned and left, but agreed to at least see some of the students' work. If I hadn't done that, I wouldn't have seen the painting of the little girl inside the window looking out. Who would've guessed that painting had held the key to my happiness?

I ran my hands up and down Hayden's thigh under the tablecloth. "Congratulations, darling," I murmured. "India just told me you've sold over ninety percent of your paintings. The remaining paintings will be sold too, as several people are bidding on them."

Hayden gave me a smile, her real one, and squeezed my hand. "So they like my paintings?"

"They adore them. When we get back to the house, I'll show you some of the reviews. And if you hear a buzzing sound, it's India's phone, hidden in Erica's pocket, set to vibrate. People keep ringing about you, and Erica wants to have her scones in peace. They want to interview you, have you on their TV show—"

"TV show?" Hayden actually looked interested. "Which one?"

"Oh, my. I'd say all of them. Why don't you ask India for a list later, and you can decide what you want to do?"

"Okay." Her eyes gleaming, Hayden gazed around the table and then locked her gaze on me. "This is wonderful. I'm happy."

I swallowed against the sudden burning sensation in my throat. I'd never heard Hayden speak of an emotion like that before. It had to be really strong for her to identify it with words. I held her hand and raised it to my lips, kissing her knuckles. "That makes two of us, darling. I'm so very happy too."

About the Author

Gun Brooke resides in the countryside in Sweden with her very patient family. A retired neonatal intensive care nurse, she now writes full time, only rarely taking a break to create websites for herself or others and to do computer graphics. Gun writes both romances and sci-fi.

Follow Gun Brooke on the web at gbrooke-fiction.com, or on social media:

Facebook: www.facebook.com/gunbach
Twitter:@redheadgrrl1960
Tumblr: gunbrooke.tumblr.com
LiveJournal: redheadgrrl1960.livejournal.com

Books Available From Bold Strokes Books

Making a Comeback by Julie Blair. Music and love take center stage when jazz pianist Liz Randall tries to make a comeback with the help of her reclusive, blind neighbor, Jac Winters. (978-1-62639-357-8)

Soul Unique by Gun Brooke. Self-proclaimed cynic Greer Landon falls for Hayden Rowe's paintings and the young woman shortly after, but will Hayden, who lives with Asperger syndrome, trust her and reciprocate her feelings? (978-1-62639-358-5)

The Price of Honor by Radclyffe. Honor and duty are not always black and white—and when self-styled patriots take up arms against the government, the price of honor may be a life. (978-1-62639-359-2)

Mounting Evidence by Karis Walsh. Lieutenant Abigail Hargrove and her mounted police unit need to solve a murder and protect wetland biologist Kira Lovell during the Washington State Fair. (978-1-62639-343-1)

Threads of the Heart by Jeannie Levig. Maggie and Addison Rae-McInnis share a love and a life, but are the threads that bind them together strong enough to withstand Addison's restlessness and the seductive Victoria Fontaine? (978-1-62639-410-0)

Sheltered Love by MJ Williamz. Boone Fairway and Grey Dawson—two women touched by abuse—overcome their pasts to find happiness in each other. (978-1-62639-362-2)

Searching for Celia by Elizabeth Ridley. As American spy novelist Dayle Salvesen investigates the mysterious disappearance of her ex-lover, Celia, in London, she begins questioning how well she knew Celia—and how well she knows herself. (978-1-62639-356-1).

Hardwired by C.P. Rowlands. Award-winning teacher Clary Stone and Leefe Ellis, manager of the homeless shelter for small children, stand together in a part of Clary's hometown that she never knew existed. (978-1-62639-351-6)

The Muse by Meghan O'Brien. Erotica author Kate McMannis struggles with writer's block until a gorgeous muse entices her into a world of fantasy sex and inadvertent romance. (978-1-62639-223-6)

No Good Reason by Cari Hunter. A violent kidnapping in a Peak District village pushes Detective Sanne Jensen and lifelong friend Dr. Meg Fielding closer, just as it threatens to tear everything apart. (978-1-62639-352-3)

Romance by the Book by Jo Victor. If Cam didn't keep disrupting her life, maybe Alex could uncover the secret of a century-old love story, and solve the greatest mystery of all—her own heart. (978-1-62639-353-0)

Death's Doorway by Crin Claxton. Helping the dead can be deadly: Tony may be listening to the dead, but she needs to learn to listen to the living. (978-1-62639-354-7)

The 45th Parallel by Lisa Girolami. Burying her mother isn't the worst thing that can happen to Val Montague when she returns to the woodsy but peculiar town of Hemlock, Oregon. (978-1-62639-342-4)

A Royal Romance by Jenny Frame. In a country where class still divides, can love topple the last social taboo and allow Queen Georgina and Beatrice Elliot, a working-class girl, their happy ever after? (978-1-62639-360-8)

Bouncing by Jaime Maddox. Basketball coach Alex Dalton has been bouncing from woman to woman because no one ever held her interest, until she meets her new assistant, Britain Dodge. (978-1-62639-344-8)

Same Time Next Week by Emily Smith. A chance encounter between Alex Harris and the beautiful Michelle Masters leads to a whirlwind friendship and causes Alex to question everything she's ever known—including her own marriage. (978-1-62639-345-5)

All Things Rise by Missouri Vaun. Cole rescues a striking pilot who crash-lands near her family's farm, setting in motion a chain of events that will forever alter the course of her life. (978-1-62639-346-2)

Riding Passion by D. Jackson Leigh. Mount up for the ride through a sizzling anthology of chance encounters, buried desires, romantic surprises, and blazing passion. (978-1-62639-349-3)

Love's Bounty by Yolanda Wallace. Lobster boat captain Jake Myers stopped living the day she cheated death, but meeting greenhorn Shy Silva stirs her back to life. (978-1-62639334-9)

Just Three Words by Melissa Brayden. Sometimes the one you want is the one you least suspect…Accountant Samantha Ennis has her ordered life disrupted when heartbreaker Hunter Blair moves into her trendy Soho loft. (978-1-62639-335-6)

Lay Down the Law by Carsen Taite. Attorney Peyton Davis returns to her Texas roots to take on big oil and the Mexican Mafia, but will her investigation thwart her chance at true love? (978-1-62639-336-3)

Playing in Shadow by Lesley Davis. Survivor's guilt threatens to keep Bryce trapped in her nightmare world unless Scarlet's love can pull her out of the darkness back into the light. (978-1-62639-337-0)

Soul Selecta by Gill McKnight. Soul mates are hell to work with. (978-1-62639-338-7)

Shadow Hunt by L.L. Raand. With young to raise and her Pack under attack, Sylvan, Alpha of the wolf Weres, takes on her greatest challenge when she determines to uncover the faceless enemies known as the Shadow Lords. A Midnight Hunters novel. (978-1-62639-326-4)

Heart of the Game by Rachel Spangler. A baseball writer falls for a single mom, but can she ever love anything as much as she loves the game? (978-1-62639-327-1)

Prayer of the Handmaiden by Merry Shannon. Celibate priestess Kadrian must defend the kingdom of Ithyria from a dangerous enemy and ultimately choose between her duty to the Goddess and the love of her childhood sweetheart, Erinda. (978-1-62639-329-5)

The Witch of Stalingrad by Justine Saracen. A Soviet "night witch" pilot and American journalist meet on the Eastern Front in WWII and struggle through carnage, conflicting politics, and the deadly Russian winter. (978-1-62639-330-1)